KISSING FROGS

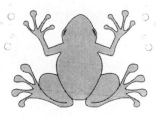

Alisha Sevigny

*Receive a signed bookplate
with proof of purchase.*

Details:

*http://
fierceinkpress.com/
collectors-edition-content/*

www.fierceinkpress.com

KISSING FROGS

Alisha Sevigny

Fierce Ink Press

Kissing Frogs
Copyright © 2014 by Alisha Sevigny
All rights reserved

Published by Fierce Ink Press Co-Op Ltd.
www.fierceinkpress.com

First edition, 2014

Library and Archives Canada Cataloguing in Publication information is available upon request.

ISBN 978-1-927746-66-0 (paperback)
Also available in electronic format

Cover design by Emma Dolan

For Aira and Nolan.

And for Gramps, the original storyteller.

"*An average of seventy-four species become extinct every day, which was one good reason but not the only one to hold someone's hand...*"

— Nicole Krauss, *The History of Love*

Chapter One

I slam the classroom door behind me. It bangs louder than expected and I dart a guilty look over my shoulder. The door stays shut as the reverberations echo down the hallway, empty except for a gorgeous guy in a tight white shirt leaning against a row of banged up blue lockers, looking like he just stepped out of a Hollister ad. My heart, still hammering from the conversation I just had with Mr. A, thumps even harder. I still can't believe that the most popular guy in school is waiting for me. Apparently he can't believe it either, because an annoyed expression crosses his face as he looks up from his phone.

"What did Mr. A want?" he asks, jamming his cell in the pocket of his Sevens.

I drop my bag and, with shaking hands, attempt to open my lock. I'm having trouble remembering the combination.

"I'm failing bio," I say, finally yanking the lock down after several tries. The statement sounds absurd to my ears.

"So?" Miles asks.

"So Miami is out," I whisper, one hand going to my mouth as if to keep the words from escaping.

"What?" His cobalt eyes take on a sharp quality, matching his voice. "What did he say?"

"He wants me to go with the stupid conservation club down to Panama, to help some endangered frogs or something." I'm not too sure of the details, having been knocked on my ass about my grade. I toss battered textbooks in my locker, and rest my forehead against the back of my hand, breathing in formaldehyde and failure.

"Did you tell him you can't go?"

Lifting my head, I look at him. "Tried, but he said if I wanted any chance at passing, I have to do a report for extra credit and make up all the missed lab time." Unfortunately Miles's free period coincides with biology, which means I don't always make it to class.

"Everything's booked and paid for, Jess," he says slowly, like I'm two years old. "The flights, the condo on South Beach." He cocks an eyebrow full of innuendo. "It's our last spring break before we graduate."

"I know, I know." My stomach churns. "It's just that if I don't get my grade up then Berkeley's totally off the table…" I examine my reflection in the locker mirror. Blue eyes bulge in a face tinged with green. I look like one of those frogs Mr. A was yammering on about.

"I thought you didn't want to go to Berkeley anymore?" Miles says. I turn to him and he tucks a piece of pale blonde hair behind my ear. "I thought you wanted to stay home with me."

I hesitate, unsure and unwilling to explain that before we met I was an entirely different person. Someone for whom Berkeley had once been the ultimate prize. Someone Miles wouldn't have looked twice at.

"It's just that my dad will freak when he finds out," I finally say. That's an understatement. I have no idea how I'm going to break the news to my father that his princess, former straight A, allstate spelling bee champ who'd skipped a year, is now failing grade twelve biology. I'm having trouble wrapping my own head around it and *I* know about the missed assignments. "He'll make me go when he hears."

Miles shrugs, his fingers sweeping hair the exact shade as mine to the side. We have the same stylist. Lorenzo's been a bit heavy-handed with the platinum lately. "Shitty," he says. Surprised, I inspect his perfect face. The incensed outrage I'm expecting on my behalf, or at the very least, at the interference with his plans, doesn't materialize. "Maybe this is a good thing," he says instead, shifting his bag on his shoulder.

"What?" I blink at him.

"Maybe we could use a break." His statement hits me in the face like a bucket of icy water.

"Are you serious?" I splutter.

"Yeah, you'll be in Panama, I'll be in South Beach — we might as well both have fun."

"Are you saying you want to hook up with other people?" My voice takes on a high-pitched frequency. I'm surprised all the dogs in the neighborhood don't come running.

He looks down at his Converse shoes then backs up. "That's not what

I'm saying."

But it is. It's exactly what he's saying.

"Miles, can we talk about this?" I struggle to bring the hysteria down a notch as pieces of my new life, the life I've fought so hard for, crumble around me.

"It's really not such a big deal, Jess."

My mouth opens and closes like a goldfish.

"All I'm saying is, it's just for a week or so, right, babe?" He follows up with a sexy smile. Scratch that — an arrogant smile.

Don't do it, Jess. Don't.

"And all I'm saying is, you're just an asshole." I shut my locker with such savagery it pops back open, narrowly missing my face. Mr. A pokes his head out of the classroom, gray irises owl-wide, framed by matching silver circles.

"Everything okay out here?" He looks from Miles to me but retreats when he sees my wild-eyed expression. "Ah, I'll just be in here if you need…" He closes the door, cutting himself off.

"Jess, wait." Miles calls after me as I start for the exit. "You're right, that was a total dick thing to say. I don't know what I was thinking." I stop, turn and look at him — the guy all the girls want to date, the guy who's supposed to take me to prom, the guy who surprised me with a trip to Miami for my birthday.

"But you were thinking it all the same." My voice cracks.

"I was just teasing you," he says, not quite able to make eye contact.

But I've been teased before. Extensively. And I know the difference between a joke and a statement that smacks of truth. The question is: do I let it go? The fact that my boyfriend just admitted to my face he wants to hook up with other girls while he's in South Beach? I should just let it go… Don't all guys think like that?

I walk back to him and pick my bag off the ground, my eyes locking with his.

"I'm keeping Lorenzo." I turn and walk away. Away from him. Away from the reality I spent the last few years creating. It's either that or drop-kick him in the balls.

I don't get far.

He grabs my arm and spins me around. "Fine. Screw biology, screw Berkeley and screw the frogs!" he says, jaw set, eyes narrowed. "Go tell Mr. A you're not going."

He marches me up to the classroom like I'm a delinquent and raps on the door. Mr. A opens it and looks at us, his left ear red from pressing it up against the wood. "Yes?"

I open my mouth but nothing comes out. Miles prods me in the back. I jump.

"Hi, Mr. A I just wanted to let you know…" I hesitate, glancing at Miles, then back to Mr. A. "…that I'd be happy to join the club down in Panama for spring break."

Chapter

Two

But I'm not happy. I'm miserable. Utterly bereft, depressed and completely regretting my temporary moment of insanity.

I'm also mother effing hot. Fanning myself, I look around the stifling van containing our driver, Hector, one oblivious teacher and six sweaty, hostile strangers. I didn't pay much attention to them on the plane, consumed with my own inner turmoil, but none seem overly familiar. Besides, it's not like we run in the same social circles — not anymore anyway. No one speaks a word to me. I get the vibe they're less than thrilled about my last minute annexation of their trip. Talk about joining the club.

I take a long drink from my water bottle, chugging hard. Sunglasses slide off the back of my head and a hand goes up to grab them.

"Better hang on tight to those Pradas, Princess," says a voice from my past.

Water sprays out my nose and mouth, splattering the backs of the two girls sitting in the row in front of me, their shrieks simultaneous.

"What the hell?" the blonde says, turning around and wiping her neck. The other girl, with the inky tresses, looks at me in disgust. I ignore them as I'm busy choking to death.

There are a few thumps on my back, and a cheery, "Easy does it, Messy Jessie." I turn my head, everything in slow motion. I'm hearing things. My disbelieving eyes rake over the boy on my right, whose once cherubic face has morphed into something slightly more … archangelic? Probably why I hadn't recognized him.

The world speeds up again.

"Panama is supposed to be pretty safe, Trav-ass," I somehow manage to gasp between coughs, eyes watering, "but I would've thought you knew that."

"Oh, I do," he says, handing me the sunglasses I hadn't been able to save from falling. "I'm just surprised you do." He pushes wavy brown hair out of dark green eyes that glint with familiar mischief.

"There happens to be this fabulous invention called Google," I retort, wiping the water dribbling down my chin. "In fact, you're there under the search term 'annoying know-it-all.'"

He grins, straight white teeth competing with a faded image of him in braces. "At least you're still aware of the fact that I do. Know it all."

Too shocked to think of a decent comeback, I face forward, staring out the bug-splattered windshield, my heart racing. You have *got* to be kidding me. Since when does Travis freaking Henley go to Cassels Prep?

"What the hell is your problem?" Blondie says, having dried herself off. Teal glasses frame hazel eyes that glower at me from under thick bangs. Both girls look like they've just turned over a large rock to expose some revolting specimen squirming in the mud.

"Sorry," I mutter, distracted, but still aware there's no way they'd ever talk to me like that at school. This only serves to remind me that I'm miles out of my realm: 3,650 of them, to be exact. They whip their heads around, whispering and throwing the occasional withering look over their shoulders.

"Long time, no talk, Messy Jessie." Travis nudges me with his elbow.

"Don't call me that," I hiss.

"So you prefer Princess?"

"I'd prefer if you stopped talking to me."

"Whatever you say, Princess." He grins and ruffles my hair. I glare at him, smooth my hair back into a ponytail and stare straight ahead. I must be hallucinating. That's the only explanation why Travis's leg is pressed against mine. Travis, who'd known me *before* my phoenixlike rise from the ashes of uncoolness. In fact, I'm clinging to the faint hope that everything since that day in Mr. A's class has been some kind of extended hallucination: Miles, Panama and now Travis? Maybe there was a chemical leak in lab and I'm in a coma right now.

"You will all love the place, I am sure," Hector yells over his shoulder as Latin music blares from the stereo. We zoom along the waterfront. Tall buildings swirl up into the sky and construction looms everywhere as Panama hurries to catch up to its reputation as a thriving metropolis.

Trying to get a grip on my shock, I turn to the girl on my left who's reading a book on Panama. "Do you know how much longer it is?" I ask. Travis leans over the seat to talk to a guy with shaggy brown hair who managed to escape being spit on. *What's he telling him?* My chest tightens.

"Around an hour, I think," she says in a soft voice, looking up from the guidebook. The dark French braids are vaguely familiar and I place them from biology class, front row. Her name's some sort of musical instrument. Harp, maybe?

My "thanks" is drowned out by an enormous truck rocketing past, inches from sideswiping us. Hector honks and gestures wildly. "*Que te pasa! Ove!*" Horns blare and fists shake. Panama traffic makes driving back home in Seattle look like meditation practice. I grab the seat in front to keep from falling into Travis as we swerve to avoid another large truck.

The phone shifts in my back pocket, jabbing me in the butt. Discreetly, I pull it out to see if Ky's texted yet. All electronics are forbidden. Mr. A has peculiar ideas about doing most of our research the old-fashioned way. Personally, I don't think he wants to be responsible if anything gets lost or stolen. Only cameras allowed. Which I, of course, didn't bring, since there's nothing I want to remember about this trip.

No new messages.

My stomach clenches. *It's fine.* I reassure myself. They're all traveling today as well. I probably won't hear from anyone until tomorrow. Ky and Alyssa were horrified when they heard the news and vowed to keep tabs on Miles. We made up after our fight, getting back together, but things are still kinda shaky. Even though he'd acted like a major d bag, some part of me is reluctant to let go after all the work I've put into that relationship. Into all of the relationships with my new friends and new life.

I cast a sidelong look at Travis. And now this. He could ruin everything.

Blondie turns to say something to him and sees my phone. "Kiki." She elbows Inky Tresses, nodding at me, then raises her voice. "Excuse me, you're not allowed to have that."

"Chrissy's right." Kiki's brown eyes are hard. "Didn't you read the waiver?"

Mr. A hears and holds out his hand. "You'll get it back at the end of the trip."

Seriously?

I grudgingly deposit my only link to the outside world in Chrissy's outstretched palm. She gives me a smug look and hands it over to Mr. A. What are we, in grade two? I open my mouth to say something when Hector slams on the brakes, my upper torso lurching forward then snapping back.

"He's got a gun!" someone screams.

The breath leaves my body as Travis throws himself on top of me.

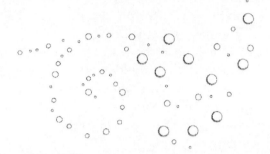 Chapter

Three

I'm sandwiched between Travis and Harp when another blast of water hits the windshield.

"Um, I think it's safe," I say, my face squished between Harp's arm and Travis's warm cheek. He gets off and hauls me up. Harp, having just had the wind knocked out of her, gasps for air.

Travis clears his throat. "Sorry about that."

"Are you okay?" I ignore him and help Harp up. She nods and we stare out the window. A mass of teeming, writhing, half-naked bodies press in on every side of the van. People shoot guns of water into the air as salsa music assaults our eardrums.

"What in the name of Albert Einstein?" Mr. A exclaims, still clutching the dashboard.

"*Perdón*, it is Carnival," Hector apologizes. "The city is crazy right now." He makes a left and we crawl through a maze of side streets, gradually leaving behind the reveling city. "This is the Pan-American Highway," he announces as we pick up speed again. "It connects most of the country."

I stare at the passing landscape. What just happened back there? Had Travis been trying to protect me? Or did he duck to save his own skin? I sneak another look at him. He's now talking to the curly-haired guy on his right, his angular profile just a few inches from my head. I'm having a hard time reconciling the Travis I once knew with this potentially chivalrous stranger. The girls in front are giggling at something Shaggy's saying and Harp is engrossed in her guidebook again, having recovered from being side-tackled.

"I don't know how you can read in the car," I finally say to her, feeling nauseous at the thought of focusing on small black-and-white type while traveling at the speed of, well, a speeding van.

"It doesn't bother me," she says.

"So you must be excited about the trip?" I venture, needing to distract myself from the boy on my right who'd tormented me for years. Besides, Harp seems okay. That and I'd just been lying on top of her a few minutes ago. The least I can do is make small talk.

"Yes," she says. "It's my first time away from home by myself."

"Like, ever?" My eyes widen.

She nods, her big brown eyes shining. "I had to beg my parents for weeks."

"Um, that's cool." My hands go to readjust my ponytail and I catch a whiff of BO. I quickly lower them. Long plane ride.

"They only let me because it will look great on my college applications," she adds, closing her book.

"Yeah," I say. I guess that's something. "Where do you want to go to school?"

"I want to study marine biology so I applied to Hawaii at Manoa, Santa Cruz and Rhode Island."

All good schools. "I'm sure you won't have a problem getting into any of them," I say, positive she gets one hundred per cent on every assignment and test she takes. Once upon a time, I had too.

"Thanks." She gives me a small smile. "What about you?"

"Maybe Berkeley?" I say, the words feeling weird in my mouth. "They have a killer sociology program." My father and great-grandmother had both graduated from there summa cum laude. Another lifetime ago, I'd planned to follow in their footsteps.

"Oh yeah?" Travis says, eavesdropping. "Juan applied there as well." He gestures to the curly-haired guy beside him who examines me as he pushes his glasses up his nose.

"Hi," Juan says. He has the startled air of someone who's recently been electrocuted. His curly black hair sticks out in a million different directions. Not that I'm winning any beauty pageants after that flight either. My eyes are dry and probably bloodshot from sleeping in contacts and my normally pale skin already feels flushed from the sun. By tomorrow I'll have a smattering of freckles across my nose, which turns up slightly at the tip. Mom used to run her finger down it and call it my ski jump nose, then wonder aloud if I should have it fixed.

"Hi," I say, then, unable to resist, turn to Travis. "What are you doing here?"

"Same objective as you, old friend." He slings a lazy arm around me.

"Helping frogs." I remove his hand from my shoulder. Ha. Shows how much he knows. Saving my grade and spiting my boyfriend are *much* less worthy goals. "Why?" He grins. "Surprised to see me?"

"Not at all," I lie. "Did you just transfer?"

"Last year," he says dryly.

"How nice for you."

"We are almost at our *casa*," Hector announces, turning down a dirt road with craterlike potholes that bounce us up and down like whack-a-mole at the fair. A thrum of energy flows through the van, resuscitating its travel weary occupants as everyone clamors to catch a glimpse of their new home for the next week and a half. Everyone but me, that is. We pull up to a thick, white cement wall encircling a large property like a concrete moat. Hector idles in front of a fortresslike gate and yells something out his window.

A wooden door swings open and a tall, dark and definitely handsome shirtless boy strolls out of the complex, heaving open the gate for the van. Tattooed arms bulge and abs ripple. The boy turns to the vehicle, giving us a friendly smile and a wave. Every female's jaw unhinges.

"My son, Enrique," Hector says.

What's the Spanish word for hot again?

"*Caliente*," Chrissy whispers.

Yes, that's it.

"*Bienvenidos a Villa Paraíso.*" Hector pulls into the property and parks. "Welcome to Paradise Villas."

We tumble out of the van and behold an Eden-like utopia. Palm trees dot immaculate grounds, swaying gently beside a crystal blue pool. Exotic birds fly between banana trees and butterflies flit among vibrant flowers. Colorful hammocks swing under a large open-air hut thing that promises shade and cool breezes. Three villas stand out on the lush property, their exterior stonework bringing to mind castles from mythical lands.

It's like something out of a tropical fairy tale.

"Wow," I say, despite myself. Nice prison.

"*Mi casa es su casa*," Hector says. "Please do not worry about the bags. Enrique and I will get them."

"Nonsense," Mr. A says, wiping his forearm against his face, scalp glistening between thinning red spikes. "Guys and gals, grab your stuff."

Enrique already has the back doors open and is unloading our luggage as we go to give him a hand. He picks up my backpack and when I reach out to grab it, he deposits the giant bag in my grasp. Our hands touch for the briefest second. A current runs up my arm and I look into eyes the color of swirled honey and chocolate. One of them winks.

"*Hola*," he says, grinning. "*Buenos días.*"

"*Buenos días*," I repeat. Wow. This guy is even better looking than Miles. "Welcome to Panama."

"Thank you. I mean, *gracias*."

"*De nada.*"

"*De nada?*"

"You're welcome."

"*Gracias*," I repeat again, a little dazed and suddenly aware the van ride has done nothing for my appearance. My hands go automatically to my pony and slide the elastic down. Subtly, I smooth my wrinkly T-shirt but refrain from sniffing my armpits this time.

"So, you are American?" Enrique raises a dark eyebrow, his voice low and husky.

"Yes, well, half. My father is American, my mother is Canadian, so I guess I'm both, but I live in the States. I go to Canada lots though. My grandparents live there and the rest of my mom's family: aunts, uncles, cousins…"

Shut up, Jess.

"We live close to the border." That last one slips out.

"Can you spare us your life story?" Chrissy says behind me. I move out of the way and she gives me another of her scathing looks before turning toward Enrique with a dazzling smile.

Walking over to Harp and Juan who are standing by the pool, I feel dizzy from the heat. Or maybe it's from talking to one of the best looking guys I've ever seen. I wonder how Miles would react if he saw Enrique. Despite his proposition, he does not share well with others. Obviously he doesn't think anyone in the conservation club poses a real threat or he never would have said what he did.

"The chytrid fungus is basically wiping them out," Juan is saying to Harp. I hadn't noticed how short he was while in the van, maybe an inch taller than my five-three frame.

"Who's covered in fungus?" My eyes go automatically to Travis, who's getting his bag from Enrique. I'm highly suspicious of this whole nice act.

"The frogs," Juan says as he adjusts his glasses, his brown eyes serious. "We're losing hundreds of species every day. It's the greatest mass extinction since the dinosaurs."

"Would a world without frogs be so bad?" I frown down at my fingernails. My polish is starting to chip. I look up. "I mean, I certainly don't miss having T. rex around."

They look at me, mouths agape, like I've just stomped on one of the things. Travis and Shaggy come up behind me with their bags, overhearing my comment.

"Hey, Princess," Travis says, "you do know you're here with the conservation club?" He pokes his finger into my side and arches an eyebrow.

I tilt my head up to glare at him. When did he get so tall? Chrissy and Kiki join us.

"Yeah, some of us actually worked our asses off to be here," Chrissy says, taking a menacing step toward me. "Do you know how many freaking bake sales we had?"

"Dude, not to mention car washes," Shaggy says. He's hunched over, like he doesn't want any credit for the six feet he's almost at.

"Yeah." Kiki sets her bag down and crosses her arms. "We didn't just luck into a free trip for extra credit." With the pool behind me, there's nowhere to go.

Several pairs of eyes laser into me as I'm surrounded. Taking a step backwards, my foot hits nothing but air and I know I'm about to fall into the water.

Chapter Four

A hand reaches out to steady me. It's Travis's. Confronted by faces ranging in expression from curiosity to severe animosity, I almost wish he'd let me fall in.

"Well, it wasn't exactly free," I say in a small voice. "I paid for my ticket."

"You mean your parents paid." Kiki narrows her eyes. "We fund-raised for half a year."

Actually, Dad and Mom did make me pay with the money I'd saved for Miami, but Kiki doesn't look like she's in the mood to hear it.

Chrissy shakes her short cap of white-blonde hair. "And that is so not the point anyways."

"The disappearance of frogs could trigger a chain reaction of unforeseen consequences, all the way up the ecosystem," Juan adds, having recovered enough to respond.

Right.

"Okay, let's get set up in our *casas*," Mr. A calls over. I slink behind the others, my new backpack feeling heavy. Chrissy whispers something to Kiki. Both of them cackle and look back. No one else meets my eyes as we are assigned our villas. "Girls on the left, boys on the right with me," Mr. A says.

"What?" Shaggy exclaims. "Dude, how come they don't get a chaperone?"

"Because we're more mature than you, Steven." Kiki flips her straight black hair and sticks out her tongue.

"Oh yeah, real mature," Travis says, giving her a light shot in the arm. Kiki stares down at her bicep then back up at Travis. Her almond eyes follow him as he walks over to Mr. A, whistling.

"Carlita will check in on the girls from time to time," Mr. A says. We've yet to meet Hector's wife, but from the mouthwatering smells coming from their villa, I gather she's busy preparing our lunch. My stomach rumbles. The last thing I ate was a stale muffin and some rubbery eggs on the plane. We separate from the boys at a fork in the path.

Chrissy and Kiki push on the door and walk in, followed by Harp. I stand back, admiring the beautiful stonework and spiraling staircase. The house is a mix of dreamy Tuscan villa, castle and tree house. It's the house Romeo would have built for Juliet if they'd run away to the jungle and lived happily ever after.

The club must have had a *lot* of bake sales.

I step inside. Burnt orange tiles pave the floor and the ceilings are high, fans blowing cool air down. The living room is to our right, along with a small dining area and kitchen, walls painted in bright yellows and blues. The staircase I'd seen from the outside leads up to a second floor. Chrissy and Kiki sprint up the stairs, probably to get dibs on the best bedroom. Harp and I follow them. We reach the landing. There are two rooms, each with twin beds, and a washroom in between.

"Kiki and I are taking the one on the left," Chrissy says, then flounces back to her room.

"I guess you're stuck with me." I give Harp a weak smile.

"Well, I snore," she says, walking into the room, "so maybe you're the one stuck with me."

"It's okay." I follow her in. "You should hear my dad."

"My dad has a sleep apnea machine," she confides. "He looks like an Indian Darth Vader."

I laugh for the first time in weeks.

We set our bags down. The ceiling in here is low, slanting down at an angle. Everything is made of burnished wood. Green curtains hang at windows that look out into gardens and a giant tree outside winds its way down and around to the ground.

"There's a balcony," Harp says. She walks over to the wooden French doors, opens them and steps out onto the terrace. I follow her. This is where Juliet would murmur sweet nothings to her Romeo under an alabaster moon.

"Nice view." I gaze over the tree line at the blue Pacific. Turquoise waters sparkle in the sunlight. Waves lap against a gorgeous stretch of sandy beach.

"It looks really close," Harp says.

I walk to the edge of the balcony, reaching out to touch branches that curl up at the ends, beckoning me to climb onto a sturdy limb. A solitary wooden swing hangs from one of the thicker boughs, swaying back and forth, pushed by a salty ocean breeze. I turn around and walk back inside the room, utterly charmed despite myself.

"So, um, which bed do you want?" I ask.

"Do you mind if I take the one farthest from the balcony door? Sometimes I sleepwalk and don't want to find myself hanging over a ledge if I can help it."

Snoring *and* somnambulism? I sigh inwardly. "Sure, I like looking out the window anyways."

We set to work unpacking. An empty closet on the other side of Harp's bed has two sets of drawers. Pulling my clothes out of my backpack, my fingers hit a small box. I examine the purple wrapping paper. Did Miles hide a present in my bag? Maybe this is his way of apologizing. My chest thuds. There's a note taped to the bottom.

Happy Birthday to our precious daughter.

My heart backflips to the floor, but I open the box anyway, breath catching. Three shimmering opals gleam back at me in an intricate gold setting. Great-grandma's ring. They had it reset. Sliding it on my finger, I admire the way it flashes in the light. It's loose but I love it too much to take it off. Gigi and I were super close when I was little. She'd left me the ring but Mom said it was too expensive for a teenager to wear. She must have felt bad about Miami. The hovering perma-cloud of despair lifts the tiniest fraction.

I bring my toiletries to the bathroom. There's an oak cabinet with five shelves, the bottom one filled with toilet paper.

"Why don't we take a shelf by alphabetical order?" Harp follows me in, seeming to have lost her initial shyness.

"Sure," I put out my face wash, moisturizer, toothbrush and toothpaste, along with my contact solution and case.

"La Mer?" Harp says, looking at my line of skin care.

"My mom bought it for me." I repeat the words she'd instilled in me from age four: "The best offense against wrinkles is a good line of defense."

"You're seventeen," Harp says, confused.

"Aaaahhhhhh!"

A piercing shriek from the next room has us racing in to see what crawled in someone's suitcase and died.

"Are you okay?" Harp asks Chrissy, who has one hand on her heaving chest, looking like someone just told her E does not equal M C squared. Kiki cowers on one of the beds.

"Huge. Spider. In corner." Chrissy points upwards.

"Don't you like all that stuff?" I say. "Frogs, bugs and creepy-crawly things?" Not adding I'm also petrified by all the aforementioned. It hits me that I'm not so sure how this whole frog thing is going to work out. I've been so upset about missing my birthday trip and Miles, I haven't given much thought to the amphibians themselves.

"Just because we're interested in saving endangered species doesn't mean I want arachnids crawling over my face when I'm sleeping," Chrissy practically shrieks.

"It's just a spider," I say with more bravado than I feel.

"You didn't see it." Hazel eyes sear me.

Gingerly, I pull back the curtain. "Don't see anything."

"I am so not sleeping in here until we find it," Kiki says, scanning the walls.

Swallowing, I shake the fabric, feeling light-headed.

An enormous black thing drops to the ground and shoots across the floor under one of the beds.

"Aaaaaaahhhhhhh!"

The four of us scream in unison and run out of the room, bumping into one another as we stumble down curving stairs. The front door flies open and Mr. A charges in, followed by the boys.

"What's wrong?" He looks around for the man with the chain saw and hockey mask.

"There's a spider in our bedroom." Chrissy pants.

The guys burst out laughing. Mr. A looks at us in disbelief.

"Aaaaahh," imitates Travis, throwing up his hands and waving them in mock horror.

"I'd like to see you get it," I say, hands on my hips. Now this is the Travis I remember.

"No problem." He grins, crossing his arms over his broad chest.

"Five minutes." Mr. A turns and walks out the door, shaking his head.

We follow Travis up the stairs, with the exception of Juan who heads into the kitchen.

"Which room?" Travis asks.

"That one." Chrissy points.

Travis and Steven go into the room while we wait on the landing.

"Don't kill it," Harp calls.

"I can't find it," Travis says.

"Check under the bed," I yell.

"There it is," Steven says, his voice rising. "He *is* a big boy. Juan, where are you, man?"

"Excuse me." Juan comes up the stairs holding a cup and a plate and pushes his way past us into the room, shutting the door behind him. After a lot of banging and shouting, the door opens and Travis emerges, his large hands cupped together, followed by Steven.

"Ewww," Kiki says, shuddering, "you have it in your hands?"

"Yup, wanna see it?" He smirks, looking directly at me.

"I'm good, thanks," I say, my mouth dry.

"Don't tell me you're afraid of a little spider?" He walks up to us. I see the old glint in his eyes. The one he used to get when he called me Messy Jessie.

"Don't even think about it," I warn him. He takes another step toward me. I back up into my room. "Travis, I swear to God — do not make one. More. Move."

He takes a quick step forward and thrusts his hands open at my face. My arms go up in a reflexive shield as I close my eyes and scream.

When no furry body smacks me in the head, I cautiously lower my arms and open my eyes.

Everyone's laughing. At me.

Juan stands behind Travis with the giant cup held tightly over the plate, spider secure.

"You're such a jerk," I say to Travis, my cheeks on fire.

"Aw, come on, Princess." His mouth curves. "I'm just playing."

"Hilarious." Spinning around, I march down the stairs and out the front door, not wanting anyone to see how close to tears I am. Walking over to the pool, I collapse onto a lounge chair.

"Boys," Mr. A yells from the villa porch, "thirty seconds!"

Steven and Juan come out of the house. I duck my head. They don't notice me as they walk by.

"Did you see her face?" Steven chortles, pulling his baggy board shorts up his lanky frame. "Priceless."

Juan gently lowers the cup and plate to the grass to release the spider, who I'm sure is every bit as traumatized as me by the whole ordeal.

"Come on, buddy," he coaxes, then straightens up and walks past me back to his villa.

Travis saunters out of the house next, Chrissy and Kiki behind him.

"Our heroes!" they call to the boys' retreating figures. Barf.

Travis turns and bows deeply, then follows the other boys.

"It's not like *you* did anything," I can't help saying as he walks by. "Juan's the one who caught the spider." He looks down, startled to hear my voice from the lounge chair. I wipe watery eyes and a look of guilt crosses his features.

"Sorry, Princess," he says, apologetic. "I couldn't resist."

"Whatever," I mumble, and start to get up. I just want to go home. He offers me his hand, but I ignore it. He's about to say something when Mr. A's voice rings out.

"Travis!"

"Coming!" he calls. "See you at lunch?" He looks down at me, an unreadable expression on his face.

"Unfortunately." I turn and walk away from him back toward the house.

Kiki stands in the doorway, arms crossed over her chest, looking like she wishes she were the one to get a fake spider thrown in her face.

"Excuse me," I mutter.

"No problem, *Princess*," she says, exaggerating Travis's insult.

He really has a knack for coming up with the most annoying nicknames.

I ignore her and walk back up the stairs to my bedroom. The excitement of the spider seems to have reinvigorated the others. All it's done for me is act as a reminder that I'm as out of my comfort zone as possible. I don't belong here with these people. A loud bell clangs, which I assume means lunch is ready.

Too bad I've lost my appetite.

***

"Are you coming down to eat?" Harp asks when I get back to the room.

"No, I'm good, thanks." I try to sound casual.

"Are you sure?"

"Yeah, I feel gross. Think I'm gonna have a shower."

"Do you want me to bring you back some food?" she asks.

"That's okay," I say, surprised by her offer, "but thanks for asking."

"Okay, see you later." She closes the door behind her.

I flop down on my bed, gripped by a sudden fierce homesickness, wishing I had my phone. I have no idea what's happening with Miles. Alyssa, Ky and the rest of the crew are probably lounging by a pool having a grand ol' time, not even missing me one bit. And I'm trapped in a foreign country with people who can barely tolerate me. Not to mention my former nemesis.

Twisting the ring around my finger, a picture of my old self pops up, entering a classroom, late and puffing, red-cheeked and frizzy-haired. The door slams behind me and everyone looks up. In the frantic run to find my class my shirt has come untucked. I look down and see a white splotch of toothpaste on my red pants. So not the impression I want to make on my first day of middle school.

I look around for a seat, feeling awkward and like a total loser. My gaze lands on a familiar face: Travis Henley. He'd been a year ahead of me in elementary. He gives a cool nod of acknowledgement. Probably still sore I'd kicked his butt in the school's Spelling Sensations contest. I'd won with 'inoculate.' He'd spelled it with two n's. The lingering smugness fades as I realize the seat next to him is the only one empty. Everyone's staring. I scurry over, arms crossed tightly over my books.

"Anyone sitting here?" I whisper.

"Well, well, look who's too smart for sixth grade." He looks me up and down, taking in my disheveled appearance. "Have a seat, Messy Jessie," he drawls.

And the name stuck. He'd teased me mercilessly right up until graduation, when he'd stuck some toilet paper on the back of my gown as I walked up to receive my award of academic achievement.

Fortunately, we'd gone to different high schools — though apparently not anymore — and I spent that summer before freshman year reinventing myself. Luckily I was a quick study, and during that first year learned to hide the fact that I had a brain. It seemed to make people feel more comfortable. Sophomore year was marginally better, and by junior year "Messy Jessie" was long gone. I applied my book smarts to carefully analyze the formulas for popularity and through strategic learning and hard work, clawed my way up out of Geeksville and into the realm of the Socially Acceptable. Thanks to my mom's Pilates connections and a bit of luck, I'd managed to befriend the popular crowd, miraculously landing in the stratosphere of the high school hierarchy.

And now it all could be ruined because of some stupid frogs. And Travis, if he decides to spill the beans about my former self. I'm sure Chrissy and Kiki would love to share the news with the rest of Cassels. Nothing like outing the phony.

Tantalizing smells waft in on the breeze through the open balcony door. My stomach growls in protest at missing the party. Laughter echoes up from the hut thingy. I feel like a child pouting and refusing to come down to eat. Which I guess I am.

Screw it. I'm not going to let them think I'm so easily affected. Besides, I need to find a phone and get hold of Ky for an update. I change into a fresh yellow sundress and pull my hair off to the side in a loose braid. After adding a touch of lip gloss and mascara, I take a deep breath and go downstairs, Havaianas smacking loudly on the tile floors.

I walk out of the villa and over to the large circular hut with a few picnic tables set up underneath. Hammocks strung around the sides alternate with swaying lanterns in the shapes of tropical fruit. A charcoal barbecue smolders and one of the picnic tables is covered in food. My mouth starts salivating. Everyone is already seated, laughing and eating. Chrissy looks up and nudges Kiki, whispering as I enter the hut. They're sitting with Travis and Steven, whose backs are to me.

God. Now I remember how it feels to be the new kid on her first day in the cafeteria — a total outsider. My gut spasms. *It's just the airplane food*, I reassure myself.

"Jess!" Harp waves as I'm about to turn and leave. She's sitting with Juan. Mr. A is at a third table with Hector and a dark-haired woman who must be Carlita, Hector's wife. I walk over to Harp.

"Hey," I say.

"That was a quick shower," she smiles, looking at my dry hair.

"My stomach got the best of me," I admit.

"Grab a plate." She senses my hesitation. "Then get your meat from Enrique." She nods in said Latin god's direction. He stands, still shirtless, by the swim-up bar area of the pool, reaching into a fridge. Pulling out a bottle of water, he unscrews the cap and takes a long drink. His throat, encircled by a puka shell necklace, moves up and down as he swallows. He finishes and wipes his mouth with the back of his hand, then looks directly at me.

Busted.

Cheeks flaming, I hurry over to the table and grab a plate.

"*Buenas tardes, señorita,*" he says, walking over to me.

"*Muy bien,*" I respond with the only Spanish phrase I know. I take French instead, so am somewhat lacking on the *Español* skills. I've always dreamed of going to France, the legacy of Geneviève, my French au pair, and have been hinting to my parents a trip would make a great grad gift. So far they aren't taking the bait, saying they want me around my last summer before I go to college. *If* I go to college.

Enrique laughs. "I haven't asked you that yet."

"Asked me what?" I say, picking up some cutlery.

"How are you?" His brown eyes take me in. "I said 'good afternoon.'"

"Oh." I flush. Dora and Boots will only get me so far here.

"Do you want some chicken?" Enrique asks.

"Um, *sí?*"

He grins. My fingers feel clumsy as I help myself to some rice, beans and salad. Enrique escorts me over to the barbecue.

"What piece would you like?" he asks.

"That one." I point, not quite able to bring myself to say 'breast.'

He puts the meat on my plate. "Here you go…" He raises an inquisitive eyebrow.

"Jess."

"Nice to meet you, Jess." He says with a languorous smile.

"You too," I say. "Thanks for the chicken." *Thanks for the chicken? Scintillating, Jess.*

"*De nada.* See you around?"

"Um, sure." I return his smile, then walk by Travis's table. Chrissy and Kiki look like they want to hurl a chicken wing at my head. I sit beside Harp.

"It's called a *bohío*," Juan says.

"What is?" I ask.

"This." He gestures around us.

So 'hut thingy' isn't the official term. I look around and then up. And up. The thatched roof goes on forever, ending in a small wooden circle at the top. Fringes of dried palm trees lift and fall with the breeze. "It's really high." I crane my neck.

"So the heat can rise," says Juan.

"I might be spending a lot of time out here." Harp fans herself.

"Your rooms don't have AC either?" Juan asks.

Harp and I look at each other. "We never checked," she says.

"That's the first thing I did when we got here," Juan says, "before saving you wimps from a spider." He puts some hot sauce on his chicken.

"Which was greatly appreciated," Harp assures him. The two seem tight.

"So what's the plan?" I ask, taking a bite of food. After a restless sleep on the plane and getting a fake spider thrown in my face, I could use a nap.

"I think we're going up to the conservation center this afternoon. It's part of a little zoo in the town of El Valle." Juan spears his food. "In the middle of the volcano."

"El Valle is in a volcano?" My fork pauses in midair. Good-bye nap, hello imminent death.

"Don't worry, it's dormant," Harp reassures me. "I can't wait to see the frogs."

"I hope you handle them better than the spider," Juan says between mouthfuls.

"That won't be a problem." Her face glows. "They're so cute."

"Cute?" I'm skeptical.

"Most of the frogs found in the tropics aren't the big ugly toads you're thinking of," she says. "Lots are pretty small and amazing colors."

"And some are poisonous," Juan adds with unsuppressed glee.

"I was reading about that." I take a sip of water. "The golden frog has a neurotoxin, right?"

Harp and Juan exchange a look.

"Yeah, it's called zetekitoxin," Juan says, "after its binomial nomenclature, *atelopus zeteki.*"

"That's its Latin name?" I ask between bites.

Harp and Juan exchange another look. "You sure you're on this trip because you're failing?" Juan eyes me.

I swallow. Something about these two lowers my nerd shield. Out of habit, I default to ditz mode, eyes going wide. "Um, aren't you super worried about the whole poisonous thing?"

"The ones at the center might not be as toxic." Juan looks thoroughly disappointed.

"Why is that?" I ask, though I'd read about that too.

"The poison comes from all the bugs and insects they eat. When there's less variety in captivity, the strength of the toxin goes down."

"Isn't that a good thing?"

Juan's face disagrees.

"So what are you writing your report on?" Harp asks.

"The golden frog," I say.

"No, like, what aspect of it?"

"Um, not too sure," I admit. My distraction over Miles and Miami has kind of taken precedence over everything else.

"Does anything about it interest you?" she asks.

I start to say, "No, actually I find frogs kind of disgusting," then see their expectant faces. They're such big fans. I think for a second.

"Well," I begin, remembering what Wikipedia had to say about Panama's national animal and beloved icon, "the myths and stories are kinda interesting. The Panamanian people believe that if you find one it turns to gold and it's supposed to bring good luck."

"Probably another reason why it's almost extinct," Juan grumbles.

"Doesn't that kind of tie into your sociology interests?" Harp says. "Maybe Mr. A will let you do something like that."

"That's not a bad idea," I say slowly. Actually, it's something I totally would've geeked out over a few years ago. And something Berkeley's soc department would eat up. For the first time in years an unexpected spurt of academic-induced excitement shoots through my veins. Easy, Messy Jessie. "I'll ask him."

Carlita must have been waiting for me to finish eating because as soon as my fork rests on the plate, she announces dessert. Going to the fridge, she pulls out two bowls, placing them on the table. She goes back and takes out a tray of fresh cut fruit with watermelon, pineapple, bananas and melon. The boys jump up and walk over to the table. Harp and I follow, Chrissy and Kiki ending up behind us. Carlita stands behind the table with a ladle.

"It is *arroz con leche*," she says. She'd bestowed her hawkish eyes on her son.

"Looks like rice pudding," I hear Chrissy whisper.

"Exactly," Carlita says, apparently having ears like most mothers.

She scoops a portion onto each plate. In the smaller bowl are cinnamon sticks, which she jabs in each of our dishes. She ladles a huge portion in my bowl.

"*Gracias*," I say, "but that's too much."

"And you're too skinny," she informs me, discussion over. Meekly, I take the bowl and go sit back down. Mr. A stands up.

"I want to thank our hosts for a delicious meal," he says. A pineapple lantern swings gently above his head. Everyone claps. Harp sticks her fingers in her mouth and lets out an earsplitting whistle.

"Where did that come from?" I gawk at her.

"My brothers." She grins.

"But since we can't have them waiting on us every night, we're going to help them out," he adds. Perfect. Cooking is not one of my strong points. My repertoire includes toast, canned soup, and mac and cheese. And I've been known to burn all three. "Guys and girls will be assigned in pairs to make dinner during the week," Mr. A continues. "I'll do Friday and Hector and Carlita will do the weekend plus breakfasts and lunches when we're not up at the center. The pair that cooks the next day does dishes the night before."

He gets out some paper and a pen and writes our names on little slips. Enrique walks over with two cups and Mr. A dumps the names in. "Enrique has also kindly consented to have his name added so there's an even number of pairs." Mr. A holds the cup out to him. "Will you do the honors?"

"*Sí*." His smile goes off like a flash. Enrique ceremoniously pulls out a piece of paper from each bowl and hands them to Mr. A.

"Steven and Chrissy," Mr. A reads. They high five.

Enrique pulls out the next two names.

"Juan and Kiki," Mr. A says.

"Remind me to order takeout that night," Travis jokes.

That leaves me, Enrique, Travis and Harp. Enrique pulls out the next two pieces.

"Me." He grins. "And…"

Please, please, please…

Chapter Six

"Harp," Mr. A reads.

I sigh. Figures.

"Okay, people," Mr. A says, "let's meet back at the van in twenty. Bring your swimsuits."

I go grab my things, the food in my stomach triggering an exhausted stupor. Between the red-eye, the jet lag and the emotional roller coaster I've been riding these last few weeks, I feel like up is down and down is sideways.

We pile inside the van. Enrique pulls back the giant gate and sends us off to the crater of a volcano with a jaunty wave. The road twists and winds its way up the mountain like a drunken snake. I stare out the window, ignoring Travis who again is pressed up on my right side. I try to focus on the scenery, which is desert-ish at first. The farther up the mountain we go, the greener and lusher the landscape becomes. Copses of thin pine trees appear, interspersed with little houses along the valleys and hills. Kids play soccer, or football I guess, alarmingly close to the road, something you'd never see at home.

"So it looks like you and me are gonna be making beautiful food together, Princess," Travis whispers, interrupting my daydreaming.

"I don't cook," I inform him.

"Relax, I'm a genius in the kitchen."

"And so modest. How'd I get so lucky?" I shake my head. "I still can't believe you go to Cassels."

"And all it took was going to a foreign country for you to notice," he says, an odd tone in his voice, then sighs. "Look, can we start over?"

"You wish, Trav-ass."

"Hey," he protests, "I'm actually a pretty nice guy."

"Ha," I say loudly.

"What's so funny?" Kiki turns and glares at me.

"Nothing," I say. "Travis just told me a joke."

"Care to share it with the whole van?" Mr. A says.

"Sure." He grins, not missing a beat. "How can you tell if someone is a boy or girl?"

"How?" everyone but me asks.

"You look in their genes."

Groans ring out. My mouth curves up the tiniest fraction.

He elbows me. "Is that a smile?"

"I don't know what you're talking about," I say.

"That's all I wanted." He pats my leg. "Lighten up, Princess."

We reach the center of El Valle twenty minutes later, driving past numerous signs for lodging, restaurants and all kinds of activity tours. The town is tiny, but cute. Hector parks the car in front of a bustling open-air market. Rows and rows of colorful stalls sell everything from fruits and vegetables to Panamanian hats and traditional dresses.

"So when are we going to the center?" Juan asks as we get out of the van.

"Believe me, I'm as anxious as you to get there," Mr. A says, a fervent look in his eye, "but it's going to be crowded today. People from the city come up on weekends to escape the heat. I thought we'd get our bearings first." He hands out a few maps. "Let's meet back here in an hour. Behave yourselves and don't get lost. Everyone got a buddy?"

Nope.

I wander along the stalls, thinking. I can't believe I'd been oblivious to Travis's existence at school until this trip. I wonder why he never said anything to anyone at Cassels about Messy Jessie. Probably waiting for the right time to drop the news. Like at prom, along with a bucket of pig's blood on my head. I stop at one stand, absentmindedly picking up different souvenirs. A bracelet made of large turquoise beads catches my eye. Ky would love it. I should bring her back something for spying on Miles.

"*Cuánto cuesta?*" I ask the man at the stall. I'd snuck a look at Harp's guidebook and memorized the one phrase I knew I'd need: "How much is it?"

"You speak Spanish?" he asks, his weathered face open and friendly.

"No, but I want to learn." It is a pretty language. It might also come in handy for my report. And for talking to Enrique.

"*Cinco dólares,*" he says.

I count on my fingers. *Uno, dos, tres, cuatro, cinco.* I hold up five fingers.
He grins and nods. Pleased with myself, I pull out a five from my wallet.
"*Gracias,*" the man says, pocketing the money.
"*De nada.*"
"*Tu español es bueno,*" he says, his eyes twinkling. Good Spanish?
It's my turn now. "*Gracias.*"
"*De nada.*" He laughs. I just had a conversation in Spanish! Granted it
only consisted of about five words. But still. I give the man a little wave,
moving through the stalls. Figuring they might come in handy, I buy a
brightly colored pen and bound notebook from another vendor, then stop
at one selling bags with gorgeous prints.
"They're called *molas.*"
I look up. Harp stands in front of me, holding one up.
"Are you getting one?" I examine the intricate hand stitched patterns.
"I want to get something traditional. These are made by the Kuna wom-
en."
"Who are they?"
"One of Panama's indigenous peoples," Juan says, coming out from be-
hind Harp. A squat lady in a long skirt and blouse, with the same bright pat-
terns as on the bags, steps forward. She wears a red head scarf and large
gold hoops impale her ears and nose.
"You like?" she asks, her smile beguiling.
"Yes," Harp says. "*Muy bonito.*"
"Twenty-five," she says.
"Should I get it?" Harp asks, unsure.
"Do you love it?" If anything makes me feel better, it's shopping.
"It's nice." She traces the geometric shapes.
"It doesn't sound like you're in love with it. Why don't you keep look-
ing?"
She puts the bag down. "Okay."
Juan rolls his eyes. "Women. I'm going to the next stand."
Harp and I browse through more bags. "What colors do you like?" I ask.
"Blue's my favorite."
"What about this one?" I hold up a design stitched on a blue background
with threads of green and yellow woven through. Two colorful birds kiss.
"I love it," she declares.
The lady steps forward with a charming wink. "You buy two, only for-
ty."
Harp looks at me and smiles. "Do you want one?"
My grin mirrors hers. "I can never say 'no' to a sale." Finding one with a
big pink butterfly stitched on a purple background, I examine it more close-
ly. Red and pink flowers entwine with green leaves and in the corner is a

tiny golden frog.

"I'll take this one," I say. We hand over our money and the lady pockets it, thanking us.

Juan wanders back over. "It's nice to see the craftspeople receiving their money directly."

"That's what I call fair trade," Harp agrees. I look at them, so different from my own friends who I'm pretty sure think 'Fair Trade' is a brand name.

"What time is it?" Juan asks Harp.

She looks at her watch, alarmed. "Shoot, we're late."

We hurry back to the van, where everyone's waiting.

"Look who finally decided to show up." Chrissy smears herself with sun-block.

"Sorry," Harp says. "We were having a retail experience." She winks at me and the pressure in my chest, there since leaving Seattle, eases a little.

"Okay, guys," Mr. A announces, "I'm taking you to see El Chorro Macho."

"Sweet, I was just thinking I could use some dessert." Travis puffs out his belly and rubs it, Buddha-like.

"Not *churro, chorro*. It's a waterfall," says Mr. A. We get in the van and Hector drives us to the waterfall, about five minutes away, up a dirt road.

"Cool, there's zip lining," Travis says as he and Steven jump out of the van.

"Your parents didn't sign waivers for those!" Mr. A calls after them.

"Aw, come on, Mr. A." Steven shoves his hands in his pockets. "I've been before. It's safe."

"Not the point, Steven," Mr. A says sternly. "That's not why we're here today."

"Today." Travis nudges Steven with his elbow.

Mr. A pays our fares and we walk down a short trail to the waterfall. Wooden slats bridge small streams and then a bigger brook. Huge boulders and fallen, moss-covered trees crisscross the creek. The water trickles and bubbles its way down over the rocks. Birds sing and the peaceful sounds of the forest soothe me. The water gets louder as we approach the falls. It flows over a rock face wall, breaking off into different paths, creating little streams through the forest floor.

"This is an example of the golden frogs' ideal habitat." Mr. A looks out at the waterfall. "You used to find them here by the hundreds." He keeps walking, mournful eyes combing the wet rocks as if to conjure one out of thin air.

"I bet it just gushes in the rainy season," Harp says, coming up beside me to take a picture. We stand on a rickety bridge facing the falls.

"So it's the dry season now?"

"You can't really tell up here, it's so green, but if you look around outside our compound you can see how dry it is."

"Didn't you smell the smoke on our way up?" Travis saunters up to us.

"Not really," I say.

"There was a small fire down the road."

"Like a forest fire?" Harp asks.

"Nah, just a little brush fire. Hector says they get tons of them every season."

"That's a little disturbing," I say.

"Hey, can I take a picture of you guys?" Harp holds up her camera.

"Sure," Travis says.

Ugh.

We face her, our backs toward the waterfall. Travis puts his arm around me like we're old friends. It's warm and wraps firmly around my sticky shoulders.

Harp takes the photo and looks at it. "How about a smile, Jess?"

I envision tossing Travis over the bridge.

"That's better." She snaps a few more. "Thanks, guys."

I'm not sure if it's my imagination or if Travis lets his arm linger for a second before taking it away. Weird.

"You guys ready for a dip?" Mr. A hollers from the other side of the bridge.

I definitely need to clear my head.

"How are we supposed to get to the waterfall?" Chrissy asks.

"We're not going swimming in the actual falls," Mr. A says. "I'm taking you somewhere Lo — my, uh, friend showed me last time I was here."

We walk back the way we came, out the entrance and onto the main dirt road. Mr. A turns into the forest and we follow him down another trail, over one more wobbly bridge and down several stone steps. We walk out to a rectangular-shaped natural pool surrounded by stones. It looks like it's been carved from the rocks. The water is a clear green color.

"It's a freshwater pool fed by the waterfall," Mr. A says.

"How deep is it?" Harp asks, an edge to her voice.

"Only one way to find out," Travis says. He tears off his shirt, revealing surprisingly sculpted pecs for a lab geek, and cannonballs in. Steven and Juan follow him.

"It feels awesome," Travis says, coming up. Chrissy and Kiki peel off their clothes and join the boys in the water. Chrissy's modest yellow-and-orange tankini and Kiki's blue one-piece also show off decent bods for supposed science nerds. Mr. A gets in the water next, his freckles prominent against his skin. There's something jarring about seeing your teacher half-naked. He's pretty white. I hope he's wearing a high SPF.

"Come on, Princess," Travis calls.

"I'm coming," I snap. My bikini was bought with Miami in mind and is a tad revealing compared to what the other girls are wearing. I hear my mother's voice. She was with me when I bought the suit. Or rather, she'd convinced me to get it, then paid for it, saying, "Jess, honey, if you got it, flaunt it, because it doesn't last forever."

I consider going in my clothes, but don't particularly feel like doing the forty minute drive home sopping wet. I take a breath, quickly shed my jean shorts and yank my tank over my head. Walking down the slippery stone steps leading into the pool, I ignore the snickers coming from Chrissy and Kiki's direction. The silver sequined bikini feels see-through as I wade into the icy water. My feet carefully pick their way over the rocky bottom, and I slide in quickly up to my chest, feeling the salt and sweat rinse away from my body.

It feels incredible.

Forgetting about my stripper swimsuit, I doggy-paddle until my feet no longer touch the stone bottom, then dive under. The water is dark, cool, invigorating. I swim to the other end of the pool, reach the stone ledge and grab on to it. To my right, water flows out of the pool and continues down around a waterwheel, dropping into the river below.

We splash around for a while until Mr. A tells us it's time to get going. Harp has stayed fully clothed in the shallow end, talking to Juan, and they get out, followed by Chrissy and Kiki, who towel off and put their clothes back on. Travis does one last backflip off the ledge. I'm reluctant to leave the fresh water.

One of the men from the zip-lining place comes down, gesturing in excited Spanish.

"What's he saying?" Steven asks, clambering out of the pool.

"He's asking if we want to come see something," Juan says, "but I'm not sure what."

Juan says something in Spanish. We catch the word 'sloth.' The man nods and points animatedly up the trail.

"Oh my God, I love sloths," Harp says, clapping her hands together.

"It's pretty rare to spot one." Mr. A grabs his camera. Everyone starts jabbering at once and scrambles up the trail after the pointing man, leaving Travis and me in the pool by ourselves.

"What just happened?" Travis laughs. He hops up on the ledge of the pool and sits there, hands in his lap, looking after everyone. Water drips from his hair onto his shoulders.

"I guess you conservationist types get excited by monkeys."

He grins. "A sloth isn't a monkey. They're in the same family as armadillos."

He'd always made me feel stupid. "How do you know that?"

Travis taps his brain. "Remember, I know everything."

"Do you know why you're such a jerk?" I dive under and swim back to the deep end of the pool. When I come up for air Travis is in the water, only a few feet from me.

"Don't you think that's a little harsh?" he says, treading water.

I grab on to the ledge with one hand. "Do you even remember tormenting me?"

"I just thought you were cute when you blushed." His arms move hypnotically back and forth under the water.

"Well, you certainly knew how to get that reaction," I say. Being around Travis reminds me of everything I used to be. A giant nerd. Someone who didn't fit in. Messy Jessie.

"I never meant to hurt your feelings," he says, his gaze intense.

"Yeah right." I look down at my hands. They're shriveling up like prunes.

Wait a second.

My ring is gone.

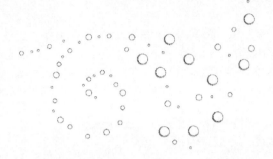

Chapter Seven

"Oh God," I panic. "No, no, no—"

"What's wrong?" Travis swims over.

"My ring." I peer down into the water. "It was my great-grandmother's!"

I dive under then realize I can't open my eyes because of my contacts. I come up sputtering for air. "I shouldn't have worn it," I say, wiping the water off my face. "It was too big." My heart breaks at the thought of losing Gigi's ring.

"Hey, don't worry." He grabs onto the ledge beside me. "I'll find it."

"No, you won't." A few tears fight their way loose, saltwater mixing with fresh. "We're in an effing pool."

"I can hold my breath a really long time," he says. "When did you have it last?"

"Just a few minutes ago." I'd felt it sliding around my finger. "It must have been when I swam over here to the deep end."

"I promise I'll find it." He gives me a reassuring pat on the back. "The pool's not that big."

"Forget it," I say, miserable. This was just the kind of day — make that month — I've been having.

"If I find it what will you give me?" He looks at me intently. A bead of water trails along his jawline, reaching the tiny cleft in his chin, and falls into the water.

"Whatever you want," I say. "I can pay you."

"I don't want your money." He gives me an offended look, one hand brushing wet hair out of his face. "How about a chance to prove I'm not as big a jerk as you seem to think I am?"

"Anything." I wipe my ringless hand on my face.

"You promise?"

"Yes." I'm devastated. Travis inhales deeply and dives down. A few minutes later, he surfaces.

"Anything?" I ask, tentative.

He shakes his head and dives down again. And again.

Gigi was the one who wanted me to go to Berkeley. She was one of its first women alumni. I still remember her proclamation on my tenth birthday. "You're smart, Jessica. You're going to change the world one day." And now her ring is as out of reach as college.

"We should probably get going," I say the next time his head breaks the water, morose. "Everyone will be wondering where we are. It's pointless."

Not answering, he dives down again. He's gone so long, I lean forward looking for him, worried. He flies up out of the water and takes a huge gulp of air, splashing his way over to where I'm still gripping the ledge. He looks at me, jade eyes the same color as the pool. Water droplets form on the tip of his eyelashes.

"Your ring, Princess." He opens his hand and my opals sparkle in his palm.

"Oh my God, are you kidding me?" Another tear falls. This time it's one of joy. "I can't believe you found it! It's a freaking miracle!" Elated, I jam the ring on my finger and tighten my fist so it can't come off.

"So you'll keep your promise?"

I don't even remember what I've promised. "What do you want?" I look at him, adrenaline pumping through my body.

"I told you, a chance to prove I'm not a jerk." He puts his hands on the ledge and heaves himself out of the water. It runs down his muscular back.

"How are you going to do that?"

He turns and sits on the stones, looking down at me. "Maybe we can spend a little time together."

Shielding my eyes from the sun, I look up at him. "Like on a date?" I'm wary.

He shrugs. "Whatever you want to call it. Three of them." He grins. "One for each stone."

I hoist myself up on the ledge beside him. "Why do you care what I think?" My legs move in the water.

A bird trills in the distance. "What can I say?" he finally says. "Maybe I feel bad for teasing you all those years ago."

I bite my lower lip. He did find my ring. But the last thing I need is to spend more time with Travis. And what would Miles say? I glance down at my reflection in the water. A mousy little girl with dishwater hair and enormous glasses stares back at me. Something Gigi used to say floats to the surface of my temporal lobe. *Always keep your word, Jessica.*

I let out a long sigh. "Can I at least think about it?"

"Sure thing, Princess." He hops off the ledge into the pool and back-strokes to the other end, getting out at as I reach my bag. I put my ring immediately into a secure pocket then grab my towel. Travis grabs his and we dry off to the sounds of the rain forest surrounding us.

"Travis." I finally look at him as he throws on his T-shirt. "Thank you for finding my ring."

"My pleasure." He takes a step toward me, his face intent. "Look, Jess … I…"

"Travis! Jess!" We hear Mr. A call our names.

"Coming!" we yell at the same time, our eyes meeting. He smiles.

"What?" I say.

"You might want to fix your makeup."

Grabbing a compact from my bag, I groan. I look like a homicidal raccoon.

After I give my face a quick wipe, we gather our things. Travis follows me over the bridge and I keep my eyes on the trail before me. We catch up with the rest of the group as they get into the van. They're still buzzing about the sloth.

"It looked like a mini Chewbacca, man," Steven's saying to Travis in the back seat. "I can't believe you missed it." Travis murmurs something in response.

"Maybe they'll have one at the zoo tomorrow," Kiki says. "I can go with you to see it."

Their voices hum around me as I think about Travis's proposal, arms wrapped around my bag, envisioning the ring safe inside. *What are you getting yourself into?* I barely speak a word the entire drive home.

***

After dinner, the others beg Mr. A to let them go down to the beach. I'm doing my best to keep from passing out in my paella.

"It's only eight o'clock," Kiki complains.

"Trust me, you guys have another full day ahead of you," Mr. A says amidst protests ringing out in the *bohío*.

"Can we just go for a bit?" Steven asks.

"Please!" everyone begs.

"Fine," Mr. A relents, "but nine o'clock curfew." He points to his watch. "And everyone better be in their houses or they're on the first plane back home."

"Is that a promise?" I murmur under my breath.

"What should we do with our dishes?" Harp asks.

"Don't worry," Carlita says. She motions toward Mr. A and Hector. "The men can do them tonight." They exchange pained looks as everyone takes off for the gate before the adults change their minds. I get up from the table, not sure if my presence will be welcome but unable to resist the lure of the ocean. The cool spray of salty air always relaxes me, and right now I could definitely use some de-stressing. I still have no idea what I'm going to do about the whole Travis situation.

"Wait," Hector yells after us. We freeze.

"You will need those." He points at a shelf in the *bohío*. Travis and Steven sprint over and grab two hanging flashlights, then race back.

"Lead the way, boys," Kiki says, twirling a long strand of hair around her finger and looking at Travis. Everyone chatters as they walk out the gate and down the path leading to the sea. I follow behind, hearing the waves clearly as we clamber down a rocky trail, reaching the ocean in only a few minutes. I inhale sharply.

The moon's bright enough to illuminate the beach, which is absolutely stunning. Diamond-black sand shimmers under our feet, sparkling like a billion tiny jewels. Azure blues and emerald greens saturate the shore, flashing and reflecting the moonlight.

"The beach must be made from volcanic ash," Juan says. Travis shines his flashlight down the length of it. Pockets of white sand swirl with the black, all of it smooth, packed down by pounding waves.

"I think the tide's going out," Juan says.

"Anyone feel like swimming?" Travis asks, looking directly at me. I look away. I still haven't decided what I'm going to do and don't want to give him an opportunity to ask.

"We don't have our bathing suits," Harp points out.

"So?" He yanks his white tee over his head.

"Easy for you to say," Chrissy says. "You can just go in your shorts."

"Well, I'm going in." Travis tosses his shirt on the sand.

"Me too," says Steven, doing the same.

They run toward the water, yelling and whooping like a couple of eight-year-olds. The rest of us follow them down. The top layer of sand crunches softly under my feet as the weight of my body breaks through the crusty upper layer. All of us wade into the sea, except Harp. Again, the water is deliciously icy after the smothering heat of the day.

"Look at the phosphorescence!" Juan points down.

I look at the water and move my foot in a slow arc. Tiny sparks shoot off all around it like fireworks.

"Harp, come check this out," I call.

"No thanks," she says, crossing her arms. "I can't swim."

"I'm not swimming. I'm standing."

"What if a wave knocks me over?" Her voice is tremulous.

"Here." I wade back to the shore. "Hold on to my arm. We won't go far."

She's silent for a minute.

"C'mon," Juan says.

"Alright." She looks at him and takes a deep breath, clutching my arm. We wade slowly over to Juan who's running his hands quickly through the water, sparks igniting everywhere.

"What causes it?" I ask.

"Microorganisms," he says.

"It's so pretty," Harp says, her grip on my arm relaxing the barest fraction.

"Look up," Juan says.

Thousands of stars shine above our heads, competing with the phosphorescence in the sparkle department.

"There's Orion," I point.

"Where's the Big Dipper?" Harp asks, scanning the sky.

"Over there," I say. "It's kinda upside down." I notice it's gotten quiet and glance over to see Travis and Steven advancing, feigned innocence across their faces. Chrissy and Kiki, engrossed in their own private conversation, spot them at the same time.

"Don't splash us!" Chrissy squeals.

Too late. They crash down, arms scooping up water, drenching us in a flurry of spray. The girls scream and splash back. Juan dives under the water. My arm feels strangely detached from my body — Harp's squeezing it so tightly I'm losing circulation.

"Stop it!" I yell. "You're freaking Harp out!" I lead her back to dry land. She grabs an inhaler from her pocket and jams it in her mouth, breathing deeply.

The splashing dies down. "Sorry, Harp," Travis calls.

"We should be getting back anyway," I say, ignoring the crescents her fingernails leave in my arm.

"Thanks." She gulps, pocketing her inhaler. We walk back along the beach as the others make their way out of the water behind us. The air is still warm and my legs dry quickly.

"Look at the cliffs." I try to distract her. The stars illuminate tall, jagged walls of rock surrounding us on all sides, forming a cove around the beach. "I bet pirates used to roam these waters, burying their treasure here."

"I didn't realize you have such a good imagination." Travis comes up behind us and I automatically tense.

"Right now I'm imagining you buried up to your neck and left for high tide." I scowl at him. "You almost gave Harp a heart attack."

"I'm fine," Harp says, breathing in through her nose.

"I said I was sorry." He looks at Harp, a chastised expression on his face.

"Don't be such a jerk," I say, "then you won't have to say you're sorry all the time."

"Did you guys used to date?" Harp asks as we walk up the trail to the villas.

"No, why?" I look at her, aghast. "Is that what people are saying?"

"No, you just seem like you're…" She pauses. "…comfortable around each other."

"Nah, I just used to tease her once in a while." Travis gently tugs the end of my braid. "Kind of like a big brother."

"Well, I don't have a brother, but they can't be this annoying," I say.

"I have two," Harp says, "and they are."

We reach the compound and go through the door beside the gate. Mr. A stands by the pool, waiting.

"You're five minutes late," he says, not looking all that concerned.

"We're on island time," Travis says. The rest of the group catches up and Mr. A does a quick head count.

"Technically, that's isthmus time." Mr. A chuckles to himself. "'Night, girls. Boys, in the villa ASAP." Everyone says their good nights and goes inside.

The fan in our room has cooled it down and I open the balcony doors to let in the fragrant night air. Chrissy and Kiki wash up first, hogging the bathroom, chatting as they brush their teeth. Harp and I wait until they are done. I let her go before me but she's only in there a few minutes.

"That was fast," I say when she comes out.

"Like I said, two older brothers. They used to flush the toilet when I stayed in the shower too long."

"Oh, the joy of being an only child," I say. I quickly brush my teeth, floss and wash my face. Exhausted, I peel the contacts from my eyeballs, which are gritty and dry after a long day of travel and tears. Did we only just get here this morning? Back in the bedroom I change into a tank and boxers, then get into bed. Harp is reading, the little lamp on her bedside table turned on.

"Does the light bother you?" she asks.

"Not at all." I yawn, exhausted. The light shuts off a few minutes later.

"Thanks," Harp says in the dark. "That was my first time in the ocean."

My bleary eyes open. "Ever?"

"Ever."

Rolling over on my side, I pull thin blue blankets up around my shoulders. "Thanks for your idea about my project. About the myths and stuff. It's a good one."

"I hope it works out," she says.

"Me too." I feel for my ring in the moonlight, now on a silver chain around my neck, and think of Gigi. Berkeley had once been everything to me. But after fighting so hard to get where I am, do I really want to start all over again and leave behind my friends, leave behind Miles? Thoughts whirl around in my head like the fan above. I wonder again what Miles would think about Travis's proposition. He'd probably laugh. I'm relieved Travis didn't press me for my answer tonight. With any luck he'd just forget about it.

Harp's breathing becomes more regular and I smile. She does snore. Here's hoping the sleepwalking doesn't make an appearance. I toss and turn, restless despite my fatigue. Unable to drift off, I get up and walk out onto the balcony. The light's still on in one of the boy's rooms across the way. Feeling like a stalker, I turn and look out at the ocean. The silvery water glints in the moonlight.

"Psst. Jess." A whisper from below interrupts my brooding and I jump. What the—? I peer down at the dark ground. Travis's outline is illuminated by the stars.

"What are you doing?" I whisper. But I know. So much for him forgetting.

"I saw you out here spying on us, so I figured you must have your answer." He looks up at me with an impish grin.

I give a quick glance back at Harp. "Look, I don't think the dates are a good idea."

"Why's that?"

"I'm seeing someone." As if he doesn't know who Miles is.

"Don't think of them as dates then, just two old friends hanging out. You're allowed to have friends, right?" He leans against the tree. "I'll even help with that report I heard you talking to Harp about, to sweeten the deal."

"I don't need your help." I sniff, disdainful.

"Aren't you failing biology?"

I wince. "That's not my fault. Well, it is, but, not because I need 'help.'"

"Okay then." He grins, his teeth white in the dark. "I guess you wanna be known as someone who doesn't keep her promises."

Thinking of Gigi, I feel myself wavering. "What will these non-dates be like?"

"A surprise, at my time and place of choosing." Moonlight reflects off his face, giving it an innocent glow.

I don't need to be getting tangled up with these people. I just need to get through this week and back to my life. Travis senses my hesitation.

"Come on, Princess, I'm not that jerk kid I used to be. People change, you know." He gives me a meaningful look.

Yes, I do know. I stare at him, the ring heavy around my neck.

"Fine." I swallow. "Three non-dates."

He grins up at me. "Great, first one's tomorrow, after we finish up at the center." Turning, he heads toward his villa, then looks back over his shoulder. "You won't regret it," he calls softly.

He slips silently back into the house, giving me a little wave before shutting the door behind him. Looking back out at the silvery ocean, I watch the waves crash in.

I'm not so sure.

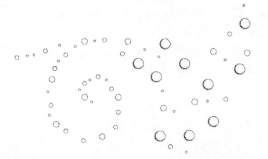 Chapter

Eight

I t's my turn to cook. I pull chrome lids off silver buffet trays. Hundreds of frogs jump from the steam. Everyone starts screaming and a golden frog lands on Travis's head, chirruping at me. The chirruping gets louder as other voices join the discordant symphony.

I sit up quickly, my heart beating fast.

I relax as I realize it's the cheeping of birds, not frogs. Hands go to my face and I groan. Do I really have a non-date with Travis today? I look over at Harp. She's still sleeping. Quietly, I get out of bed. Too tired to shower last night, I sneak into the bathroom for a quick rinse. Shampooing my hair, I sigh. So much for not getting tangled up. Wrapping a towel around my body and hair, I go back to the bedroom to get dressed. Harp is awake.

"Nice turban," she says sleepily. "Anyone in the shower?"

"All yours."

"Thanks." She yawns, gets out of bed and heads for the bathroom.

I throw on dark denim cutoffs and a tangerine shirt. I need to find a phone and call Ky, ASAP. I haven't communicated with anyone in over twenty-four hours and want to hear exactly what's been going down in Florida. I also want to ask Mr. A about my research paper. Now that I'm officially stuck on this trip, I suppose I may as well give this whole save-the -biology-grade thing a shot. I walk out of our villa into warm, fragrant air, up to the boys' door, and knock.

Travis answers. His hair is messy from sleep and falls in front of foggy eyes. He's wearing *Angry Birds* boxers and a blue T-shirt. "That eager to start our non-dates, huh?"

I roll my eyes. "Is Mr. A here?"

"Try the *bohío*." He yawns, one of his large hands pushing the hair out of his eyes. How can guys look so good after rolling out of bed, when it takes me twenty minutes in front of a mirror? Minimum. Turning around, I head toward the large hut. "You could've given me a little more warning," he calls behind me. "These aren't my nicest underwear."

I'm happy he can't see the corners of my mouth lift.

Mr. A is sitting and drinking coffee with Hector and Carlita. There's an enormous array of food on the table.

"I was just going to ring the bell for breakfast," Carlita says, getting up.I smile at her. "Hey, Mr. A," I say.

"Hi Jess, you're ready bright and early." He sips from a chipped blue mug.

"Can I ask you something?" I take a breath, unexpectedly nervous.

"Sure, what's up?" He gives me an encouraging smile.

"About my project. Does it have to be a typical science report on the golden frog? Like, you know, what it eats, its habitat and all that?"

"Well, it should be mostly scientific," he says. "It's for biology class."

"I know, but I was wondering if I could maybe weave some other stuff in there as well."

"Like what?"

"Like some of the myths about the frog and its cultural significance and stuff."

He thinks for a second, taking another sip of coffee. "Just make sure you cover the biology," he says. "The other stuff should just be the icing on the cake."

"Cool. Thanks." For the first time I feel optimistic about actually being able to pull this off. With the exception of bio, I got straight A's. Of course, nobody knows that but my teachers and parents.

"No problem. Help yourself to some huevos rancheros." He gestures at the buffet.

"Sure." I walk over and serve myself, then sit down at a table as everyone else wanders in, lining up for food. Shoot, I forgot to ask about the phone. I get up from the bench.

"Oink, oink. Looks like someone was hungry," I hear Chrissy say.

"I thought we might see a pig today at the zoo but I didn't know there'd be one at breakfast," Kiki adds and Chrissy shrieks with laughter.

I freeze. I want to defend myself but can't think of anything to say. What's wrong with me? My crew would normally eat these girls for, well, breakfast. I sit back down. Mr. A's talking to Hector and doesn't hear.

"And I didn't know there'd be any hyenas here," Juan says.

I look up. He stands behind the girls, casually spooning fresh fruit onto his plate.

"Why are you defending her?" Chrissy challenges him. "Do you like her or something?"

"I don't even know her," he says, "and neither do you."

"I don't have to," she says. "I know exactly what she's like. Her and all her friends who think they're so much better than us."

"Hey, guys, can I just get some breakfast?" Travis complains from the end of the line. "It's a little early for all this drama."

"Yeah, guys," Harp adds, "haven't you heard the early bird gets the worm?"

Chrissy and Kiki ignore her and sit at their table from yesterday. Juan comes and sits at my table. Harp follows him. Steven goes and sits with the girls. Travis serves himself last. There's space left at both tables. It looks like he's heading for ours when Kiki scoots over to make room for him.

"There's a spot here, Travis," she calls, flipping her hair back.

He hesitates, then turns toward her. "Cool," he says, sitting down. Whatever.

"Thanks," I say to Juan after a few minutes.

He stuffs some eggs in his mouth with his fork. After chewing, he takes a drink of orange juice and sets it down. He picks up his knife and fork again. "People used to call me 'Little Juan', you know, like 'Little One' because I'm so short." He takes another bite and swallows. "It was annoying, you know?"

"I know."

"Really?" Harp arches a thick brow. "And how would you know that?"

I glance over at the other table. I don't mention Messy Jessie. "Travis calls me Princess."

"That's not that bad." Harp rolls her big brown eyes. "At least people don't call you 'Curry Breath' and avoid sitting beside you because they say you stink."

"I guess everyone has their own stuff." I shift in my chair. I hope none of my friends ever said that to her. I may be a bit of a shallow fake, but at least I'm never intentionally cruel to anyone.

"It's just high school bullshit," Juan says, looking at her. "Wait 'til we get to college."

"Did you ask Mr. A about your report?" Harp changes the subject.

"Yeah," I say, taking a bite of watermelon. "He said it's fine as long as I have the science facts in there."

"Cool. So how are you going to do your research?" she asks.

"Well, lots of sociologists use qualitative research, which is like interviews and pictures and stuff." They look interested so I continue.

"And regular science uses mostly quantitative research, which is like numerical data and facts. Both have pros and cons."

Harp takes a drink of orange juice. "So you're going to interview Pana-manians?"

"I guess so," I say, then remember something. "Except I don't speak Spanish."

"I can help translate if you want," Juan offers.

"Are you sure?" I smile at him. "That's really nice of you."

"You can always start with Hector and Carlita. Their English is really good," Harp says as Enrique walks into the *bohío*. He says hello to everyone as he grabs some breakfast. His eyes search me out, and I wave. Harp gives me a shrewd look. "I'm sure their son wouldn't mind either."

"Yes, it'd be great to have the younger generation's perspective," I say, all innocence. "From a purely scientific perspective, of course."

"Of course," Harp says, and we both giggle. Juan makes a gagging motion with his spoon.

"Hey, do you guys know where those phones are that we're supposed to be able to use?" I say. There are probably a million unanswered texts on my confiscated cell. Everyone probably thinks I'm dead or something.

"No idea," Harp says. "And I wonder if there's a computer where we can check our emails?"

"Mr. A," we call out together.

He turns around.

"Do we have a phone?" Harp says. "I need to call my parents before my dad has a heart attack. He's got high blood pressure."

"I emailed all your parents last night, but yes, you should give them a call yourselves." Mr. A looks at Hector.

"*Sí, sí.* I have a phone." Hector pulls it out of his pocket and puts it on the table. "It has already some minutes but if you are calling much long dis-tance you will need to buy another card."

"Great, thank you," Mr. A says.

Kiki jumps up from her table and races toward the phone.

But I'm closer. And I want that phone.

I hop up from the bench and sprint toward Mr. A and Hector, reaching them a split second before she does. My hand snatches up the cell. Hers closes tightly over mine, and nails dig in. Hard.

"Easy, girls," Mr. A says, sliding his coffee mug out of harm's way.

I am so not giving up the phone.

"I had it first," I say.

"So?" she challenges, tugging on it.

"Give it up, Kiki," Travis calls. "Jess beat you fair and square."

Surprised, I look up. Did Travis just stick up for me?

Pouting, she lets go and walks back to her table. "Whatever, it's like from 1998 anyway."

Triumph fades to dubiousness as I look down at the phone in my hands. It does look pretty prehistoric.

Hector tells us how to dial and writes down the number for us.

"What about internet?" Harp calls.

"There is wireless in the *bohío*," Hector says, "and we have a laptop you may use."

"One laptop and one phone for all of us?" I ask in disbelief.

"You'll just have to share. We'll get a sign-up sheet going," Mr. A says. "Besides, there'll be some free time to use it."

I perk up.

"Free time?" Steven asks.

"Right, listen up guys. This is the schedule," Mr. A says, clapping his hands. "Up at six thirty, in El Valle by eight thirty. Whoever's turn it is to cook that night gets their groceries later on in the afternoon, and everyone else has free time. You can go to the beach, relax by the pool, work on your tan…" He waves his hand.

This isn't sounding too terrible. Aside from the six thirty wake-up.

Mr. A looks at me. "Or on your report."

Right.

"Make sure you're ready to leave in half an hour." He adds, "Chrissy and Steven, you guys cook tomorrow night, so you're on dishes today."

"I thought it was just dinner," Steven complains, twisting his ball cap around on his head.

"Nope, breakfast too, but lunch you're on your own," Mr. A says, benevolent.

"What!" Chrissy says.

I stand up, phone in one hand, dish in the other, and walk over to their table.

"Happy washing." I set the plate down in front of her with a sweet smile. Then turn and walk out of the *bohío* with my prize.

Chapter Nine

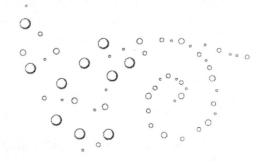

I sit down on a white plastic lounge chair by the pool. My stomach tightens as I dial Ky's number, chewing the nail on my left pinky.

No answer. I stare at the phone, spit out the piece of nail in my mouth
and dial Miles.

The phone rings.

No answer.

Juan walks by, huffing on and cleaning his glasses.

"Hey, Juan, what's the time difference between Panama and Florida?"
My chest feels tight.

"Don't think there is one." He slides the glasses back on his face, looking like an owl caught in a lightning storm.

Okay, so maybe it's a bit early. They both like to sleep in. Feeling des-
perate for some contact with the outside world, I try my parents next. Even
though I think it's like five in the morning there.

"Hello?" my mom answers groggily.

"Mom!"

"Jess! How are you? How was the flight? You were supposed to call last
night."

"I know, sorry, we just got the phone today."

"Alan," she says, "Jess is on the phone."

There's some static and fumbling as Dad picks up the other cordless.

"Jess? How you doing sweetheart?"

"Thank you guys so, so much for Gigi's ring. I love it."

"You weren't supposed to open that until your birthday next weekend,"

Mom chides.

"Sorry, couldn't help it."

"You like it?" She's unable to hide the pride in her voice.

"It's gorgeous." I neglect to mention I almost lost it.

"How's Panama and the report coming along?" Dad tries to sound casual. Though he'd been devastated to hear about my grade, I know he's pleased I'm on the trip. Guess he thinks it means I'm still considering Berkeley. Like Gigi, he's always had such high hopes for me.

"It's okay, I guess. Hot. Our place is pretty nice."

"See any frogs yet?" he asks.

Travis walks by with Kiki. She stares up at him, her hands moving animatedly.

"Just a couple toads," I say.

We chat for a few more minutes then say good-bye, and I promise to call them in a few days.

I try Alyssa this time, but again no answer.

Knowing Harp's waiting to call her mom and dad, I trudge over to our villa and up the narrow, winding stone steps to our bedroom.

"All yours." I hand her the phone.

"Thanks," she says. "Guess I should let my parents know I haven't drowned yet."

I manage a half-hearted smile, bummed about not getting ahold of any of my friends. I pack a small bag then go outside to wait by the van. It's early but the sun's already scorching. Enrique strolls toward me. Black-and-red board shorts sit low on his hips, skimming a tanned washboard stomach.

"*Buenos días,*" he says. Dark hair hangs around his face, dripping like he's just been for a swim. Why couldn't my non-dates be with him?

"*Buenos días,*" I say, feeling shy. "Are you coming with us to the center?"

"Not today," he says. "I have some work to do."

"Here?"

"*Sí,* I must make the grounds *bonito* for you." He gestures around us. "*Bonito?*"

"Beautiful," he says, staring at me. His eyes are more honey than chocolate this morning. They're framed by thick dark lashes most girls would kill for.

I realize I'm staring, and my cheeks redden.

"It's hot," I say, blaming the sun for my flush.

"*Sí,*" he says smiling. His teeth are blinding against butter toffee skin. "Don't worry, you will get used to it."

I'm not sure I will.

Voices ring out behind us as people walk up to the van.

"See you later, Jess." It sounds like a promise. He gives me a wink and strolls away, whistling.

"Everyone ready?" Mr. A asks once we're all assembled. "Today's the day we've all been waiting for. Let's go see some frogs!"

"You ready for our non-date this afternoon, Princess?" Travis whispers as everyone gets in the van.

"Can barely contain myself," I say, climbing in. "What exactly do you have in mind?"

"It's a surprise."

Yippee.

I notice Juan looking a bit green as we wind our way up the mountain-top.

"Are you okay?" I whisper to him. I'm sitting between him and Harp.

"I get car sick," he says, breathing heavily through his nostrils.

"So what did you do yesterday?"

"Gravol," he says. "Couldn't find it this morning."

"Well, if you're going to barf, would you mind aiming it out the window?"

"Do my best," he says, leaning forward, head in his hands.

We make it up to El Valle without me being sprayed by vomit, the only upside to the morning besides Enrique's abs, reaching the zoo after a few agonizing miles of bumpy potholed asphalt. Juan is beyond pale when he gets out of the van — especially considering he's half-Hispanic. I give him a supportive pat on the back and he manages a wan smile.

We pile out of the van and a striking woman walks toward us. Mr. A's positively vibrating, like a hummingbird that's been sipping on Red Bull.

"Kenny!" the woman cries as she reaches the dusty van.

Everyone looks at each other. *Kenny?*

"Lola," he breathes, sweat glistening on his forehead. Is it the heat or is he nervous? A cool breeze blows through the trees around us and I side with the latter.

"It's so good to see you." She embraces him tightly, kissing him on both cheeks. Turning, she faces the rest of us, holding Mr. A's hand. "Thank you so much for coming here." She tucks a silky strand behind her ear. "I am Lola, lead research associate. I help run things around here."

Dark hair hangs to her waist. Her face is a work of art: high cheekbones, sculpted nose, full lips and deep brown eyes speckled with Aztec gold. This woman spends her time helping slimy frogs? She looks like a contestant in a Miss Panama pageant.

"So, how do you guys know each other?" Chrissy asks. "Lola and I went to college together," Mr. A says, not taking his eyes off her.

"Kenny was just the sweetest thing," Lola confides. "I had trouble with my English and he tutored me every night so I could improve."

"Isn't that sweet," Kiki coos.

Mr. A actually blushes. "She was a natural."

"Obviously." There's a whisper in my ear as Travis appears beside me, a bemused look on his face.

We walk through the entrance under a wooden archway. The property is bordered by a fence made out of sticks and branches.

"Welcome to El Níspero Zoo." Lola gestures around her. The landscape is dazzling with hundreds of shades of green set against a dramatic backdrop of volcanic hills covered with trees. No animals are immediately visible. "We have several endemic species here," she continues. "Some of the cages aren't too big but we try to do our best for the animals."

"What's endemic again?" I whisper to Juan, who stands beside me, an ear-to-ear grin on his face.

"Native," he whispers back. I'm glad he's feeling better.

We follow her along an uneven path. Footsteps have worn down the grass, creating a gravelly trail over roots and stones that skirts several enclosures. The first few cages hold exotic birds, which I guess, being endemic, are not really exotic at all. We reach the end of the trail. A strong smell emanates from one of the larger enclosures.

"What is that?" Chrissy's hand goes to her nose.

"A tapir." Lola clucks lovingly to the massive mammalian beast. It looks like a giant mutant hog crossed with an anteater and smells about the same.

I fervently hope I will not have to clean out that cage.

We continue our tour and see more birds. Colorful toucans, parrots and peacocks that caw, whistle and strut. Rows of plants and flowers are everywhere, giving the impression that El Nispero is more elaborate garden paradise than zoo.

Lola reads my mind. "We have a plant nursery as well as a small zoo." She turns and smiles, holding Mr. A's gaze. "And, of course, there's the conservation center and our beautiful little frogs."

We reach the building housing the hallowed creatures. The center itself is almost anticlimactic after hearing how supposedly important the frogs are. Three sides are bare cement, resembling a bunker. Its only redeeming feature is a vibrant mural painted on the front, depicting the mountain forests of El Valle, waterfalls and several species of frogs frolicking in rivers and lounging on lily pads.

"It is so good of you to come to help us keep up the place," Lola repeats. "It is always nice to have an extra set of hands."

"Well, you have eighteen of them." Mr. A holds his up. "I mean eighteen hands, so nine sets," he corrects himself.

Lola giggles like it's the funniest thing she's ever heard, her laughter tinkling like bells in the wind. Travis rolls his eyes good-naturedly and winks at me. I hide a smile so he doesn't think it's for him. Because it's not. Mr. A is just hilarious right now. We follow them inside the center. It's clean and cool, the air tinged with bleach. I don't know what I expected but the habitats actually look decent, each terrarium resembling a mini rain forest.

"The center is sponsored by several zoos around the world, and our partnerships have allowed us to rescue many of our frogs," Lola says. "Most are critically endangered, and some, like the golden frog, are thought to be extinct in the wild."

"That's the step before an animal is extinct and gone forever," Harp says softly in my ear. Everyone's whispering, like we're in some sanctuary.

We walk around, looking at the different species. It hits me that I'm staring at some of the last survivors of their kind. They're not as disgusting as I imagined they'd be. Harp was right. Some are even kind of cute, coming in all colors of the rainbow. I read the different names. There are tiny florescent-green, neon-blue, and midnight-black poison dart frogs. Slightly bigger is a horned marsupial, lime green with eyes that bulge from the sides of his head, making him look wise and quizzical at the same time. Miniature red harlequin frogs, the size of a thumb, hop around, blissfully ignoring the giants looming over their pimped-out homes. Signs list every species as critically endangered, the primary cause being the chytrid fungus Juan mentioned. Other causes listed are habitat loss and pollution.

Lola walks up to where I'm standing by the harlequin frogs. "We've lost over two-thirds of this species," she says. "That is why we need places to keep and study the frogs that remain. There is still so much we don't know about them."

"How did the disease get so out of control?" I ask, looking at her.

"Some think that changing air and water temperatures caused by global warming allow the fungus to thrive and spread very quickly."

"There's no cure?"

"It is very hard to save a frog in the wild once it has chytrid." She rests her fingertips lightly on the glass. "Their skin is like their lungs, thin and extremely sensitive to even the smallest change in the environment, making it very susceptible to the fungus."

Juan walks up to us, holding a very small, very expensive looking camcorder.

"Where'd you get that?" I ask.

"Mr. A," he says. "The club is making a documentary to spread the word about the frogs. We're calling it *A Ribbeting Cause*." He zooms in on the glass. "I know you have your research paper, but do you want to help out?"

"Sure," I say, surprising myself.

"Cool," Juan says. "And if you need to borrow it to record stuff for your paper just let me know."

"Thanks," I say, touched by his generosity.

"That is wonderful," Lola says. "Most people don't realize how important frogs are to biodiversity. We are just now discovering their uses for medicines and cures for things like cancer and AIDS."

"And because they're not as cuddly as other endangered species, most people don't pay them any attention," Juan says.

"*Sí*," Lola says, "but luckily this one over here has become a symbol for the whole species." She walks up to the largest exhibit that dominates the entire middle of the room. We follow, about to get our first glimpse of Panama's golden frog.

Chapter

Ten

I nside the clear glass is a stream flowing down a rocky mountainside, with plants and little pools of water, a mini version of El Chorro Macho. I look to see what all the fuss is about, but there's not a golden frog in sight.

"This is as close to their natural habitat as we can get," Lola says. "We try to imitate the perfect conditions so they can not only survive, but breed, though we give them some help with that." She smiles. "Maybe one day we can reintroduce them back into the wild."

Everyone comes to stand around the exhibit, trying to spot the tiny frogs amidst the foliage. I catch a flash of gold under a large leaf.

"There's one!" I point, walking around to get a better look. Panama's revered icon appears fragile and small as it looks up at me and blinks. "I read that people collected them because they thought they were good luck," I say.

"Yes," Lola says, "the indigenous people of Panama believed they were holy. They would trek once a year to the slopes of our mountains to perform sacred rituals."

"Do you think this started the myth that the frog turns to gold when it dies?" I ask, thinking of my report. Juan's filming our conversation.

"Perhaps. People also believe you will be blessed with good fortune if you have the opportunity to see the Panamanian golden frog alive." She looks over the group, her eyes finding Mr. A "So now you are all blessed with good fortune. Unfortunately, all these things likely contributed to their disappearance from the streams of our rain forests."

"To quote a wise Muppet, it's not easy being green." Travis walks over to us. "Or gold, I guess."

"Over collecting may have been the first threat to the frog, but chytrid is now the deadliest," Juan summarizes for the camcorder as he focuses in on the bright yellow-orange frog with black spots.

The somber mood is broken by Lola. "So why don't I explain what you'll be doing around here," she says, leading us back out into the sunlight. I blink against the brightness.

"The frogs, of course, are important, but there are many areas we could use assistance."

Mr. A clears his throat. "You guys will be on a rotation schedule, like dinner duty. There are three stations: one in the center with the frogs, another in the nursery looking after the plants and the third taking care of the animals."

"Are we picking names out of a bowl again?" I ask.

"You can just pick who you want to partner with. There'll be one group of three."

Obviously Kiki and Chrissy pair up, as do Travis and Steven. Harp and Juan come and stand on either side of me.

"Okay, let's get the Jess sandwich with Lola at the center today," Mr. A says. "Kiki and Chrissy follow me to the nursery, and then I'll take you boys over to make friends with the tapir."

"So are you like the foreman?" Steven asks.

"No, Lola is, I'm just your supervisor."

Juan, Harp and I stay with Lola, while the others follow Mr. A, who shoots a yearning look over his shoulder.

"Are you ready to jump right in?" Lola asks, holding his gaze.

Harp and Juan nod. Lola claps her hands together as if ending a trance, all business.

"First we need to do spot checks. Every day we visually inspect the frogs, clean their cages, and on some days we give them their vitamins."

We follow her into the center through a door leading behind the scenes. There are several metal sinks and sanitary stations with long counters. Everything's clean, well-lit and organized.

"Every few days all the greenery in the habitats is checked or replaced. Today I need help cutting up fresh greenery for the tanks. When you work in the nursery tomorrow, one of the things you will be doing is harvesting plants for the habitats." She smiles. "And lots of watering."

She leads us to a counter covered with an enormous pile of bamboo. "Remind me of your names again?" Her eyes examine our faces as we introduce ourselves. "Great. First, please cut the bamboo into smaller pieces. After that I'll show you how to clean the cages."

Just like that? We glance at each other. Juan looks like he's died and gone to frog heaven.

We spend the first few hours of the morning cutting up bamboo. It's tedious but talking to Juan and Harp helps distract me from thinking about my non-date with Travis later. Or that I haven't talked to my friends in almost forty-eight hours. Harp tells some hilarious stories about her brothers and Juan does great impressions. He's nailed Mr. A. Both are surprisingly funny. Lola comes to check on our progress.

"You are almost done!" she says. "This would've taken me all morning." She hands us each a pair of rubber gloves. "Now we are ready to clean some tanks."

"We won't hurt the frogs, will we?" I'm nervous. She's putting a lot of faith in a few teenagers handling species on the verge of extinction.

"I certainly hope not," she says. "You are here to help save them, no?"

Juan and Harp nod.

"Now, all you have to do is make sure they don't escape while you are cleaning out the poop."

Yuck.

"Sounds easy, right?" she asks. "Well, it is not. The frogs are very good at hiding and jumping."

We wash our hands and put on our gloves. Lola leads us to the first habitat.

"Watch me." She opens the tank, deftly checking the frog for any signs of fungus or injury while keeping it in the enclosure, and quickly wipes the cage down with a special solution and cloth.

"Now you try," she says to Juan and me.

"This isn't the poison dart frog's tank, is it?" I ask.

She laughs her tinkling laugh.

"Not your first day," she teases. "Maybe next time."

I look at Juan. "Why don't you do the honors while I make sure the little guy doesn't make a break for it."

Juan looks thrilled. He opens the cage to clean it while I stand there with my hands up to block, linebacker style. After a few minutes of grunting and wild maneuvering, Juan finishes up. Lola double-checks his work.

"*Perfecto*," she says to Juan. "You are an expert frog-poop cleaner."

Juan's chest puffs out like she just told him he was Master of the Universe.

"Can I try next?" Harp asks.

Lola purses pouty lips. "Yes, but maybe this is not the best use of resources. Why don't two clean cages and another can sweep and mop the floor?"

Sweeping and mopping sound fine to me. And hey, if I miss a spot, no frogs will die. Besides, I know how eager Harp and Juan are to work with the frogs. This is their Miami Beach.

"I'll mop," I volunteer.

"Wonderful! You can start back here. The center is closed to visitors today so you don't have to worry about tourists."

She sets me up with a broom, mop and bucket, then leaves me to clean the floors. I sigh. I'm sweeping while my friends are chilling on the beach, playing volleyball, meeting other people. I gulp. I wonder who Miles is meeting. And why I couldn't get ahold of anyone this morning.

I picture them laughing in their bathing suits. A busty redhead spills out of her bikini top as she rubs Hawaiian Tropic tanning oil all over Miles's back.

I look down at my own lack of boobage and swallow.

Mr. A walks in, interrupting my décolletage examination.

"Hey, Jess, how's it going?" He looks at me strangely, then around the room, anticipation all over his face.

"Good." I pretend to wipe a speck off my shirt. "Lola's in the back."

"What makes you think I'm looking for her?" he asks, crossing his arms over his blue checkered shirt.

"Aren't you?"

He clears his throat. "I just came to check up on you guys."

"Oh. Harp and Juan are cleaning out some cages."

Lola walks out. "I thought I heard your voice."

Mr. A's face lights up.

"How's everybody doing?" he asks.

"They've been great. Very helpful. Poor Jess here got stuck with the cleaning."

"I don't mind," I say. "Besides…" My voice trails off. Neither one is listening. They stare at each other, funny looks on their faces.

"I'm … just gonna go talk to Harp for a second…" I slowly back out of the room, broom in hand.

The second I'm behind the door, I put down the broom and go look for Juan and Harp.

I find them sitting on a bench. Juan is showing Harp some footage on the camera.

"Hey, guys," I whisper. "Lola and Mr. A are having a moment out there."

"Shut. Up." Harp's brown eyes go wide.

We run to the door and open it a crack. They stand there, holding each other, talking softly. Oh my.

"We should probably give them some privacy," Juan whispers, uninterested in the romance unfolding before our eyes.

"Ssshh!" we both say.

We can't make out what they're saying but it looks serious. Juan sneezes and Mr. A's head swivels toward us.

Chapter Eleven

W e quickly shut the door and race out the back entrance where supplies are brought in, laughing and out of breath.

"They're in love!" I say.

"It's so sweet." Harp sighs. "Mr. A deserves someone great."

"Too bad they don't live in the same country." I look at the green peaks surrounding us.

Distance is so not great for relationships. "True love kept apart because of a few frogs."

"Like you and that Miles guy?" Travis says. He has the worst habit of sneaking up on people. He walks over with Steve. Both look hot and sweaty and smell of tapir.

"Phew." Harp waves her hand in front of her face. "You guys are pungent."

"Who's Miles?" Juan adjusts his glasses.

"Jess's awesome boyfriend." Travis stretches his arms up and brings them behind his head to cradle it.

Not really, I almost say, but the words stick in my throat.

"Does he know about Enrique?" Kiki says, walking up with Chrissy.

Everyone seems to be finished with their chores for the day.

"Excuse me?" I ask.

"We've seen the way you look at him," Chrissy adds.

"I barely know him," I say. They look at him too. Any warm-blooded female would look at him. You can't help it. It's just nature.

"You practically drool." Kiki flips her hair over her shoulder.

"Kind of like when you look at Travis?" I snap back, losing it.

Kiki goes white. She shoots a mortified look at Travis and hurries off, mumbling something about forgetting her sunglasses in the nursery.

"You're a cow," Chrissy says, hurrying after Kiki. Everyone looks stunned.

There's an uncomfortable silence. "You didn't know?" I venture.

"Kiki and I used to date." Travis runs a hand through his hair, pulling out a piece of hay. "I didn't know she still has feelings."

Whoops. "I guess I should go apologize."

No one says anything.

Awkward.

I walk away from the group, heading in the direction I'd seen Kiki and Chrissy go.

Great. Just when I was starting to make friends with Juan and Harp and reach some kind of twisted truce with Travis, I go and screw it up.

I spot the girls sitting on a bench near the entrance of the zoo. Chrissy's arm is around Kiki's shoulders and their heads are down. Steeling myself, I walk up to them.

"Um, hey, Kiki."

Both of them look up at me. It feels like I'm facing a firing squad.

I take a deep breath. "Sorry for outing you to Travis."

"You humiliated me," she says, her cheeks tearstained.

"I'm sorry, but it's not like you've been all that nice to me either," I can't help saying.

"Why should we?" Chrissy sneers. "You and your friends think you're so hot, you treat us like crap every day back home."

"I don't think I've even talked to you before this week." I'm taken aback by her venom.

"Exactly. It's beneath you to acknowledge losers like us."

"That's not it at all—"

Kiki interrupts me, standing up, fists clenched at her sides. For a second I think she might hit me. Or pull my hair or whatever girls do when they fight. Not that I've ever been in one — though it appears that streak may be over.

"Then you get to come on this trip we worked so hard for." Her eyes are like scalpels. "Treating it like it's a punishment, like you're too good for it too."

"Just stay away from us." Chrissy stands up as well. "Go get bitten by a snake or something." They storm off and I realize I'm shaking a little.

They hate me.

I look up to see Mr. A leading everyone toward the van. Nobody looks at me.

Everyone hates me.

"Jess." Mr. A waves me over dreamily, still wrapped in his love cocoon. "It's time to go."

I walk to the van, staring at the pebbly ground. Part of me feels like Kiki brought that on herself. Then I think of the embarrassment that flashed across her face and a bigger part feels like a steaming pile of tapir dung.

Aside from Juan's dry heaving, it's a long and silent trip back to the compound.

***

After we get back, I decide to go for a swim to get away. I change into my suit and purple sarong, then head for the bright blue pool that curves like an 'S.' Spotting the laptop all alone on one of the picnic tables, I hurry over and sit down in front of it. Half the letter keys are worn off and it's covered in scratches and nicks. Still, it works, although I could send a postcard faster than it takes the internet to connect.

I log in to my email account.

My heart constricts. There's one from Miles. Finally.

I open it.

To: jessscotchsundae@casselsprep.com
From: milesfrommars@casselsprep.com
Hey Jess,
Hope you're having fun and the freaksters aren't boring you to death. Florida's awesome. I'm moving here after high school. Ky's cousin ended up getting fake IDs for everyone and the clubs down here are crazy insane. Anyways been doing a lot of thinking and not sure I want to get serious with anyone right before grad, you know? I kinda think the break thing was a good idea. I'm not sure what I'm doing and I think we should experience as much as we can while we're young, right? I still think you're an awesome girl and can't wait for you to see my sexy tan when you get back.
Later babes,
Miles

My heart is hammering. Well, that was pretty clear. He's found someone, then. I log on to Facebook, ignoring all my messages, heading straight for Miles's account. Pictures. So many pictures. Each takes an eternity to load. Him, Alyssa, Ky, Danny, Jason. Random girls. Girls in bikinis. Everyone lifting up red Solo cups. Feeling like I'm suffocating, I slam the laptop lid down.

On autopilot, I walk over to the pool, take off my sarong and dive in.

Surfacing, I wipe the water from my face, wade over to the swim up bar and take a seat. My elbows plunk down on the wet blue tile, head resting on fingertips, and I breathe in and out through my nose. So. It's officially over. After all that time invested. I don't know how to feel, what to think. Just numb.

"Would you like some pineapple?" A deep voice interrupts my dark thoughts. I peer under dried palm fronds. Enrique walks toward the bar in his trunks, holding a bowl. Doesn't he ever wear a shirt? He offers the fresh cut fruit, holding my gaze, eyes intense.

"*Gracias.*" I give him a weak smile and take a chunk. It somehow manages to get past the lump in my throat. "It's delicious."

He laughs. "Your face does not agree."

"No, really, it's very good." My eyes fill with tears and Enrique gets blurry.

His tone is gentle. "Panama wins awards for the sweetness of its pineapples." He puts the bowl down, his elbows on the bar, and leans forward. "Do you know how to tell if it is ripe?"

"No, how?" I offer another watery smile. *He's trying to distract me.*

He lowers his voice as if relaying a huge secret. "You pull one of the green leaves at the top. If it comes out easily, it is ready to eat."

"Oh?" I take another bite, this time really tasting it. It's juicy and sweet, better than any pineapple I've ever had.

"Why are you swimming all alone?" He looks around. "Where are your friends?"

Good question.

"I'm not sure," I say.

"So you are all by yourself?" He raises an eyebrow.

"Looks that way." I try to keep the pitying tone from my voice.

"Do you want to come surfing?"

Surprised, I look up from the blue tile of the bar. My first instinct is to say no. I'm not feeling up to much more than curling into the fetal position on my bed. Besides, something about Enrique makes me a little jumpy. It's probably because he's older and just so … hot. Miles would definitely not approve.

Something inside me crackles. Then again, his approval is no longer my concern.

"Sounds great," I hear myself say, "but I don't know how."

"It's easy," he says. "I can teach you."

I think for a half-second. I can interview him for my report. Then it'd technically be research. Not to mention going surfing will give me something to tell everyone back at home. Maybe I'll get Enrique to take some pictures and post a few of my own. Serve Miles right.

"Sure, let's go. Just let me grab something." Galvanized, I hop up from the stool and get out of the pool, tying my sarong around my neck. I dash up to my room and grab the pen and notebook I'd bought at the market and shove them in my new bag, nerves going berserk. The compound is silent. Everyone must have gone into town with Mr. A. There's no one to ask permission to go. Better to seek forgiveness than permission anyway.

Feeling reckless, I go back outside and walk up to Enrique who's waiting by a battered red Jeep, two surfboards strapped to the roof, the gate open. *Be cool, Jess.*

"Ready?" he says, one tanned forearm on the hood of the car, leaning back to offer me a full view of his swimmer's body. I don't think I've ever known anyone with an eight-pack before.

I nod. What am I doing?

"Then let's go, *bella.*" He holds out his hand to help me up into the car.

I take it.

Chapter

Twelve

W e speed down the dirt road out to the highway. Enrique turns on his music and Bob Marley croons from the speakers. I rack my mind for something interesting to say.

"How long have you been surfing?" I ask. Not fabulous, but not terrible either.

"All my life," he says. "It's the best. Nothing but you and your board in the ocean."

"Is it hard?" My hands fiddle with my sarong beads.

"Where we're going is good for beginners. The waves are small."

"Oh." For some reason, my acquired repartee skills seem defunct around Enrique.

"So you are in Panama to help your little friends?" he says.

"Harp and Juan?"

He laughs. "No, the frogs."

"Oh, right, yes." I clear my throat. "Actually, can I ask you a few questions about that?"

"You can ask me anything you want." He punctuates his words with a suggestive look.

I take the primitive recording materials from my bag, feeling a little foolish as I uncap my pen. "So, um, why are the frogs so important?"

"They are Panama's national symbol," he says. "You can find them everywhere — on our lottery tickets, our signs, but to tell you the truth, I am not sure how much the average Panamanian thinks about them."

"Yeah, that's kind of like back home," I say. "Everyone says how important something is and it gets all this attention in the media, but most people forget pretty fast."

"But there are people like you who work hard to make a difference, no?"

"Well, the people I'm here with do. I didn't really have a choice," I confess.

"You are here against your will?" His tone is teasing.

"Kind of."

"So you are my prisoner." He turns his head again and winks at me.

"Um, I guess so." I tame a piece of hair behind my ear that the wind has blown astray, glad that sunglasses hide my face.

We turn off the highway onto a dirt road and bump and bounce down to the beach. The sand here is pure ivory powder, and blue-green waves crest frothy white, like an aquamarine cappuccino. We park and Enrique gets out of the Jeep and hauls down the surfboards.

"Can you carry yours?" he asks.

"I think so," I say, not really sure how.

"Just pick it up and balance it on your head. Hold the sides."

He helps me hoist the board up and onto my head. It's heavy. My head sinks down on my neck and into my body. I'm positive I now resemble a turtle. He swings his board easily onto his head and we walk down to the water. The heat of the sand sears my feet.

"First we will have a little lesson on the beach." He puts his board on the sand then helps me, his arms coming up to take the weight off. He smells like pineapple.

"Most important thing: safety first. When you fall off the board, duck your head and cover it with your hands." He demonstrates, bulging tattooed arms coming up to encircle his head.

I nod, obedient.

"I've seen lots of people lose their front teeth and break their noses," he says.

I'm not sure that would be a good look for me.

"Look here." He points at his jawline where I can make out a long faint scar. "Twenty-two stitches." He looks into my eyes. "You don't want to damage that beautiful face."

He called me beautiful.

"Make sure your board is never sideways. The tip goes straight into the wave." He steps on its edge, all business. "And when you fall off, get your board back as fast as possible — you don't want to hit anyone else. *Entiendes?* Do you understand?"

"*Sí.*" I resist the urge to salute.

He holds up a long rope tied to my board. "This goes around your ankle." He lies down on the board. "Deep strokes to paddle, chest lifts up high and toes hang off the edge of the board." He demonstrates. "You try."

I lie down on my board and start paddling in the sand, feeling self-conscious.

"Chest more up."

I correct myself.

"Good. Let's practice pop-ups."

I look up, squinting against the bright sun behind him.

"You pop-up in one motion." He demonstrates, graceful as a jungle cat. "One leg in front. Never put your knees down first, just straight up. Try."

I try. It's harder than it looks.

"Again."

He makes me practice paddling and pop-ups for the next ten minutes. I'm exhausted and we haven't even hit the water yet.

"Tops of your feet must touch the back edge of the board," he says, "not just on top."

He makes me do a few more drills then finally pronounces me ready for the water.

"Grab your board," he says.

"What about yours?"

"First I will help you a few times."

I wade in up to my thighs then lay the board in the water and get on top. Enrique grabs one side of the board and walks me out deeper. I'm exceedingly aware that my scantily clad butt is mere inches from his face. He turns the board around.

"Okay, when I say 'paddle,' you must paddle very hard. I will tell you when to pop-up. There's a set coming now. Ready?"

I'm really not, but find myself nodding.

"Paddle!"

I paddle furiously. Enrique holds on to my board and pushes me with the wave.

"Harder! Chest up!"

I feel the wave swell underneath me.

"Pop-up!" he shouts and lets go of my board.

I pop-up … and promptly fall into the ocean, my surfboard flying out from underneath me. I stand up sputtering, coughing up salty sea water that burns my nostrils and the back of my throat.

"You need to cover your *cabeza*," he yells as he wades over.

"My bathing suit's too small!" I yell back, checking to make sure it's still there.

"No, your head." He points. "Your board was very close to slicing it open. Like this." He demonstrates again, ducking his head into his chest and covering it with both arms.

Oh. Right.

We try a few more times. Each attempt ends with me falling straight into the water.

"Okay," Enrique says, wiping water from his face, "this wave coming — it's your wave. Now focus."

I focus.

"Paddle!" he shouts.

I paddle.

"Pop-up!"

I pop-up and … don't fall over!

"Yeahhh!" Enrique yells behind me.

"Whoooo!" I scream, balancing precariously as I ride the wave all the way into shore, feeling like a rock star. I hop off the board when it gets too shallow to keep going.

"I did it!" I yell, turning to face him.

"Grab your board!" he yells.

Whoops.

I scramble to grab my board just as Enrique reaches me.

"*Fantástico*," he says, wrapping one arm around my shoulder, half-hugging me.

"I surfed!" I say, beyond proud of myself. Take that, Miles.

"You surfed," he agrees, looking down at me.

"Let's do it again!" I look at him. The sun illuminates the drops of water dripping down his broad shoulders. His dark wet hair curls slightly, white teeth gleaming in his tanned face.

"Okay," he agrees, laughing.

I'm hooked.

Chapter Thirteen

I smell dinner cooking as I hop out of Enrique's Jeep.

"Thanks for the lesson," I say, grabbing my bag and shutting the door.

"My pleasure, *bella.*" He winks.

"Well." I adjust my sarong. "I better get back before anyone realizes I snuck away."

"I'll sneak you away any time." His dark eyes watch my hands re-tie the purple fabric around my neck.

"Really? How about to the airport?" I say, half-joking.

"Where do you want to go?"

"Miami?" The word pops out of my mouth. It's only a three-hour flight. I'd checked.

"What's in Miami?" he asks.

Everything. My friends, my old life, my boyfriend — make that ex-boyfriend — all just slipping through my fingers like sand.

"Forget it," I say. "I'm just kidding." Surfing had temporarily distracted me but now my heart is heavy.

"Good." He smiles, eyes crinkling around the edges. "I'd hate to see you go."

Unsure of how to respond, I settle for an eloquent "Um, thanks." Giving him a quick wave, I speed walk back to my villa, keeping my head down, hoping no one noticed my disappearance.

"I thought we had a non-date," a voice says from the shadows beside the pool.

I jump, my hand flying to my chest. Travis sits on a chair, chin resting on folded hands, elbows on his knees, looking up at me. So much for escaping undetected.

"You scared the crap out of me!"

"Sorry." His green eyes look like the surf.

"I didn't think you'd still want to after … everything," I say, walking over.

"With Kiki?" He shrugs. "I can kinda see why you lost it."

"Does anyone else feel that way?" I gnaw on a fingernail.

"Not her and Chrissy, but maybe the others." He looks up, his expression indecipherable.

"Can we do it tomorrow instead?" I offer a tentative smile.

"Wouldn't want to force you to do anything you don't want to do, Princess."

"I said I would."

"Whatever." He lies back on the lounge chair, hands going behind his head, and looks up at the sky. I've been dismissed.

"Okay, see you at dinner." Disconcerted, I leave him lying by the pool and go up to my room. No one's around. I catch a glimpse of my shoulders in the bathroom mirror as I get in the shower to rinse off. They're a bit pink, probably from being on the water in prime sun time.

I scrub the salt from my skin. Surfing had been a distraction but the lump in my stomach is still there. If anything, it's bigger. Probing it internally, I try to figure out what the main cause is. Could it be door number one: things are a mess with Miles? Or maybe it's door number two: what happened with Kiki today. Then I think of the look in Travis's eyes when I ran into him by the pool. Door number three: could I actually be feeling *bad* for standing him up? That can't be it. I get out of the shower and throw on a black cotton sundress over a dry bathing suit. Sighing, I comb out knotty blonde hair. Whatever it is, there's definitely no shortage of options to choose from.

The bell sounds for dinner. I square my shoulders and walk out of the villa and into the *bohío*. Chrissy and Steven are busy cooking and Harp, Juan, Travis and Kiki are playing cards.

"You're the asshole," Kiki says.

I freeze. Is she talking to me?

"Aw, man," Travis complains, picking up the deck.

It's just the game.

I go and sit at the table. Harp's guidebook is on it and I thumb through, hoping I'm giving the impression of being thoroughly engrossed. Mr. A walks in with Hector and Carlita. Enrique's nowhere to be seen.

"Dinner's ready!" Chrissy calls, and we line up. She glares at me as she scoops some limp noodles and shrimp in tomato sauce on my plate and I go sit back down. To my surprise, Harp and Juan come sit beside me. I let out a breath I wasn't aware of holding.

"So you got out of touching any frogs today," Juan says, forking a giant shrimp into his mouth.

"I never mentioned I live to mop?" I say, taking a bite.

He grins. "Thanks."

"No problem."

I look at Harp. "What do you think of the pasta?"

"If I were you, I'd check yours for an extra side of spit," she says.

I look down at my plate, feeling ill. I thought that was Parmesan.

She giggles. "Kidding." I look up at her dark eyes, sparkling and full of mischief. "You should see your face."

"You didn't know spaghetti and spitballs were on the menu tonight?" Juan blinks at me as they both laugh.

"Very funny." But I can't stop the smile spreading across my face. I look up and catch Travis's eye. He doesn't smile back.

***

After dinner I join Harp and Juan by the pool. We lay on the hammocks, watching the last of the sunset. The sky is cotton candy pink tonight, the moon out and almost full.

"It gets dark so early here." Swaying, I can't help but wonder what Miles and everyone are doing right now.

"Sunrise at six thirty and sunset at six thirty," Juan calls from his hammock.

"It's kind of nice, you know?" Harp says, her hammock swinging evenly.

"What is?" I say, preoccupied. I really need to get a hold of Ky.

"Your body following the rhythms of the day, up with the sun and down with the sun."

"Just like Mother Nature intended," Juan says.

"Not too many people live like that." I think of the frenetic pace of life back home.

"Here, people work to live; there, we live to work," Juan says. "At least my mom and dad do."

"What do they do?" I ask.

"They're both lawyers," he says.

"Cool."

"Not really," he says from his hammock, face partially hidden. "I never see them."

"That's better than having them breathing down your neck every minute of every day," Harp says. "Mine are always asking me what I'm doing, where I'm going, what my plans are for the future. It never stops."

"At least they care," Juan says. "I'm not sure if my parents even know I'm in Panama right now."

"They don't know you went on a trip?" I ask, incredulous. My mom can be a superficial pain in the ass but at least she cares what continent I'm on.

"Nah, they probably know I'm off somewhere," he says, "just not what country."

"What about your parents?" Harp asks me.

"They're alright, I guess," I say. "Dad's pretty cool. He used to be a sociology professor at Seattle U."

"Nice," Juan says.

"Mom's a bit of a piece of work," I say, gently rocking in the cozy woven fabric.

"You guys fight a lot?" Harp says, picking up on my tone.

"Not really. More like, I don't know, growing up sometimes I felt like she was maybe a little jealous of my relationship with my dad." And Gigi.

I've never said that out loud before and wonder why I'm sharing these intimate details with virtual strangers. But something about Harp and Juan makes me feel comfortable, like I can tell them my secrets and not have to worry about them judging. "Mom's his second wife. He was married to his high school sweetheart before." I look up at the stars. "She was one of the youngest women in the country to earn a PhD in astrophysics. Then one night a drunk driver thought it made sense to cross over into their lane of traffic."

Harp and Juan are quiet.

"Dad escaped without a scratch but she was killed instantly. I think he was pretty broken up about it. He never talks about her." It's weird to think he'd had a whole other life before us. "Sometimes I think it bothers Mom a little. She takes very good care of herself. And by very, I mean weekly facials, hair appointments, spa retreats — she's into all that." She'd been much happier accompanying me to a mani-pedi than a spelling bee.

"That's shitty." Juan interrupts my thoughts. He lowers his foot down out of his hammock and pushes it off against the ground, making his hammock swing faster.

"Life can be shitty," Harp agrees.

I laugh.

"What's so funny?"

"You, saying shitty." A light shines in my eyes.

"Does anyone want to go down to the beach?" Travis walks toward us holding a flashlight. He's alone.

"Sure," says Juan, getting out of his hammock.

"I'm in," says Harp. "Jess?"

"Um, sure," I say, getting out of my hammock, careful not to get tangled in the netting. The lump, partially dissolved, re-hardens. I wonder if Travis plans to confront me.

"Does Mr. A know we're going?" Harp asks.

"Yup, I told him." Travis swings the flashlight around his finger.

As we walk down to the beach, Travis, Juan and Harp talk about El Níspero and Juan's documentary. I think about my conversation with Harp and Juan. Dad and I'd been close when I was little. I don't think he'd ever considered his daughter might not attend university. To be fair, I'd also thought the same thing for most of my life. Mom was more understanding. She'd met him as a young receptionist working in his department and that was the extent of her post-secondary experience. From what I gather, it was quite the scandal around campus. Even now, at forty-two, she looks like she's in her early thirties. We often get mistaken for sisters, which of course she absolutely loves.

I was having second thoughts about Panama when Mr. A called to break the news. Panicking about the insanity of what I'd done, I tried to get out of it. Mom was on my side for once.

"It is her last big trip with her friends," she'd said to my dad. Both had been in my room since Mr. A's phone call. "Besides prom's just months away and Florida's a great place to work on her base." She turned and examined me. "You're positively pasty after the winter we've had."

As if it's my fault Seattle's cloud cover is a permanent part of the landscape.

Dad had looked up from my computer, glasses perched on his forehead. "I'm sure Panama's just as good a place for her to work on her tan, dear," he said, not budging an inch.

"It's only eight degrees from the equator. I'll probably fry to a crisp," I complained, lying on my bed. I glanced up at the ceiling where faded yellow stars no longer glow. "And what about my birthday trip? I've been looking forward to it forever."

"Fine, then stay at home and go to one of the local schools," Dad said. "Gigi'd be so proud."

Ouch.

"What good is school if she has skin cancer?" Mom said, still obsessing about my dermatological status. I watched her examine her own immaculately bronzed face in the mirror above my dresser. "I can get her a job at the studio."

"Dad's right." I sighed, not quite willing to completely flush Berkeley down the toilet. "Mr. A just may let me scrape by with a decent mark if I do this extra report."

"On frogs?" Mom scrunched her nose. She actually made it look cute.

"Golden frogs," I said.

"What's so special about them?" she asked. "Frogs are … icky."

"Did you just say *icky*?"

"Well they are! You'd better not touch one," she said. "It might give you warts."

"Pretty sure that's a myth," I said.

Dad chuckled and Mom flushed a dusky rose that spreads down to her ample cleavage, artificially enhanced, of course. Unfortunately, I inherited her pre-surgery cup size. Still, I'm too deathly scared of scalpels and needles to ever want to do anything about it.

"You're not too far off, sweetheart," Dad said, scrolling down on the keypad. "It says their skin secretes a poison, which could perhaps cause a lesion resembling a wart."

Dad's always trying to make Mom feel better about her lack of education. She never finished high school. She'd been thinking of going to night school to get her GED when they met, but that had fallen by the wayside after the wedding, and me, I guess. And I'd already checked out the Wikipedia page for some background research. The poison is a neurotoxin, so most likely no blistering.

"They can also wave." I tried distracting her.

"Wave?" she said.

"You know, like move their arms back and forth." I demonstrated.

"I know what waving is," she snapped. "I just meant why would a frog wave?"

"To get attention," Dad said.

"Are you two making fun of me?" she asked, suspicious.

"No really, Ellen, come see right here." Dad gestured at the laptop. "They have no eardrums so they use sign language. They wave to attract mates or to warn off rivals."

"So it's either I want to *frog* you or I want to kill you," I said. "Wouldn't want to get those two mixed up."

"So you're sending our daughter off to the jungle to be poisoned by frogs?" she said.

"Nah, she has more chance of being bitten by a snake," he said, scrolling. "Still it's better than the alternative — losing out on her dream." He turned to look at me, his gaze falling on the shelves above my head. Pictures take up every square inch, snapshots of me and my friends, me and Miles, happy faces laughing and completely unconcerned with things like bad biology grades. The same shelves had once been full of trophies, awards, certificates and ribbons for every kind of academic achievement possible. Those are now in boxes at the back of my closet.

"What if Berkeley's not my dream anymore?" I said, my voice soft.

"Is that you or your friends talking?" his eyes lingered on a shot of Miles and me at a concert.

"Does it matter?" I said.

"You should just make sure that the people you give up your dreams for are worth it," he said finally, looking back at the computer screen. "We shouldn't have to compromise who we are for others."

The sound of the waves brings me back. It's low tide. The sand goes out much farther than the night before and is just as sparkly. The moon is brighter, lighting up the whole beach.

"Look at all the shells." Harp picks some up and examines them. "They're so pretty."

"Hector said people come down in the morning at low tides to collect oysters," Juan says.

"To eat?" I ask.

"I guess so." He looks around in the sand.

"Yummy."

Wanting to see the phosphorescence again, I take off my clothes and move into the water, thankful I'd put on the clean bathing suit. I swim out a ways, admiring the flash of florescent lights in the water. There's a splash and I look up to see Travis swimming toward me. I try to swim out farther but the wind has picked up and the waves are starting to swell.

I'm trapped.

Chapter Fourteen

"Hey, Princess," he says, swimming over to me.

"Hey," I say, avoiding his gaze.

A wave swells up and under us as we bob in the water.

He doesn't say anything and I finally break. "Look, sorry about forgetting our ... thing today." I borrow a term from Harp and Juan. "It's just been a real shitty few weeks, you know?"

The swells are getting bigger. He just keeps looking at me so I continue.

"I'm supposed to be in Miami with all my friends for my birthday and instead I'm stuck here." I tread water. "My boyfriend just dumped me, half these people hate me and I might still fail biology."

He's quiet for a few seconds. Water swooshes. "'Hate' might not be the right word," he says, his tone thoughtful. "Probably more along the lines of 'loathe' or 'despise.'"

I stare at him. Then burst out laughing.

"Look, I just feel sorry for you and thought the non-dates would be a good way to make you not feel like such an outcast, you know?" he says, arms moving back and forth in the water.

"Why would you care whether I feel like an outcast?" I search his face for any signs of insincerity.

"Like I said, people change." His green eyes hold mine for a heartbeat then go to my hair. "Plus, you've definitely lost a few brain cells from all that bleach, and are obviously going to need help with your report."

I look down my nose at him, slightly difficult when treading water. "I assure you all my brain cells are intact."

"Really?" His tone is light. "Wouldn't have guessed that from the company you keep."

"And you're so much better?" I can feel the tug of the tide pulling me into the current. We've been carried a good distance from Harp and Juan, who are stooping to pick up shells along the beach.

"I guess you'll never know now, will you?" One of his hands brushes mine underwater as the waves push us closer together.

"Fine." I'm unable to resist the quiet challenge in his voice. "Why don't we have our first non-date tomorrow and you can show me the 'new' Travis?"

"Sure thing, Princess. You don't have to beg." He sends a lazy grin my way.

I splash water at his face but he sees it coming and dives down.

"We better get back before we're swept out to sea," he says after popping back out of the water. He's right. The current is much stronger now.

I swim away from him toward shore. Travis must see me struggling because he swims up beside me. "You okay?"

"Fine," I pant.

"Don't worry, I won't let you drown," he says.

"How sweet." I focus on my strokes.

We touch down on the bottom of the ocean at the same time and I walk up the beach breathing hard, emotions tumbling in my body like a starfish tossed around in the surf. We reach our clothes, where Juan and Harp sit on the sand examining each other's seashell treasures.

Travis picks up my dress, brushes the sand off and hands it to me.

"Thanks." I say.

"How were the waves?" Harp asks.

"Rough," I say.

"Amazing," Travis answers at the same time.

She looks confused.

I know how she feels.

***

I wake the next morning on my stomach, stiff and crispy like a strip of overcooked bacon. My skin feels stretched too tight, like the bad facelift my mom's friend Cheri had last July.

"Ouch." My voice is muffled in my pillow.

Harp comes in from the bathroom and I turn my head. She's in shorts and a T-shirt, braiding her hair.

"Ooooh, you're red," she says, fascinated.

"It burns."

"Yes, that's why they call it a 'burn.' Do you want some of my aloe vera gel?"

"Please."

I get up slowly, wincing with each move. I take the gel into the bathroom and look in the mirror. My front isn't too bad, but that's not where I feel the heat. I turn, craning my neck.

I groan. I look like a giant red pepper.

It must be from lying on the surfboard yesterday, water amplifying the UV rays. Mother is not going to be impressed with my base tan. I slather the cooling green gel all over me and get an Advil from my Marc Jacobs bag on the bathroom shelf.

There's a knock on the door.

"Are you okay?" Harp's voice comes through.

"It looks like I've been smacked by a thousand angry octopuses."

"Do you think you'll be able to come today?"

"I think so." There's only so much time to work on my report. Plus I can't ditch Travis two days in a row. I coat myself with sunblock and head on out.

He gives a low whistle when he sees me by the van after breakfast. "Who ordered the lobster?"

"Ha-ha."

"Does it sting?" he asks.

"About as much as owing you three non-dates."

"Zing." He grins.

The ride up is torturous. We reach the zoo and I peel myself off the seat, leaving behind a layer of skin. It's my group's turn in the nursery today but Mr. A takes one look at me and tells me to stay out of the sun. This means I get stuck sweeping and mopping for a second day, while Chrissy and Kiki work with the frogs. Both still aren't talking to me.

Travis finds me after the morning's work. The plan is for everyone to explore El Valle some more on our own, and nobody notices us walk off together. Gravel crunches under our feet as we head for the shed. Lola showed us the caretaker's shack yesterday, saying we could help ourselves to the bikes inside whenever we wanted.

"You still up for this?" he asks, inspecting my skin as he picks a rusty red Schwinn the same color as my shoulders.

"Yeah," I say, looking dubiously at the rickety contraptions. "Where are we going?"

"I had to change our itinerary a bit, but you should be able to do it." He hops on his bike.

"Do what?" I ask, carefully straddling mine.

"You're not scared of heights, are you?" he says, riding slowly ahead.

I stop, one foot on the pedal. "Yes."

"Well, today's the perfect day to get over that," he calls over his shoulder.

"Please don't tell me we're going zip-lining." I pedal up to him.

He grins at me as we ride out onto the road. "Okay, I won't tell you."

"Travis, I can't." I swerve around a larger crater. "Seriously, I'll have a heart attack. And I really planned on living until my seventeenth birthday."

"That's right, your birthday is coming up." He looks over at me. "What day?"

"Saturday, but don't tell anyone. It's not a big deal."

"Since when are birthdays not big deals?" he says, grabbing a branch above our heads, skinning the leaves off.

"I'm trying to fly under the radar here." I look down at the chain, which is making squeaking noises.

He laughs. "That went out the window the minute you joined our little expedition."

I sigh. "I prefer to blend in." Travis snorts. "I do. Being different just calls attention to yourself." I give him a pointed look. "All being super smart ever did was get me picked on."

"Yeah, about the whole Messy Jessie thing." He puts his hands back on the handlebars and looks at me. "I didn't know the name would take off like that."

"Yeah, well, it did." And precipitated my entire metamorphosis.

"You seem to have recovered from it." His tone is dry. "Do your friends even know you skipped a year?"

"No — something else that's not a big deal." A piece of hair blows across my face and I puff it away.

"It's not so bad to be different, Jess." He gives me a sidelong look.

I wait for the punch line, but it doesn't come.

"Since when did you grow up?" The light breeze feels heavenly on my hot skin.

He shrugs, green eyes shaded by the brim of his cap. I eye him covertly as we ride. It's weird, but talking to him like this, it feels like deep down he has direction. He knows where he's going, unlike the rest of us, who just wander around aimlessly.

"Are we there yet?" I ask, my skin tingling.

"What are you, five?" He laughs. "But yes, we are."

We round a bend in the road and I realize we're at the waterfalls and the pool where I'd lost my ring. Which he saved when he didn't have to. Bringing me to this very bizarre moment where I am about to risk my life with a boy I've disliked for years. We hop off our bikes and lean them against a thick tree.

"I hope they don't get stolen," I say. We don't have locks.

"They'll be fine," he says, glancing back. "We'll just ask those guys to keep an eye on them." He nods at the men standing behind the counter. I read the signs. There are warnings in five languages.

"*Hola, señores.*" Travis says a few more words in Spanish. They nod and he pulls out his wallet. I feel uncomfortable, and not just because I'm char-broiled.

"Here." I hold out the money for our fare. "Since you found my ring." The guides approach to suit us up, holding out complicated-looking harnesses.

"Don't worry about it. I'm the one making you do this, remember?" He squints at the ropes currently being attached to our bodies by the nimble-fingered men. They sure don't waste any time. One of the guides hands me a helmet and a pair of thick gloves.

"I'll tell you what." Travis grimaces as a thick cord comes up between his legs. "If we survive, you can leave the tip."

Swell.

Chapter Fifteen

We start up the trail to the top of the mountain with our guides. I assume they don't speak much English, as they've yet to speak directly to us. Or make eye contact. They set a snappy pace as Travis and I follow behind.

"So, any accidents?" I can't resist asking over the noise of the waterfall, not quite managing to keep the sliver of hysteria out of my voice. One of the guides turns around. He's average height with muscular forearms. Dark hair grazes pantherlike eyes.

"No," he says and turns back around.

Chatty fella. The roots of trees curl under our feet as we climb higher. I try again, this time with the other guide, a man of about thirty and hefty, which is somehow reassuring. If the lines can support his weight…

"Are you from Panama City?" I ask, inhaling the fresh air.

"No, *aquí*," he says, pointing to the forest pressing in on all sides.

"That means 'here,'" Travis translates. "El Valle?" he asks.

Hefty nods. Despite his large frame he moves up the tree line like a model on a catwalk.

"Why is everyone's Spanish better than mine?" I say, slightly breathless as the incline steepens.

"We had some time to prepare, seeing as how we've been planning this trip since last year." Travis rolls his eyes upward in mock exasperation. Wooden steps appear built into the side of the mountain and we begin to climb them.

"I guess I get why the girls are pissed." I pant. "They've been waiting and dying to do this and I just get to—"

"Crash it?" Travis supplies from over his shoulder, helpful as always.

I stick my tongue out at his shoulder blades but don't disagree. "What's Mr. A thinking?"

"Mr. A's a good guy," he says, "and you have to admit this is a pretty cool way to make up extra credit." He spreads his arms at our surroundings. "You're in a beautiful country doing something noble."

"Not so noble." I step over a large jagged boulder. "I'm doing it so I won't fail biology and screw myself out of college."

"Well, consider the nobility a positive side effect."

Birds sing in the trees. With so many different calls, trills and whistles, it sounds like an avian orchestra warming up for an impromptu concert.

"How did that happen anyway?" Travis asks, stopping abruptly to turn around. I'm watching my feet and bump into him. I take a step back. He slides his ball cap around backwards. "The Jess I knew was a genius. Hell, you skipped a grade."

"I don't know." I look up at him. "It's not a big deal."

"You keep saying that." His green eyes dissect me. "Is nothing a big deal, then?"

"It's just a grade."

"Really? Don't I remember you crying one time when you got an A minus on an English test?"

"Never happened." It was history. "You know, you sound a lot like my dad," I say, putting my hair into a low ponytail, avoiding his gaze.

"And what does he think of your friends?" The guides stop to wait for us so Travis begins climbing again.

I shrug and follow. I get the feeling Dad doesn't especially love them. Mom, on the other hand, was thrilled when I started hanging out with Alyssa and Ky. She'd actually been the one to introduce us. Both of their moms were in her Pilates class. One day they all went for manicures after class and brought the three of us along. For some reason, Ky and Alyssa had immediately adopted me as their makeover project, which was a step up from being Mom's.

"Whatever happened to those two girls you used to hang out with all the time in elementary?" Travis asks.

Wow. He remembers Sara and Annika. I try not to think about them too often. "Which girls?" I say, casual.

"There were three of you, always bouncing around together," he says. "Didn't you guys call yourselves something?"

"The Three Claras." I cringe, but can't help smiling at the same time. "That was it."

"We all played clarinet in band," I explain the ridiculous name as I step over an army of industrious ants carrying pieces of leaves above their heads.

"They were a lot different from your new crew."

That's putting it mildly.

"You know what happens when you go to different schools," I say, my tone clipped. I'd been terrified to skip. Everyone was older and cooler than me. Dad had been so proud, and when Mom found out it was one of the best schools in Seattle with the right kind of people, she was on board as well. I didn't get much of a say. "Why the interrogation?" I ask.

"You just seem really different from middle school."

"So?"

"Like, *really* different."

The satisfaction I feel at his comment is laced with the bittersweet reminder of my old friends.

"Like you said—" I lift a branch out of the way and turn to give him a small smile "—people change."

"It must have been rough," Travis continues, "missing out on your last year of elementary and getting the chance to be king of the school." He looks over his shoulder. "Or queen."

Where did Sir Sympathy come from? The trail peaks and we start to head down.

"It was." The words slip out.

"You don't talk to them anymore?" Travis persists.

"We still send each other the odd message and email." I pause. "I guess friendships are like fires: they eventually burn out without anything to fuel them."

"That's pretty profound for a sixteen-year-old." Travis grins.

"Almost seventeen," I correct.

The guides ahead of us stop, putting an end to our disconcerting heart-to-heart. We've reached the first station. It's one thing to talk about zip-lining, but standing at the edge of a cliff — it's all too real. I shiver despite the warm air.

Panther Eyes and Hefty demonstrate what to do and attach us to a cable with a thick pulley. One hand up on the cable acts as a brake. The other holds on to the wires connected to the cable. Pull down on the cable to brake at the end of the line. End of instructions.

"That doesn't seem very comprehensive." I gulp down giant breaths of mountain air.

"It's easy," Travis says. "Just don't put the hand on the cable in front of the pulley." He demonstrates.

"Why?"

Travis and the guides exchange a look. They nod seriously.

"Just don't do it."

"Do you know someone who lost a hand? Oh my God, you do, don't you?"

"Not personally," he says, walking back over to me.

"What!"

"I'm sure it's just an urban legend." He pats me on the head. I am not reassured.

"I can't do this."

"You can," he says. "Think of how awesome it'll be to say you went zipping along the canopy of the Panamanian rain forest."

"Can't I just say it and not actually do it?"

"You have witnesses though," he says.

The first guide hooks himself to the cable and steps off the edge of the platform that looks out on to the forest below. He shoots down like a rocket.

"You." Panther Eyes points at me. "Go."

"Okay, see you later." I turn and walk back up the trail.

A hand reaches out and grabs my wrist. "Very funny." Travis turns me around to face him, looking into my eyes, gripping both arms. "It'll be fine, I swear."

I hate the fact that he might think I'm a coward. Besides, I tried surfing, didn't I? Granted, I have a mild fear of heights, not water, but I shove down the dread and nod.

"Fine, you first."

"As you wish," he says, bowing.

He turns back around and the guide hooks his pulley to the cable. Travis sits back, testing his weight. He looks over his shoulder.

"See you on the other side, Princess." He grins. Then he's gone.

"Whoo!" He screams all the way down until reaching the other end. He puts his feet up to brace against a large pad meant to cushion your faceplant into the tree it's strapped to. "That was amazing," he shouts up at me, his voice echoing over the valley below. "Come on!"

Okay. I can do this.

Panther Eyes looks at me.

"What's your name?" I ask, stalling. My life is in this man's hands, I should at least know his name.

"Arturo," he says.

"Okay, Arturo." I swallow. "Please, be very, very careful."

He nods and hooks me up to the cables. I don't think he has any idea what I'm saying. What's the word for 'careful'? I improvise.

"*Me nervioso*," I say, hoping that's the word for nervous. I imitate biting my fingernails. He finally cracks a shy smile.

"*No hay problema*," he says, stepping back after checking all my wires and cables.

"You can do it, Jess!" Travis shouts from below.

I stand on the edge of the platform. The more I think about this the harder it's going to be. I take a tiny step forward and close my eyes.

"Okay?" Arturo asks.

"*Un momento*," I say, holding up one gloved finger, and gulp down more air.

"Is like flying." He gives another of his bashful smiles.

You can do this.

I take a giant breath, close my eyes and step off the edge of the platform into oblivion.

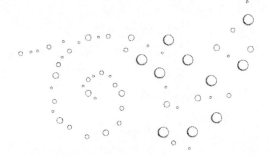 # Chapter

Sixteen

I swoop down over treetops at breathtaking speed. I open my eyes and don't take them off the landing area or stop screaming the entire time. When I get close to the end, I pull down on the cable to slow myself and put my feet up, bracing for impact. Hefty helps me brake, and before I know it I'm touching solid ground again.

My stomach is in my chest. My heart is in my throat.

"You did it!" Travis grabs me and gives me a hug. "That wasn't so bad, was it?"

It wasn't.

In fact, it's the biggest rush I've ever had.

"Let's do the next one." I look up at him, eager to continue the tour.

He laughs, his eyes sparkling. "Knew you'd love it. This time try to look around and take in the scenery."

We do two more lines, each one steeper and longer than the last. It's exhilarating to soar through the canopy, over streams and trees, the wind rushing in your face. It really is like flying.

"This is the last one," Travis says as we reach the fourth line. "It goes by the waterfall."

"Can I go first this time?" I ask, feeling brave.

"But of course, Princess" he says, one hand showing the way.

"Cut it out," I say, too euphoric to mind much.

Our other guide, who Travis introduces as José, goes first again. He flies down lightning fast until he's just a speck below.

I step up to the final wooden platform. It's scarier knowing Travis won't be waiting on the other side. I hear the waterfall to my right. This time I look down. And down. It's the steepest and longest cable yet.

"I can go first if you want." Travis senses my hesitation.

"No, I'm okay," I say, exhaling deeply.

Arturo hooks me up and steps back, holding the cables tight.

I walk off the edge of the world.

Remembering to look around, I drink in my surroundings. Then I feel myself stop even though I'm not braking. What's happening? Terror blooms. Maybe there's something wrong with the wires. I come to a complete halt, stuck halfway between both platforms. Oh God. I *knew* this was a bad idea. My eyes clench and my breath hitches. I'm having a panic attack. I'm going to die.

"Jess," I hear Travis shout. "Open your eyes."

I peer through slit lids. El Chorro Macho gushes down the rock face in all its regal glory. Water splashes through a dazzling rainbow arcing over the falls. I can almost reach out and touch it. Arturo just stopped me so I could get a good look at the falls. I'm not going to die after all.

"Okay?" Travis shouts.

"Okay," I shout back.

Arturo releases the cable and I'm flying again, over the wide river, whizzing through trees. I pull down on the wire to brake almost gracefully at the end.

"*Algo natura.*" José smiles at me.

I'm beaming as he unhooks me from the cable. Travis goes next and Arturo stops him in the same spot. Travis snaps a few pictures with a small camera from his pocket.

He reaches us a minute later.

"Did you see the rainbow?" I dance from foot to foot, buzzing.

"Yeah." José unhooks Travis and he takes a step toward me, smiling. "Pretty sweet, huh?"

"Sweet? It was amazing!" A surge of adrenaline propels me into his arms, my legs wrapping tightly around his waist as I leap up. His arms go to catch me and he holds me there a few beats, our faces inches apart. I feel his heart pounding in matching rhythm to mine. Suddenly aware this is a very intimate position, I drop to the ground.

"Sorry." My face is hot. "I just got a bit carried away."

Travis smiles. "No problem." His voice is soft.

I see José hide his own smile. A few minutes later Arturo is at our side.

"You want photo?" he asks shyly.

"Thanks, buddy." Travis holds out his camera. He stands beside me and I look at the camera, a giant grin on my face. We both give a big thumbs-up.

We walk the rest of the way down the trail, reaching the forest floor. The guides go ahead and indicate we should have a look around the waterfall.

"That was so fun." I'm unable to keep a goofy smile off my face.

"So you're an adrenaline junkie now?" Travis asks, his voice teasing.

"First surfing, now zip-lining." I do another little dance. My arms go up in an arc, my feet skip along the ground as I spin. A tree root catches between my flip-flop and the bottom of my foot. I pitch sideways. Two warm arms encircle and right me.

"Careful," Travis says. "You don't want to survive zip-lining to be taken out by a root." He grins at me and my heart does a little twirl.

I feel like an idiot. "Thanks." My chest thuds. Must be the adrenaline.

"Is that what you were doing with Enrique yesterday? Surfing?" Travis asks, curious. "That's why you forgot our non-date?"

For some reason his question rankles.

I step back. "We should get going. Everyone's probably wondering where we are."

"Look, you don't have to tell me what you were doing. It's none of my business."

"You certainly ask a lot of questions about things that aren't your business." I think of Sara and Annika, and a guilty feeling that's becoming all too familiar arises, accompanied by annoyance. The guy's nice to me for a few days and I'm confiding in him like some sappy Dear Abby reader? Not to mention literally throwing myself into his arms.

"It's called conversation, Jess." He scratches his arm.

"Well, can we end it?" My good mood has fizzled.

"Whatever you say." A baffled expression crosses his face.

We reach the entrance. I go leave Arturo and José each a five dollar tip, say *adiós*, then hop on my bike riding in the direction we came. I reach a fork at the end of the dirt road and brake, unsure of which way to turn.

"It's left," Travis says, riding up behind me.

"I know," I lie, staring straight ahead, my chin high.

***

We ride the rest of the way in silence, reaching the center of town. The van is parked in front of the El Valle market. Harp and Juan are already there. Juan has his camcorder out and is filming.

"Hey, guys!" Harp waves.

"Hi!" I say.

"We just got back from the Serpentario." Harp looks at us curiously.

"How was it?" Travis asks.

"Sweet. They had some super deadly snakes," Juan says. "I put a giant boa around my neck. It was huge." He demonstrates with his hands.

"Crazy! Did you hold it?" I ask Harp.

"Actually, I did." She looks pleased with herself.

"You guys have to check it out," Juan says. "What were you up to?"

"Jess begged me to go zip-lining with her." Travis doesn't bother to hide that we'd gone off together.

"I did not!" I glare at him.

"Didn't what?" Mr. A comes up behind Harp.

Shoot. Mr. A will kill us if he finds out. Fortunately, we're saved by Chrissy, Kiki and Steven, who walk toward us with Lola in tow.

"Hey, Mr. A," Chrissy says in a singsong voice, "look who we found."

"Lola!" Mr. A's face lights up like a kid on Christmas. "You don't have to be at the center?"

"I'm finished for today." She frees her hair from her bun, noticing Juan filming our surroundings. "Juan, over there." She points at the mountainside. "That may be something for your documentary."

We all look at the hills.

"I don't see anything," he says.

"It's La India Dormida — the Sleeping Indian Girl," she says, tracing the outline of a hillside that vaguely resembles a sleeping woman. "One of our most famous local legends."

Juan turns the camera on her. "Can you tell us the story?"

She laughs, her eyes glowing. "*Sí*, right now?"

"*Por favor, señorita*," he says.

"Well, since you ask so nicely…" Taking a deep breath, she begins. "A long, long time ago there was a beautiful princess called Flor del Aire. Her father was Urracá, the leader of her tribe. He led his people in many great battles against the Spanish conquistadors, who came to Panama to seize the riches of the land. Unfortunately for Flor, she fell in love with one of the Spanish soldiers." She interrupts herself. "It's always unfortunate when we fall for someone it is impossible to have, no?" We nod, like schoolchildren getting their story before nap time. I sneak a peek at Mr. A. He's absolutely spellbound.

She continues. "One of her own tribesman, Yaraví, the bravest and fiercest warrior among her people, also loved Flor. When he discovered she did not return his affections but instead loved the soldier, he fell into great despair. He went up to those mountains and jumped to his death before the princess's very eyes."

"A bit dramatic, don't you think?" Steven leans over and says to Travis.

"Ssshh!" the girls say in unison.

"Flor was so anguished at betraying her people, she left her soldier and wandered the mountains in sorrow, weeping until at last, when she had no tears left, she lay down on the mountainside where her spirit left her body.

The mountains felt such compassion for the girl they covered her body and took her shape forever, in a shrine to lost love."

We stare out at the rolling hills, all of us as bewitched as Mr. A.

"It's actually a very good hike." Lola breaks her own spell. "It has a beautiful view of El Valle."

Juan lowers his camera.

"We'll all have to do it some time," Mr. A says, though I'm sure he'd like nothing better than to ditch the rest of us and have Lola to himself.

I'm struck by an idea. "Mr. A, why doesn't Lola come for dinner?"

"I'm sure she already has plans." Mr. A hasn't taken his eyes off her.

"No plans." She smiles at him.

"Whose turn is it to cook tonight?" He asks no one in particular.

"Juan and I." Kiki holds up a bag of groceries. "We're having fajitas."

She could have said we were having tapir for all the attention Mr. A pays her.

"How will we all fit in the van?" Juan points out.

"I have my car," Lola says.

"Why don't you ride with Lola, Mr. A?" I say. "You can show her how to get to our place."

"*Sí*, I am not so good with directions." Lola holds up her hands in a helpless gesture.

"Shotgun!" Steven shouts.

Chapter Seventeen

Dinner is actually pretty good. At least with Juan helping Kiki I don't have to be on guard for any nasty surprises in my fajitas. The sun sets as we lounge by the pool and soak up its final rays before it dips below the horizon. Lola and Mr. A are still in the *bohío*, talking animatedly. Their laughter drifts over the water.

"Nice move, Princess, getting Lola to come to dinner." Travis lies back on the lounge chair, hands clasped behind his head.

"Thanks." I'm surprised he's talking to me after my little outburst. "Do you think they ever dated?"

"Dude, look how hot she is," Steven says from a couple of chairs over. "Mr. A probably choked every time he tried to ask her out."

"Mr. A has potential," Chrissy defends him. She and Kiki are on Steven's other side, as far away from me as possible.

Steven snorts.

Enrique and Harp walk toward us after finishing the dishes.

"Hey, *amigos*, no swimming in the pool tonight. I have to put the chemicals in."

"No problem." Chrissy sits up. He walks over to the shed and comes back with some bottles. She watches him as he fiddles with the solution. "So what do you do around here for fun, Enrique?" she asks as he bends over to pour some liquid in the pool.

He looks over and flashes one of his lethal smiles.

"Many things. Surfing, parties." He straightens and looks at me. "Spending time with our interesting guests."

Travis murmurs something that sounds like, "I bet."

Enrique catches it. *"Perdón, amigo?"* He screws the cap back on a bottle.

"I said I bet you spend time with a lot of guests." Travis says, stretching on the chair. "Female guests."

"Why? Would you like to spend time together, my friend?" He bats his long lashes and we laugh, with the exception of Travis. "This Friday some of us are going to a nightclub at one of the resorts," he continues, smoothing over the tension. "You should come."

"Like all of us, go to a club?" Kiki asks, looking excited.

"Aren't those only for the people staying there?" Harp says.

"Our friends work at the security gate," he says, pouring a different solution into the pool.

"That sounds like so much fun." Kiki bites on the arms of her sunglasses.

"I might be able to get some of you in." His eyes linger on the girls.

"What about ID?" Juan asks, ever practical.

"Nobody checks ID in Panama," Enrique scoffs, putting the bottle down.

"Sounds dope, man," Steven says.

"Yeah," Travis says, sitting up on the chair. "And what better way to kick off Jess's birthday this weekend."

I give him a look. Big mouth. Guess I deserved that.

"It's your birthday?" Harp asks.

"It's not a big deal," I say.

"Birthdays are very important." Enrique sits down beside me. "We must have a party."

"Perfect," Chrissy says with a fake smile. "We can all go with Enrique to the club for Jess's birthday." She grimaces at the last few words but gets them out without gagging.

"I guess I could try to get you all into the resort." He looks around at us. "But it might be a bit dangerous."

"Dangerous how?" Harp asks.

"If we get caught."

"What happens if we get caught?" Travis crosses his arms over his chest.

"Why? You scared, *compadre?*" Enrique says, turning hawk eyes on Travis and mirroring his posture.

"I think it'll be fun," Travis responds evenly.

"Me too." Chrissy looks at Kiki, who nods her assent.

"Sweet," Steven says.

Harp sighs. "I've never been to a nightclub before."

"None of us have," Juan points out. "We're in high school."

"You are on vacation, no?" Enrique asks. He'd definitely be a part of the crew back home.

"Sort of," Juan says.

"Then it is the perfect opportunity for you," Enrique declares as if that solves everything.

Juan gives Harp a look.

I watch the proceedings unfold, amused. Sneaking out and into bars underage? This is more my crowd's scene than theirs. Maybe the heat of the Panamanian sun inspires a little rebellion. Obviously they've never done anything like this before. Not that I have either. Miles was working on getting us all fake IDs before we left. My smile fades. Well, he has them now. They all do. Except for me. Guess when we get back I'll be spending a lot of Friday nights alone.

"Let's do it!" Chrissy's practically jumping up and down.

"It *is* Jess's birthday." Enrique gives me a wink.

Perfect. So now it's on me if anything goes wrong.

"Whatever." Juan looks at the ground. "But nobody's going to think we're legal."

"Don't worry so much, my friend." Enrique puts a friendly arm around him. "Everything will be fine. Trust me."

We work out the details. We'll have to sneak out somehow. Enrique's friend will meet us outside our compound down the road. Some of us will go in Enrique's Jeep and the others with his friend.

Plans made, the girls and boys separate to their own villas. Washing up for bed, I hear Chrissy and Kiki jabbering about what they're going to wear. Harp is quiet. I can tell she's nervous. She goes to the bathroom to shower after I come out. After slathering on aloe vera gel, I throw on my pj's and gingerly climb into bed.

I lie there. I tried calling Ky and Alyssa again after dinner, but no answer. Maybe they didn't recognize the strange number. No emails either. And nothing from Miles. Are things really over just like that? What am I going to tell Mom? She loves Miles. She doesn't know what a jerk he is. I snort. Not that she'd care. He's handsome, charming and has the right pedigree. *And proof of how far Messy Jessie's come?* I turn over to get away from the voice.

Harp walks into the room in her shorts and T-shirt, drying her hair with a towel.

"What do you think about this whole scheme?" she asks.

"It could be fun," I say, cautious.

"And you trust Enrique?" She combs out wet hair.

Good question.

"He seems like a cool guy."

She stops brushing and looks at me. "You know he's a player, right, Jess?"

I look at her, my mouth open.

She laughs. "I may not have tons of experience with guys, but I'm not blind."

I have to laugh. "Okay, he might be a bit of a player." I think of Miles. "What is it about bad boys?"

"Not sure. I've never seen the appeal myself."

"Really?"

"I'm more attracted to the intellectual type," she says. A blush spreads up her cheeks and she turns out the light.

I smile in the dark. A certain intellectual type with glasses and curly black hair, perhaps? "Well, then you're smarter than most of us." Present company included.

"It's common sense. 'Bad boys' usually treat you badly." She crawls into bed. "Why would I want to waste my time with someone like that?"

Another good question.

"By the way…" Harp's tone is mischievous. "How was zip lining?"

"Fun," I say. Until I sabotaged it by being a drama queen.

"I didn't know you and Travis were friends."

"We're not." Are we? "He used to tease me a lot when we were younger, that's all."

"Mmm-hmm," Harp says.

"What?"

"Nothing." I can feel her smiling. "'Night, Jess."

"'Night." I lie on my stomach, irritated. And not because of my burn.

Chapter

Eighteen

After a breakfast of plantain pancakes, it's Travis's and my turn to wash dishes.

"Sorry I was so prickly yesterday," I start out as we sort the sticky plates.

His eyebrows rise. "That's okay."

"You hit a few sore spots, that's all." He doesn't comment, waiting for me to elaborate. "It was … difficult adjusting to a new school."

"I imagine being yanked out of your comfort zone isn't the easiest thing to deal with." He walks over carrying a stack of cups as I run more hot water to rinse them. "And, again, I'm sorry for giving you a hard time back then." He bumps his hip against mine as he stands beside me. "But how else was I supposed to get your attention?"

I'm not sure how to respond to that.

"So, are you excited about seeing the frogs today?" I ask instead, shifting gears.

"Can't wait." He looks at me with a warm smile, handing me a dishrag. We pass the rest of the time in civil conversation, and I find myself wondering if Travis and I actually are becoming friends.

***

Today at the center, it's my group's turn with the animals. Luckily Travis and Steven cleaned out the cages the other day, so all Juan, Harp and I have to do is make sure everyone's bellies are full. We're walking up to the habitats to feed the birds when a sexy, feminine voice calls out, "*Hola.*"

We look around, but there's nobody here but us.

"*Hola,*" the voice says again.

Juan laughs. "It's the bird."

We are standing in front of the parrots' cage. One cocks his or her head and climbs down the fence using its claws to get to eye level.

"*Hola,*" I respond. It's followed by another parrot and the two poke their beaks through the wires. They're a vibrant red and blue, with bright yellow heads. Each has a tiny band encircling its leg.

"*Hola,*" they repeat.

"They sound exactly like Lola," Harp says. "Hey, do you think she's as in to Mr. A as he is into her?"

"Definitely," I say. "As if she didn't know her way to our villa. How long has she lived in the area?"

"You women and your feminine wiles." Juan shakes his head and walks over to Harp, procuring the keys to the cage he received earlier from the wily woman herself.

"We should try to set them up on a date," I say, then am struck by a thought. "It would be perfect if we could get him to take her out Friday night. He'd be so distracted he'd never know we were gone."

"About that," Harp says. "Are we sure it's a good idea? If we get caught, we're putting our entire trip in jeopardy." She picks up some seed and holds her hand out to the Lola birds. Sticking out their short stubby tongues, they eat ravenously from her outstretched palm.

"Then it'll be the frogs who suffer," Juan agrees.

Harp and Juan look at me. I feel like I need to reassure them. After all, this is who I'm supposed to be: popular party girl.

"It'll be fun and make a great story," I point out. "And you'll probably never get a chance to do something like this again."

"Great story," one of the parrots squawks in agreement.

I laugh. "See, even he thinks it's a good idea."

"I guess." Harp looks a bit more relaxed as she brushes her hands off.

"These are the experiences you're supposed to have your senior year." I push down my own apprehension, like I've ingrained myself to do. You don't get cool by playing it safe. "Let's feed these birds before they start pecking our eyes out." I pick up my bucket and steel myself for an on-slaught of psychedelic wings.

***

The rest of the morning passes quickly. Dappled sunlight splays through the birds' enclosures, illuminating the brilliant shades of their plumage. One of the peacocks takes an intense disliking to Juan. He walks up to the cage and the affronted bird shoots his iridescent feathers out and up. Harp and I laugh as Juan leaps back. Long, thick quills extend from a white tuft on the peacock's behind, creating an arc eight feet across. Any time Juan takes a step forward the bird shakes them in warning, luminous blues, greens and turquoises bristling in indignant fury.

Juan watches from a distance while we feed the virile bird and its harem. "Now I know where the expression 'shake your tail feather' comes from," he calls.

"Don't you think it's funny that in nature, the males are the one who get all the looks while females are the plain Janes, but with us it's the opposite?" I say. "The girls are the ones expected to get all done up to attract a guy."

"I guess there are other qualities men have besides looks that women find attractive," Harp says.

"Like money!" Juan calls.

"Yes, that explains perfectly why Lola is interested in a high school biology teacher." I roll my eyes. "Why do all men think women are gold diggers? How is that different from them dating hot young girls half their age?"

"Both are equally superficial," Harp agrees.

"Are you guys almost done?" Juan puts his hands to his throat in a choking motion. "I'm suffocating in estrogen over here."

"This guy's got enough testosterone for the both of you," I say over my shoulder. Harp laughs as Juan throws some birdseed in my general direction.

We take a break, admiring a little crocodile lounging by a tiny murky pond. "It's a spectacled caiman." Juan takes out his camcorder to film. Her cute underbite belies the ferocity of her jaws, as she stands guard over a nest containing several large eggs that look almost ready to hatch. "They have amazing maternal instincts."

"She'd also make an amazing clutch," I coo through the cage, "or a great pair of boots." My eyes travel lustfully down the length of her body.

"Jess!" Harp admonishes me, giggling.

Whoosh! A much larger caiman explodes out of the water, landing in a flurry of spray, as if my words summoned it from below.

Harp and I jump, both drenched. Juan laughs, holding his camcorder on us. "I don't think he liked that." The crocodile eyes me as if to say 'Back off.' The cage is made of very thin chicken wire.

"Easy, Papa." I hold my hands up in surrender. "Only kidding."

We finish feeding the animals and walk back to meet the others. The *meh* -ing goats are in serious conversation, each voice distinct and plaintive. Their pens, along with the chickens', are directly in front of the jaguars. The giant cats stalk back and forth, listening to the mindless bleating and clucking. They stare at the pens, licking their lips, long pink tongues glistening.

"That seems a bit unfair." Juan nods at the scene, holding up his camcorder again. "It's like being on a diet and having fast food constantly paraded in front of you."

"They don't look all that secure either," Harp says. Most of the cages at the zoo have seen better days. A white placard hangs lopsided on the jaguars' cage. A blue marker has written the obvious for the tourists: "Don't get too close!" Half of the words are faded and smudged.

"I guess when you don't have a big budget, maintenance tends to slide," Juan says, "which is why it's good we're here."

"How's the doc going?" I ask, breathing in the earthy tang of the goats.

"Pretty good. Got lots of great footage. What about your paper?" he asks.

"I was thinking I'd just gather my materials then write it when we're back home."

"Are you taking notes?" Harp asks.

"Do the ones in my head count?"

They both laugh.

"Kidding. A few." I feel awkward at the admission. But then remind myself that Harp and Juan are not Miles and Ky.

Sure enough, they both nod in approval. "Have you talked to any of the locals?" Juan asks as Lola walks out with Travis and Steven.

"Just Enrique and Lola." I wipe the dampness off my forehead. "I plan on asking a few more."

"How were the frogs?" Juan asks Steven and Travis.

"Awesome," Travis says, his body language ebullient. He sends me a quick smile, and I feel myself responding in kind. "We handed out their vitamins today."

"There are so many cool species in there." Steven pulls the rim of his ball cap around to shield the bright sun. "Hey, Juan, I have a sweet idea for the doc." The boys discuss filming, and Harp and I turn to Lola.

"Hey, Lola, can I talk to you a bit more about the golden frog?" I feel shy. "I'm doing a report on it."

"I'd be honored, *chiquita*." She beams at me. "When did you have in mind?"

"Um, today?" I venture.

"I'd love to, but today I am going to the hot springs." She thinks for a second. "Why don't you girls come with me and we can talk there?"

"Sure, but I think the van is leaving soon to go back down to the villa."

"I can give you a ride and drop you off to Kenny later," she says.

I smile at Harp. "Sounds great."

"I have to go shopping for groceries," says Harp, glum. "It's my turn to cook dinner tonight."

"That's too bad," Lola says. "Why don't we ask the other girls to come?"

"Uhhh…"

The girls in question stroll around the corner of the building.

"We saw the cutest monkey," Kiki exclaims to Lola, "with the tiniest face and the hugest eyes. I want to take him home."

"That must be our Panamanian night monkey," Lola says, brushing the hair off her face. "Did you know that, unlike other monkeys, they are monogamous animals?"

"That's pretty rare in the animal world," Harp says.

"Pretty rare in the human world as well," I mutter. I've been trying very hard not to think about what Miles is up to right now.

"The father is also very involved with the babies," Lola says. "He carries them from one day old and passes them to the mother when she needs to nurse."

"That's so sweet," Kiki says.

"*Sí.* Perhaps not so sweet is they like to wash their hands and feet in their urine." Lola laughs. "Speaking of bathing, I invited the girls to come to the mud baths with me." She glances at her watch. "Would you like to join?"

"Mud baths?" says Chrissy, looking down at her arms.

"It's very good for the skin. The mud has special mineral properties, then you bathe in therapeutic waters from the volcano." She pats her glowing cheeks. "It's my beauty secret for keeping my skin looking young and fresh."

Chrissy and Kiki look torn between getting beautiful skin and spending time in my company. Vanity wins out.

"Sure," they say.

"Wonderful, I'll get my bag and meet you back here." She heads back into the center.

Done talking camera angles, the boys walk over.

"What's the story?" Travis asks with an easygoing smile I'm becoming accustomed to.

"We're going to the mud baths," Kiki says. "Wanna come?"

"Like a spa thing?" Travis looks at the guys. "We'll leave you ladies to it."

"We're going to check out the square trees." Steven says, yanking up his shorts.

"Square trees?" I ask.

"You know, like the opposite of circular?" Chrissy says, outlining the shape with an aggressive finger.

Sometimes I want to slap her.

"El Valle is famous for them." Juan pushes his glasses up his nose. "Although I hear they're actually more rhomboid in nature. We're getting some more B-roll for the doc."

"Am I the only one going back with Hector?" Harp sighs martyrlike and looks at me. "Bring me back some mud? I want gorgeous skin too."

"You're going to cover your faces in mud?" Steven asks.

"That'll be a definite improvement," Travis teases.

"Very funny." Kiki pokes him in the stomach. She's definitely recovered from her discomfort around him. Travis doesn't appear to mind the attention. I look away from them, wondering if they're going to get back together. Not that it's any of my business.

Lola comes back with her bag. "Alright *chicas, vamonos!*"

This should be interesting.

Chapter Nineteen

I look in the mirror hanging on the tree outside. A green alien stares back, blue eyes the only recognizable feature on my face. The mud's drying fast, turning green, tightening and making it difficult to move or talk without it cracking. After smearing mud all over our bodies while trying to avoid trashing our bathing suits, we stand sentinel still, arms away from our trunks as we dry.

"The mud is drawing toxins from the body," Lola says, barely moving her lips.

"It feels really cool." I try not to move my jaw. It's a weird sensation. My body feels heavy and tingly all over.

"How often do you come here?" Chrissy asks Lola, her mouth a thin slash across her face.

"I try to come every week," she says.

"It's so beautiful here," Kiki says, and for once I have to agree with her.

We'd walked across a wooden bridge spanning a bubbling stream, tall green trees and flamboyant flowers blooming everywhere. Hundreds of bird species fly from treetop to treetop, singing and calling to one another. Inside the grounds are pools of different sizes and color. The biggest is filled with steaming water the color of rust.

"The color is due to the different minerals," Lola says when she sees me eyeing it.

"My mom and her friends would pay a fortune for this stuff," I say about the mud.

"Why don't you bring some home for her? A jar only costs two dollars,"

Lola says. Even covered in mud she looks stunning.

"Seriously? I could repackage this stuff and sell it for a hundred bucks a pop," I say. "Organic volcanic mineral mud? People would go crazy for it."

"Maybe that can be your new business if Berkeley doesn't work out for you," Chrissy says. I give her a look. Talk about having the whole passive aggressive thing down. Though … her idea is not a bad one.

Lola misses the sarcasm. "You're not going to college, Jessica?"

"Um, no, I'll probably go to college," I say, uncomfortable discussing my personal failings in front of two people who probably take great pleasure in them. "Just not sure if it'll be Berkeley."

"But Berkeley is a good school, no?" Lola asks.

"One of the best for the program I was interested in," I admit. And somewhere Messy Jessie had once badly wanted to be. I'd gone with Gigi and my dad a few times when I was younger and fell in love with the campus, not to mention California's gorgeous weather.

"It is so important to go to school. They were the best years of my life. It was when I discovered who I really was as a person," Lola says. "What makes you consider not going?"

"Well, none of my friends are going," I say, "and my boyfriend's sticking around home as well." I don't mention that he just dumped me.

"And he is worth it?"

Once I'd thought so. I look down at the dried mud that's cracking in places. "None of it matters unless I pass biology anyway."

"Jess is here to do a report for extra credit," Chrissy says. "Mr. A's being super nice, letting her come on this trip. She's not even a member of our club."

"Is that why you wanted to ask me questions about *la rana dorada*?" Lola asks.

I look at her, confused.

"Golden frog." Kiki rolls her eyes.

"Yes, for the report," I say.

"Then ask away. I will do everything to help you pass and go to university."

"She just said she might not go," Chrissy points out.

I open my mouth to protest. That's not what I meant. Or was it? Somewhere along the way did I manage to convince myself that Berkeley didn't matter? But then, if that's true, why am I here? Maybe the old Messy Jessie isn't as dead and gone as I'd once thought.

"Thanks, can we start now?" I ignore Chrissy's comment, determined to get some good information.

"*Sí*, but let's get this mud off first."

We lumber like zombies over to the fountain and Lola pumps thermal water up from the ground to rinse ourselves off. The mud that's dried to green clay immediately reverts back to its original state of grainy gray-brown and washes easily from our bodies. My skin feels unbelievably silky. It's never been so soft and smooth. I follow Lola into the rust-colored pool, admiring her perfect body, wishing I filled out a bikini half as well as she does. I don't think my mother would be overly fond of Lola.

The water comes up to my shoulders and has the same mineral smell as the water pumped from the ground. As Kiki and Chrissy finish rinsing off, a busload of blue hairs pulls up and forty elderly ladies hightail it toward the baths, chattering like the birds above. They remind me of Gigi.

Lola sees me watching the grannies.

"They are birders. Panama is a very popular destination for bird-watchers, El Valle especially. It has a large percentage of the world's species."

The ladies, and some men as well, order their mud and smear it over their wrinkled bodies with gusto.

"I hope I'm doing trips like that when I'm their age," I say. Chrissy and Kiki join us in the pool, talking by themselves at the other end.

"Youth has no age — it is a state of being." Lola treads her hands in the water. "So what do you want to ask me?"

"Um, so what makes the golden frog special to Panamanians?"

"It is a symbol of the country itself. It represents something precious that is rapidly disappearing, like the traditional way of life, as we become more westernized." I focus on her words, wishing I hadn't left my pen and paper at the villa. Not that they'd do me much good in a mineral bath.

"Doesn't Panama have a long history of that?" I say.

"*Sí*. Overall we have a very good relationship with the US, which is why we have developed more quickly than some of the other countries in Central and South America. We have your medicine and healthcare. Our education is good. The country is also fairly safe when compared to others down here."

"What do you think will happen if the frog disappears?" I ask.

"What happens when any species disappears?" she says softly. "A piece of us will be lost forever and we can never get it back. The repercussions of that loss are like throwing a pebble in a pond. We have no idea how far the circles will spread."

"Do you think there's any way to save it?"

"The most important thing is education." She smiles at me. "Exactly what you and your group are doing here now. Learning about the wildlife and bringing back that knowledge to others."

"I'm not sure too many people care about frogs." I look down, not wanting to hurt her feelings. It's her life's work, after all.

"It's true there are many other species in danger just as worthy of attention," she agrees. "Each is important and they are all connected. If people can save one species, they can save others. It requires a change in our way of thinking, in the way we view our planet. We are not the only ones entitled to survival here."

Chrissy and Kiki wade over, making room for some of the elderly ladies who join us in the pool.

"Oh, that feels good on the old bones." A woman with short curly white hair sighs in bliss. She glances at us. "Did you girls look like me when you got in here? If so, I ain't ever getting out."

We giggle.

"Why don't we finish our conversation later?" Lola says. "We'll leave the ladies to enjoy the pool."

Chrissy exits first. As I watch her climb up the ladder, I'm struck by a memory from last year's gym class. A girl had bailed off the diving board, much to the hysterics of Alyssa and Ky. They'd called her 'Dive-Bomb' for the rest of the year. Any time she was up to bat, or about to kick a ball, they'd scream it out and she'd mess up.

Chrissy. Dive-Bomb.

No wonder she hates me. My friends and I laughed at her, and I didn't even remember doing it. I get out and towel off, feeling light-headed from being in the warm water, equal parts heavy minerals and shame.

"Are you going to bring some mud home?" Lola asks.

"Right, I forgot." I walk over to the stand selling it and ask for three containers, one for me, one for my mom and one for Harp. Chrissy and Kiki buy some as well. I want to say something to Chrissy but don't know if it'll make things worse. I, of all people, know no one likes to be reminded of past humiliation.

We walk back to Lola's car. It's a tiny white thing with a bumper sticker that reads "Save the Golden Frog" in Spanish. The satisfaction I feel at reading in Spanish is diminished by the realization that maybe Chrissy and Kiki aren't entirely off base in resenting me.

I get in the front and Chrissy and Kiki sit in the back.

"Thanks for answering my questions," I say to Lola, going over her answers in my head so I won't forget them.

"Not a problem." She adjusts her rearview mirror, glancing at the girls in the back seat. "Since you are in Kenny's biology group, I'm sure you must be very smart," she says.

"Thank you," Chrissy says. "We have the top marks in our class." She sees me glance at her in the mirror. "In all our classes," she adds defensively.

I can't believe I didn't recognize her until now.

"Then you must help Jessica with her report," she declares.

Chrissy's about to protest, then changes her mind. "Sure, we'll help her." She looks conspiratorially at Kiki.

Help me right off a cliff.

"*Perfecto.*" Lola turns the key in the ignition, starting the car. "We girls have to stick together."

Or as my mother would say, keep your friends close and your enemies closer.

Chapter Twenty

We get back to the villas just in time for dinner. I try Ky on the phone one more time. No answer. Big surprise. I walk out to the *bohío* where Harp's running around frantically, checking on pizzas that Enrique's barbecuing to crispy spheres. She looks frazzled. Wisps of hair escape her normally impeccable French braids. Maybe cooking is also not her thing. Travis sees me enter and sends an affable smile my way. I return it.

"Okay, I think we're ready." Harp's out of breath. She grabs the inhaler from her pocket and takes a quick puff.

We sit down to eat in our usual spots, with Lola joining Mr. A and Hector and Carlita for the second evening in a row.

I take a bite of my pizza. "Mmm, yum," I assure Harp who looks anxiously at me. Then laughs.

"What?" I say.

"You have something," Enrique murmurs, reaching across the wooden table. He's joined us since he helped with dinner. His fingers lightly brush against my cheek and come away with a gooey piece of cheese string, which he surreptitiously wipes off on his plate. I want to die.

"Yeah, relax. It's pizza, not rocket science," Juan says to Harp.

"Rocket science is easier," she informs him.

"It's okay, *bella*," Enrique says. "I told you my secret sauce would be amazing."

"It's really good," I say, hands going to my face with a napkin, discreetly seeking out any more rogue cheese. "What's in it?"

"If I told you, I'd have to kill you." Enrique grins. "Or marry you. It's a family recipe only Gonzalezes are allowed to know."

"I think I'd prefer the second." I lick my fingers.

"Get in line," Chrissy calls. "This sauce is incredible."

"How were your square trees?" I ask Juan.

He shrugs. "Cool. The bases were more square than the tops but we got some great shots. How were your mud baths?"

"Good. That reminds me," I say to Harp. "I brought you back some mud."

"What? None for me?" Juan affects a wounded look.

"You don't need it," I assure him.

"You ladies don't either," Enrique says. "Your skin *es muy hermosa.*"

I look at Harp.

"Gorgeous," she mouths silently.

We finish up dinner. It's tricky to look gorgeous while eating pizza with your hands, but I do my best. People bring their plates over to the outdoor kitchen area of the *bohío.*

A smooth voice comes up behind me. "Can I sneak you away for another surfing lesson?"

I turn. "Uh, I'd love to but—"

"She's got dish duty." Travis walks between Enrique and me, thrusting an apron into my arms.

"Sorry to hear that," Enrique says smiling, keeping his eyes on me. "Another time then?"

"Um, sure."

Travis makes a rude noise and the tendons in Enrique's neck tighten, but he's all smiles as he waves good-bye to everyone and leaves the *bohío.*

I'm left standing with Travis, holding my apron. "I'll wash, you dry this time," he says as we walk over to the mini kitchen. He's already wearing his apron, the sink filling up with water and soapy bubbles.

"See you after dishes," Harp calls, walking off with Juan, Steven and my two nemesises. Nemesisi? I wonder what the plural form is...

"Hey, what's the plural form of 'nemesis'?" I ask, tying up my own apron, ignoring the currents running through the air after that little confrontation.

"Um, 'nemeses,' I think," he says, handing me a plate, "after the Greek goddess of retribution."

How fitting.

"Why?" he asks.

"No reason." I put the plate in the stainless steel rack. He really does know everything.

The *bohío*'s empty except for the adults who talk at their table. Hector and Carlita face Mr. A and Lola, who sit so close together you couldn't slide a litmus paper between them. I squint — is her hand on his leg under the table?

"Did you have fun today?" Travis asks, sounding oddly formal.

I pull my focus away from the love scene unfolding before me. "Yeah, we saw some cool animals," I say. "What about you? How were the frogs?"

"Awesome." His tone relaxes. "I got to pick them up and inspect them. I can't believe they're letting us do all this stuff."

I finish drying another plate and Travis hands me the next one.

"So this trip is going well for you then?" My voice is friendly. Aside from our civil dishwashing session this morning, the Chrissy flashback has me realizing that calling someone 'Messy Jessie' or 'Dive-Bomb' may not be so very different. Despite feeling rotten for going along with my friends when they called Chrissy that, I know deep down I'm not a bad person. And if I'm giving myself a break then maybe I should be giving Travis one too.

He looks mildly taken aback that I've initiated polite conversation. "So far, so good. It's a pretty great experience."

"Helping out at the conservation center?"

"No, washing dishes with you," he teases.

I focus on a spot on my plate. "Harp said universities love this extracurricular stuff."

"They do. It'll make a difference on your application. You should have no problem getting into Berkeley."

"As long as my report doesn't totally suck." A thought strikes me. "How does everyone know I want to go to Berkeley?"

"You told Harp in the van, remember?" He passes me two forks. "We're scientists, highly skilled in the art of observation."

"More like skilled in the art of eavesdropping," I say wryly. He laughs.

A few minutes pass in companionable silence. Crickets chirrup as the sun begins its familiar dip into the horizon. The light grows softer as dusk filters through our piece of paradise.

"Where do you want to go to school?" I finally say, placing a cup in the rack.

"I got early acceptance into UCLA. Their biology sciences are kick-ass."

"Congrats."

"Thanks," he says. "I guess that means we'll both be in Cali."

"Well, one of us anyway." I suddenly feel really sad about the prospect of not getting in. My conversation with Lola earlier that day made me realize that I do still very much want to go.

"Have a little faith, Jess." My name sounds strange coming from his lips. I look at him. "You're a smart girl." He gazes down at me. He hands me another plate and our fingers touch. His thumb lingers and something in my stomach flutters. "Except for maybe your taste in men," he says with a grin, breaking the spell.

"Are you referring to Miles?" I say, drying the plate.

"You said it, not me."

"Well, that's over," I say, feeling hollow.

"Should I say I'm sorry?" he says. "'Cause I'm not. That guy's a d bag."

"And how would you know?" I say.

"We were on the same club ball team. He says some pretty crazy stuff in the locker room."

"About what?" I ask, holding my breath. The crickets chirrup louder.

Travis is silent as he washes another dish, then says, "Did he ever date someone named Candice?"

Candice is his ex. I've heard about her, but we've never actually met. She goes to a different school than us. "Maybe," I say.

He whistles softly. "She sounded pretty wild."

My face grows hot for the second time that morning.

"Did he…" I pause, my hands wringing the dishtowel. "Did he ever say anything about me?" He'd slept with Candice and made it clear he'd like to do the same with me. I know he'd been expecting something to happen in Miami. I have no clue what I would've done. Deep down I wanted to be in love, and I didn't know if I was in love with Miles. Which — according to my au pair Geneviève — meant that I wasn't.

"*Ma chérie*, when you know, you know. Otherwise, it's not love," she'd always said with an authoritative hair toss.

Well, going to Panama had got me out of that one. I'll die if Travis says Miles talked about me in the locker room. I bite my lip, waiting for him to respond.

"He was on my team the year before you started dating, so I didn't hear anything," he says finally, "but thought you should know he likes to talk."

My grip relaxes a fraction. "Since when are you so concerned about me?"

"You deserve better. All girls do."

"What do you know about that?" I look at him, curious. He hands me another cup. "You missed a spot," I say and pass it back to him.

He looks down at the cup. "My mom's a single mom. Dad left when I was little. All my life I've seen her get treated like crap, one guy to the next." He turns the cup over in his hands. "The latest one thinks he's a real Romeo. You can just tell he thinks she's lucky to have him."

"Sounds like most guys." I'm only half-kidding.

"Not all guys," he says, face serious. I refrain from saying anything. "And when he thinks she isn't looking, I see how he acts around other women, the vibe he sends out, that he's up for whatever opportunity wants to present itself."

He's still scrubbing the same cup. "She deserves more, you know? She's just afraid to be alone." I see something in his eyes and put my hand tentatively on his arm, feeling the strength of it beneath my palm.

"She's lucky she has you watching out for her," I say quietly. He doesn't respond. I gently take the cup from his hands. He gives me a small smile.

"Not all of us are jerks, you know. Even though I teased you when we were little, I never meant it in a mean way."

So that's why he wants the chance to prove he's a nice guy. He can't stand to be lumped in with the men his mother dates. I should feel relieved at the reasonable explanation, but there's an empty feeling in my chest.

I dry the cup and look up at him.

"Apology accepted," I say.

***

"There's an iguana in our swimming pool," I announce to no one in particular the next morning. An enormous green lizard paddles leisurely around the pool, its short front legs in a perfect front crawl, its tail swishing lazily back and forth in the water.

"Perfect, now we don't have to figure out what to cook for dinner tonight," Travis says, coming up behind me and peering over my shoulder.

"Are you serious?"

Hector must have already seen the iguana because he's walking over with a large net. He hears Travis's comment and chuckles. "*Sí*, in Panama we call them *pollo de palo.*"

"It means stick chicken," Enrique follows his dad. "They're delicious." He smacks his lips together noisily and gives me one of his winks.

"You can't kill him," I protest.

"Why not? What's the difference between eating him and the chicken we had the other night?" Enrique says.

"I don't know." I cringe as Hector leans over and neatly scoops out the iguana like he's done it a hundred times before. Which I'm sure he has. "He swam in our pool? Guest rights and all that?"

Hector laughs. "Alright, *señorita*. For you, I let him go. But next time the only thing he will swim in is Carlita's stew."

I shiver as father and son walk off with the reptile.

"Aw, now we have to go and buy groceries," Travis jokes.

After dishes yesterday, we seem to have reached an unspoken truce. He's back to his teasing self, all traces of last night's vulnerability wiped clean away.

***

The trip up to El Valle passes quickly. It's our turn with the frogs again. Juan, Harp and I wash out the temporary tanks that the frogs are placed in whenever they're removed from their exhibit. Lola comes in to grab us.

"Are you sweeping today?" Lola asks.

"Um, maybe I'll help with the frogs if that's okay?"

"*Muy bien.*" She gives me an approving look.

Juan has his camera ready. "Do you mind if I film?" he asks.

"Of course not," Lola says. "Okay, wash up and meet me by the terrariums."

We scrub our hands at the sink. Harp and I put on gloves.

"Here we have two members of our team about to examine and clean the frog habitats," Juan says into the microphone on his camcorder. "The El Valle conservation center acts as a mini Noah's Ark for several endangered species of amphibians, which are disappearing as fast as they're discovered."

We walk over to Lola. She addresses the camera. "Today we will be carefully inspecting and replacing the greenery. My two assistants will join me in this process."

I gulp. Of course Juan has to be filming this.

Harp pulls back the lid of one of the cages slightly and pokes her head inside. "This is the habitat of the horned marsupial," she says for the camera's benefit.

"Its eggs are the largest of any amphibian species," Lola adds. "They are fertilized externally and the female carries them in a pouch on her back."

Harp gives me an encouraging look. "I'll scrub, you stand on guard for runaways. Ready?"

I nod. She quickly sets to work, spraying the inside of the habitat with mild disinfecting solution. Her hands fly as she wipes up frog poop and scrutinizes the vegetation, making sure everything is clean and cozy for the little guy. Feeling slightly unnecessary, I hold my hands out protectively over the cage in case the frog decides to make a break for it. I've mastered this stance.

Harp finishes without incident and closes the lid of the cage.

"Smooth," I admire.

She shrugs. "It's a calling."

We clean a few more cages, then Harp offers to let me do the next one.

"Maybe next time." I worry I might accidentally squish the frog or spray it in the eye or something.

We finish up and Juan turns the camera back to Lola, who distributes bugs covered in calcium powder to keep the frogs healthy. "Lola, can you tell us a bit about the efforts to save the frogs?"

"When something happens to frogs it is a warning sign that something is off balance in our environment," she says. "Right now there's a massive extinction going on, so biologists and conservationists are building arks like this one all over the world in a race against time."

"How can people help?" Juan asks.

"Just like these wonderful ladies are doing now." She nods at us, and Juan pans the camera in our direction. We smile and wave. He pans back to Lola. She continues. "By learning about the frogs, volunteering, fund-raising or donating money to the center — there are so many ways. Just go online and check the information on our website."

"Saving the world, one frog at a time," Juan intones then turns off the camera.

"Thanks, Lola," he says.

"It is I who should be thanking you," she says. "All of you." She brushes back a few tears, unashamed. "I am so happy you all are here. Some days it is very hard to stay positive, but when I see people like you who care, it inspires me all over again."

I walk over to Lola and give her a hug. She squeezes me, then holds me away from her by the shoulders. "*Muchas gracias*," she says, her eyes slightly red.

Harp and Juan walk over and put their arms around us. Nothing like a group hug covered in frog poop.

***

"Where are you guys buying groceries?" Harp asks after we wash off and are sitting outside the center on the grass.

"No idea. I don't even know what we're making. Travis is supposed to be a guru in the kitchen — according to him, of course."

"Speak of the devil," Harp says as Travis and Steven round the corner of the building.

"You ready to blow some minds tonight, Princess?" he calls out.

"I guarantee I'll blow something up," I say. "Maybe the oven?"

Harp laughs, then stands and brushes herself off. She holds out her hand to pull me up.

"What are you up to?" I ask her.

"Juan and I are going to see the petroglyphs," she says.

"Cool. Have fun!" Travis says. "Let us know how it is."

"See you guys later!" I wave at them as Travis and I head toward El Valle's outdoor market.

"So where'd you learn to cook?" I ask him.

"My mom was out a lot. I got tired of cereal and instant noodles," he says.

"Do you have anything particular in mind?" I notice his olive skin is tanning nicely in the sun, in direct contrast to mine, which is still pink and now peeling.

"Let's let the ingredients speak to us," he says as we reach the market.

"You do realize how ridiculous that sounds, right?"

He walks over to one of the stands and lifts up some green leaves. "Basil." He shoves it under my nose. "Smell," he commands, looking down at me.

I inhale the fragrant leaves. They smell spicy and sweet at the same time. "Mmm," I say.

"We'll have risotto with pesto shrimp." He picks out more of the basil.

"Sounds hard. I believe I mentioned I'm a disaster in the kitchen?"

"Can you stir?"

"Possibly."

"The trick to a killer risotto is constant stirring and adding the liquid slowly. Piece of cake."

"If you say so."

We gather the rest of the ingredients: garlic, rice, fresh mushrooms and onions. I'm actually having fun shopping with Travis. He talks with the vendors, asking about this and that in a mix of Spanish, English and a lot of hand gestures.

"We need vegetable broth." Travis looks across the street at the convenience store that also sells alcohol. "And white wine."

"I dare you," I say.

"Fine, you pay for the veggies and meet me in front of the store."

"I was kidding!" I shout after him, but he's already crossed the street. I look around. If Mr. A sees us buying alcohol we'll be in so much trouble. Hastily, I pay the lady. It's less than five bucks and all organic. She takes forever to count out my change. After thanking her, I rush after Travis, crossing the road, not paying attention. He comes out of the store with a bag and, lifting my hand to wave, I hurry toward him.

There's an endless honk and a screech of brakes.

"Jess, watch out!" Travis shouts as I look up to see a giant bus barreling down on me.

Chapter Twenty-One

My arm is jerked out of its socket as Travis yanks me onto the curb. The bus carrying the seniors from yesterday's mud baths whizzes by, missing me by inches. The driver honks again and I make out a few canes shaken from behind tinted windows.

My heart's pounding. That was close.

"Are you okay?" he asks, looking worried.

"Fine. Just glad I'm wearing clean underwear today," I joke weakly as I sit on the curb. Then realize what I've said. "Not that that's something I don't do every day. Wearing clean underwear, I mean."

Oh God, shut up, Jess.

Travis gives me a funny look. "You sure you're okay?"

"It's just something my mom always said to me when I was little." I'm mortified. "Always wear clean underwear in case you get hit by a bus."

"That's what she was worried about?" he asks. "That if you were in some horrific accident you'd be wearing clean underwear?"

"That's my mother." I attempt a half-smile, noticing the bags in his hands. "You didn't have any problems buying the wine?"

"They didn't even blink an eye." He smiles and there's that flutter again. I ignore it, blaming it on the near death experience.

"I wonder what the legal drinking age is here."

"Eighteen, but I don't think it's enforced," he says, "especially for tourists."

"So all we need is the shrimp? Where are we going to get them?" I ask.

He grins and my heart does an involuntary flip-flop. This is getting seriously annoying — I do not like Travis. I will not like Travis.

"The fish market. You ready for our second non-date?"

***

The fish market isn't really so much a market as it is a lady with a calculator sitting on a smelly dock while beat-up boats tow in their wares of the day. An enormous tractorlike machine tugs the boats up the sandy beach while giant flocks of screeching birds chase the ships, torpedoing them like fish-seeking missiles. I duck as one almost scalps me.

"You sure know how to impress a girl," I say, pinching my nose with my fingers. Ky and Alyssa would be hysterical.

We walk over to a man standing by a net, just releasing his catch. Different types of fish are being separated. A baby hammerhead shark spills out and onto the ground and I jump back.

Travis moves forward to get a closer look. "It's dead."

"Poor thing." I take a step forward. It's so tiny. Its little hammerhead flops pitifully over to one side. Travis squats down and touches the baby shark. It's no bigger than the length of his forearm.

He looks around at the villagers buying fish. Two men on our right bid on the shark. "At least it won't go to waste." He gestures to the scene around us. "This is nothing. Huge commercial fishing boats rake in millions of sharks and other species every month."

"What do you mean?" I ask.

Through no fault of his own, Travis sometimes leaves me with the vague impression I'm completely clueless.

"They catch them by accident. Billions of fish, seabirds, mammals and turtles are caught in nets or whatever and just thrown away if they're not exactly what the fishermen want." He looks up at me from his position on the ground. "It's pushing many species to the brink of extinction."

An unexpected wave of despair washes over me and I turn and walk away, thinking of the fish, the turtles, the frogs. Travis follows me.

"What's wrong?" he asks.

I face him. "How can you stand it?" I ask, tears in my eyes, my voice rising. "Everything on the brink of extinction, our environment disintegrating. Don't you get sick of hearing about this all the time?"

"What should I do instead? Go to the mall? Ignore it all and watch some ridiculous reality show?" His tone is unexpectedly biting.

I'm taken aback. "If you're saying I don't care—"

"I'm saying it's easy to be apathetic, Jess."

"I'm sorry we can't all be saints like you," I retort. "Walking around like you're better than everyone."

"I am better than the people you hang out with. We all are," he says, referring to the members of the conservation club.

"Oh, yes, Chrissy and your little girlfriend Kiki have been so kind and welcoming," I shoot back.

"She's not my girlfriend. And they do a lot of good work."

A flash of unexpected jealousy at his defense of them has my blood fizzing.

"You're a hypocrite!" I put my hands on my hips. "If you care so much about the planet, why aren't you a vegetarian?"

"I am!" he yells in frustration. "And if you paid any attention to anything but yourself, you'd know that."

"Last time I checked, fish were still animals," I say. The villagers are staring.

He takes a calming breath. "You're right."

"Excuse me?" His admission pops the bubble of my own anger.

"I try and make sure my fish is from sustainable sources, but you're right. I never said I was perfect."

We're silent for a minute, the storm passing as quickly as it'd sprung up. Travis looks at me.

"It makes me angry too, Jess," he says, putting a hand on my shoulder. "I didn't mean to call you apathetic."

"It's okay," I say, my voice almost inaudible. "You're right."

"Look, you're not a bad person because you have fish or meat now and then," he says.

"Really? Because I kinda feel like one."

"All I'm saying is you could be a little more informed about what you eat, that's all."

"So what, it's just pesto risotto tonight?"

He shrugs. "Up to you. It'll be amazing either way." His eyes have lightened to a translucent emerald.

"We've eaten a lot of seafood since we got here." I look around and my eyes fall on the corpse of the baby hammerhead. "Let's take a night off."

Travis looks at me, surprised. An approving smile spreads across his face, warming me like the sun. "Whatever you say, Princess."

We turn away from the fish market and walk toward the highway to catch a bus back to the villa. I can't stop thinking about the little shark. About all the animals I've seen so far. Lola's words come back to me. *We are not the only ones entitled to survival here.*

"I'm going to try it." I look to see his reaction.

"What?"

"The whole vegetarian thing."

He raises an eyebrow. "Just like that?"

"Just like that." I mentally say good-bye to all the delicious animals I'll never eat again.

"You don't need to go that drastic. If everyone just cut back on how much meat they ate it'd make a huge difference." He puts a hand on my shoulder.

"We'll see how it goes." I look at his hand, my mouth dry, then into his eyes. "And by the way, I hate reality shows."

***

Dinner's phenomenal. And not just because I helped cook it. Or more accurately, helped stir it. The risotto is creamy, the texture is perfect, and the flavors of the pesto burst in my mouth. We serve garlic bread and a green salad as sides. Travis and I receive a ton of compliments. We look at each other from across our tables and he lifts his glass of OJ in a mock toast. I lift mine in response and take a sip.

"That was amazing," Harp says, taking a final bite. Her plate, along with Juan's, is spotless. "Travis wasn't exaggerating when he said he was good in the kitchen."

"For once." I can't help saying, but have to agree. The boy does have some serious culinary skills.

"You guys make a good team," she says.

For some reason a panicky feeling spreads through my body at her words. "What's that supposed to mean?"

"Nothing," she says, wide-eyed innocence personified. Juan hides a smile behind his glass.

The three of us bring our dishes to the washing station and leave them for Chrissy and Steven, who are back on duty tonight. I follow Harp and Juan out of the *bohío* and we retire to our usual spot by the pool.

"So how were the petroglyphs?" I collapse on one of the plastic lounge chairs. Cooking in the heat is hard work.

"Fine," Harps says, casting a wistful look at Juan. I turn, hiding my own smile. Juan really has no idea that his best friend is into him. Something will have to be done about these two.

Enrique walks by carrying some buckets and gives me his usual wink. I wave back. He's chatted with the group a few times about Friday, all the while staring at me with those hawk eyes. I get the feeling that he'd like nothing better than to swoop down and ensnare me in his talons. I'm not sure whether to be flattered or terrified, though I suppose it is a bit soothing to the ego after getting dumped.

"Did you know there was an iguana in our pool this morning?" I ask, giving my head a shake.

"Really?" Juan says, interested. "What did they do with it?"

"Hector says they eat them, but I convinced him to let it go."

"Saving the world one animal at a time," Juan says in the same newscaster voice he'd used while filming Lola today.

"On that note…" My voice is casual. "I decided to give vegetarianism a shot." Both Harp and Juan look up at me, surprised.

"And what precipitated this?" Harp asks.

I shrug. "Just been thinking a lot about things since I've been here."

"Hey, Jess." Our heads swivel as Travis approaches. He pushes too-long hair out of his eyes. "Nice work with the risotto."

"I did master the clockwise rotation, didn't I?" I feel a happy glow at his compliment.

"Can I talk to you for a second?"

My heart speeds up. "Sure."

We head in the direction of the girls' villa and walk over to the big tree beside it. It's so large the branches canopy our entire balconies. I sit down on the swing, stomach in knots.

"You're a natural in the kitchen," he says, walking behind me and giving me a small push. A couple of blue butterflies flit past.

"Thanks," I say, breathing in the fresh air.

"You still bummed about Miles?"

"I'm surviving." The initial hurt I felt has turned into the beginnings of reluctant acceptance. He and everyone else seem so far away. That whole life does.

"Like I said, it's probably for the best." He gives me another push.

"What makes you so sure?" Each time the swing rises I catch a glimpse of the ocean beyond the fence and trees.

"Just a feeling," he says, not pushing me this time, and the swing slows.

"Oh?" I say, my feet brushing the ground.

"So, I was thinking." He walks around to face me.

"Don't hurt yourself." My voice is playful. Travis's teasing is catching.

He laughs. "Since today's non-date was kind of a bust, can I get a do over?"

"A do over?" I say, not horrified by the idea of another non-date with him. "What do you have in mind for next time — the local sanitation plant?"

"Well, it can't smell much worse than the fish market," he says, a chagrined look on his handsome face. Whoa. Do I really think that Travis is handsome?

"What smells bad?" Kiki stands on her balcony, staring down at us like she wants to wrap the swing around my neck. How long has she been there?

"Um, cleaning frog cages," I say the first thing that leaps in to my head, not quite sure why the lie slips out. It's not like Travis and I have anything to hide. We were just shopping for dinner. But something about our fishy non-date feels … special. Something I don't want Kiki knowing about. Or rubbed in her face either.

"Yeah, you wouldn't want to wreck your manicure." Her pretty face twists in a sneer and she looks at Travis. "She's not like us."

He doesn't say anything. I dig my feet into the ground and the swing comes to a halt. I hear the balcony doors slam shut.

"Travis!" Mr. A hollers over from the front steps of his villa.

"She's wrong, you know." Travis touches my shoulder then takes a step back toward his villa. The grounds are floodlit by a bright moon, making his outline glow against the sky.

His gaze holds mine, searing me. "See you tomorrow."

I sit on the swing for a few minutes after he's walked away, then slowly pump my legs, taking myself higher with each motion. Travis has been the enemy for so long. But was that all in my head? Had he really just been trying to get my attention all that time? Well, he definitely has it now.

"Jess!" Mr. A pops his head out a window. "In your villa please."

I startle, then slow the swing and get off, almost stepping on a giant toad as it hops by.

"Ack!" I squeal, my heart racing. The frog lets out a disgruntled croak. "It's not my fault you're camouflaged," I whisper to it.

It gives me a stare that suggests I look more closely next time.

"I'm working on it," I say, and it hops off into the night.

Chapter

Twenty-Two

riday is hot. The cool mountain air we've become accustomed to re-
fuses to make an appearance and sticky humidity settles into the volcano's valley. I'm covered in dirt from repotting plants in colorful
plastic garbage pails, and my back aches from being bent over half
the day.

I stand up and put gloved hands on my lower spine, leaning backwards
to relieve some of the tension.

"So how long has this volcano been dormant?" I ask.

Harp looks up. "About thirty-five thousand years."

"Oh. Good."

"But you experienced ongoing volcanic activity the other day," Juan
says.

"I did?" I don't remember seeing any molten lava spewing over the
landscape.

"The hot springs." He stands and guzzles from his aluminum bottle.
"Red-hot magma passes through a fissure, miles below the surface. When it
hits the subterranean river beneath the valley it mixes with cold fresh water
and produces warm mineralized water."

"Thank you, Boy Science!" I salute. "How'd you get so smart anyway?"

He takes another drink. Water dribbles down his chin and he wipes it
away. "I read a lot."

"I read a lot too but trashy tabloids don't really have the same quality of
information."

"If I ever have any questions on celebrity baby names, I'll know who to ask," he assures me.

"Aw, thanks, Juan. You sure know how to make a girl feel less superficial," I tease.

He blushes.

"You guys ready for Mission Resort Crash tonight?" I ask. To my surprise they both look excited.

"Should be fun." Harp plays with the end of a braid.

"If we don't get caught," Juan adds.

"I have a plan," I say. "It involves a little distraction on Mr. A's part." Since it looks like we're actually going through with this, I've decided to foolproof the plan as much as possible — for their sakes. I guess it's my little way to thank them for the unexpected good time I've been having.

"How do you plan on doing that?" Juan asks, readjusting his glasses.

"Not me." I give him a mischievous wink. "Lola."

***

We finish up our work for the morning and walk back to our usual meeting spot at the center. Mr. A's talking to Travis and Steven. Sweat runs down Travis's face, his hair is mussed and there's a smudge of dirt on his cheek. He looks hot. In more ways than one.

Lola comes out, humming softly to herself, her high ponytail swinging. Chrissy and Kiki follow close behind.

"Thanks again for taking us to the hot springs," I say, "and for talking to me about my report." After we returned to the villas I wrote down all her comments. There's some good stuff in there.

"It was my pleasure." She smiles.

"The mud really soothed my burn." I give Mr. A a guileless once-over. "Speaking of burns, you're looking a little red, Mr. A."

He's flushed, but no more than he's been all week. His pale skin, freckles and red hair don't exactly make him the best candidate for the Panamanian sun.

"Hmm?" he says absentmindedly, staring at Lola.

"Hey," I say as if a brilliant idea has just occurred to me. "Why don't you go with Lola to the hot springs tonight? It's so great for your skin."

It's a pretty obvious ruse, but both of them are so infatuated that the tiniest push is all that's needed.

"I have been feeling a little overcooked these past few days," he says slowly.

"Some time in the hot springs is just what you need, then." Lola smiles at him, her bronze cheekbones glistening.

"But it's my turn to cook," he remembers, shoulders slumping.

"I will help you," Lola declares. "Come, let us go buy the groceries. We will make *sancocho*."

I smile. Too easy.

***

Dinner and dishes are long done and Lola and Mr. A are off for a romantic evening under the stars. When asked what our plans were, we murmured something noncommittal about lounging at the beach. Enrique's parents are also out and the group is getting ready for our big night. Volts of electricity run through the compound.

"I have nothing to wear," I complain to Harp, clothes strewn all over the bed. She looks over at the pile with an arched brow.

"Really?" Her tone is dry.

"What are you wearing?" I ask, not sure why I'm feeling so anxious.

"This." She gestures at her beige shorts and blue T-shirt.

It's my turn to raise an eyebrow. "Really?"

She laughs. "Not impressed?"

"It's fine, but doesn't exactly scream 'party.'" I smile. "I have this cute skirt that would look great on you, and actually my black tank top with the sparkles…"

Ten minutes later Harp's decked out in my jean skirt and black tank, her hair swept to the side in a low ponytail.

"You're missing something…" I go to my bag of accessories and pull out a pair of silver hoop earrings, holding them up to her lobes. "Perfect." That ought to wake up Boy Science.

She shakes her head and takes them from me. "You're sure I don't look ridiculous?"

"Are you saying my clothes are ridiculous?" I tease.

"No, I'm just not used to … to…" she stammers.

"You look fantastic," I assure her. "Who knew you were hiding such a great bod?" Blushing, she examines herself in the mirror.

"Now, what am I going to wear?" I throw some more clothes around until I find something that might work. It's a white dress with a halter top that cinches at the waist and flares out inches above the knee.

"You brought that on a conservation field trip?" Harp asks when I hold it up.

"A girl never knows when she'll need a great outfit," I say. "Besides, it's getting worn tonight, right?"

She laughs, her brown eyes sparkling. "You have a point."

I slip on my opal ring, now a proper fit with a wad of tape around the band, and a glittery gold headband, leaving my hair down.

We go downstairs to meet everyone. The boys are sprawled on the lounge chairs, all wearing shorts and assorted T-shirts. Chrissy and Kiki are talking to Enrique. Chrissy sports a red tank top and jean shorts, her short blonde hair pinned back. She's traded her teal frames for contacts. Kiki wears a purple sundress, her shiny black hair up in a high pony.

Enrique sees us first and gives a low whistle. "May I say that you ladies look *muy bonitas* this evening?" he says to Harp and me.

"You may." I make a curtsy, aware of another pair of eyes on me. "Glad to see you boys didn't go all out," I say.

"They'll blend in," Enrique says, wearing a tight black shirt. "Tourists don't always dress so nice at the resort."

"Did he just insult us?" Steven asks Travis.

"Huh?" he says, eyes still following me. I pretend not to notice.

Bass pumps and gravel crunches as a vehicle pulls up outside the compound and gives a few quick honks.

Enrique looks at us. "You ready?"

Everyone nods.

"Girls with me, guys with Carlos," Enrique instructs.

As we load into their Jeeps, I hear Travis mutter something like, "Figures."

I sit in the front and the other girls get in the back. Enrique has the top down and the warm night air blows around us. The atmosphere in the car crackles with excitement. We follow Carlos closely. Juan turns around and waves at us out the back window.

"So how is this going to work?" I try to appear casual, smoothing my dress down.

"Carlos works at Crystal Shores. Our *amigo* works the security gate."

"How far away is it?" Chrissy says from the back.

Enrique looks at her in the rearview and smiles. "Fifteen minutes."

In no time we're making a left down a long and winding road bordered with palm trees. Five minutes later we see a ginormous sign lit with twinkling lights that spell out 'Crystal Shores.'

A few feet ahead, a security gatehouse with a long horizontal pole on each side barricades the entrance and exits. Carlos's Jeep pulls up to the window. Harp inhales noisily. The guy at the security gate shines his light in Carlos's window. Harp exhales loudly when he gives Carlos a fist bump and the Jeep continues on through.

We pull up next. The guy nods at Enrique, saying something in Spanish. He crosses meaty arms over his chest. His voice rises and Enrique looks surprised, his tone becoming insistent.

"What's wrong?" I ask.

"It's not our *amigo*. This guy knows Carlos but doesn't recognize me."

Enrique looks grim. "He says we can't come in."

"Oh God," Kiki whispers from the back, "I knew this was a bad idea! We're going to get in so much trouble!"

The guy looks menacingly into the Jeep and barks something into his walkie-talkie.

"Maybe we should just go," Chrissy says, panicked.

"It's too late." Enrique clutches the steering wheel. "He's called for backup."

Chapter

Twenty-Three

"Oh God," Kiki wails again.

Enrique bursts out laughing and so does the guy holding the walkie-talkie.

"We are just playing! It's cool." Enrique dispenses one of his disarming grins.

I put my hand on my chest. My heart's pounding.

"Not funny," I say.

"*Sí, muy* funny." The security guy scratches his generous belly. He gives Enrique the same fist bump as Carlos and waves us on in.

Enrique's still grinning as we drive down a lane lit with soft fairy lights wrapped around palm trees spaced perfectly apart. We reach a parking lot and pull into an open spot.

"You should have seen your faces," he says as we get out of the Jeep. All of us are so relieved we giggle along with him, the tension fueling our giddiness.

The boys stand in a dim corner of the lot and start over.

"We'll go down through the back path," Carlos says. He's almost as good-looking as Enrique, with a shaved head and goatee. "But first you need your bracelets." He holds up a bunch of plastic orange wristbands.

"What're they for?" Harp asks.

"It's what guests wear when they stay here. It's all-inclusive so if you have one of these you don't pay for anything."

"So we can just order whatever we want?" Steven asks. Travis looks skeptical, his face shadowed in the moonlight.

"That's the idea." Carlos puts on our bands for us.

Chrissy and Kiki exchange excited looks.

"Remember," Enrique says, "act like you belong."

The open-air lobby of the hotel is stunning. Huge arches inlaid with gorgeous tiles whisper of opulence and luxury. Carlos and Enrique lead us down a dim path. Music and laughter float on the warm breeze. We pass by a restaurant where people enjoy a late dinner. Men with guitars strum romantic up-tempo music, keeping the diners entertained. The grounds are exquisitely manicured, stretching on forever. We follow our smugglers as they guide us down to the beach where it's darker and we're partially hidden by palm trees.

"It's best if we have some drinks down here and relax for a while until the club gets going," Enrique says. "We will be less obvious if anybody's looking for people who don't belong."

"So is this a common thing to do around here?" Travis shoves his hands in his shorts pockets.

Carlos shrugs. "Most of the staff won't care, but there's always a chance one of the bosses will be around and recognize us."

Enrique laughs. "Relax, *amigo*, we should have no problems."

"What do you guys want to drink?" Carlos asks. "Enrique and I will get the first round."

"*Una cerveza por favor,*" Juan pipes up. Travis and Steven echo his sentiment.

"Ladies? *Piña coladas* all around?" Carlos asks.

"Sure," we chime.

They go get our drinks and the seven of us look at each other.

"This is awesome," Steven says. I look around at everyone's faces. The full moon reflects their exhilaration. I catch Travis's eye. He shrugs and gives a small smile.

"So far, so good," Harp says. She's been quiet since the joke Enrique and Carlos played. I give her an encouraging smile. They come back a few minutes later with the drinks and hand them out.

Enrique holds his Corona aloft. "Let the party begin!"

We hold up our glasses.

"What's the word here for 'cheers'?" I ask.

"*Salud,*" Enrique says.

"*Salud,*" we echo.

We take a drink. It's delicious.

Harp whispers in my ear, "This is my first drink."

We spread out on the cool sand. The waves brush gently against the shore in lazy strokes. Chrissy and Kiki go with Enrique and Carlos to get more drinks. Travis, Steven and Juan sit with me and Harp. We talk about

El Níspero, offering opinions on Lola and Mr. A, while catching glimpses of the onstage entertainment. Tonight's theme seems to be Africa.

"So how's *A Ribbeting Cause* coming along?" I ask, as costumed dancers gyrate to tribal beats.

"Why, Princess," Travis's expression is alight with mischief, "are you actually starting to care about the fate of frogs?"

I kick some sand at him, but can't help smiling as he looks into my eyes. "They've been growing on me." So is he.

Enrique comes over with another round. The tasty drinks are strong but go down way too easy. I can already feel a buzz flowing through my body. The music is loud and infectious. My feet start tapping in the sand.

"This girl wants to dance!" Enrique winks at me.

The night has settled upon us and the alcohol is working its way not only through our small crowd but through the rest of the guests at the resort as well. People dance to the band that has replaced the performers and shrieks of laughter ring out in all directions. Tiki torches light the beach and the stars shine down on throngs of raucous vacationers having a good time.

"What do you say we hit the club?" Enrique stands up and brushes the sand off his shorts.

We follow him and Carlos in the direction of the thumping beats. Chrissy and Kiki walk beside them and Harp with Steven and Juan close behind. Travis and I trail.

"How's your pre-birthday bash going so far?" he asks me.

"Ssssh. I think everyone's forgotten." I hold a finger to my lips.

He looks at my hand. "Your ring looks pretty in the moonlight."

"Thanks to you."

"Glad to be of service." He bows, less mocking, somehow — almost charming.

"Speaking of which, I *do* think our last non-date deserves a do over," I say, the alcohol making me magnanimous.

"Sweet." He grins. "The fish market wasn't up to my usual standards."

"Oh?" I say. "You do this a lot then?"

Kiki turns around at that exact minute and spots us talking. She looks back at Carlos and laughs loudly at something he says.

"I think she's trying to make you jealous," I say.

"That only works if you have feelings for the person." His voice is soft.

"You don't?"

"She's a nice girl, but not really my type."

"And what's that?"

He smiles, mysterious, and avoids my question. "Speaking of, Enrique keeps staring at you," he says. "Is there something going on between you guys?"

"We're … friendly," I say.

"I think he'd like to be more than friendly," Travis whispers.

"Don't be ridiculous. Enrique flirts with everyone." But something about what Travis says unsettles me.

We reach the club entrance. It resembles a cave from prehistoric times, a place the Flintstones would come to party. I turn the conversation back to him. "You never said what your type is."

"It seems I have the same taste as our gracious host." He looks at Enrique, who's holding the slab of a door open for us to walk in. I stop suddenly at his remark and he bumps into me, not expecting my abrupt halt. I twist my head to look up at him.

He swallows and looks down at me. "Can we go for a walk?"

At the exact same time Enrique calls, "Jess, are you coming?"

Everyone else has gone inside. The moon glints off of Travis's green eyes while sultry music beckons from behind Enrique. I look back and forth between the two.

"Are you coming?" Enrique repeats. His broad tanned shoulders go up, questioning.

Travis doesn't say anything, but stands there looking at me.

"I, um…"

Harp pokes her head out. "Jess, get in here, quick."

"Coming." Flustered and grateful for the out, I shoot Travis an apologetic look and follow Harp inside. It takes a few minutes for my eyes to adjust to the dark and my ears to the drum-bursting speakers. I look to see Enrique and Travis enter behind me. Travis doesn't look happy. Confused by the sudden turn of events, I let Harp guide me to the bar where the bartender lights drinks on fire. He slides a flaming drink down the length of the bar to Juan, who catches it and deftly shoots it back to the cheers of the crowd.

"That's his third," she says.

Juan places the empty shot glass upside down on the bar and turns to us. "This place is awesome." His eyes are glassy under the strobe lights.

"Maybe you should slow down," I shout over the music.

"I've never felt like this before."

"You've never drank before either?"

"Not even a little bit." He hiccups, swaying.

Momentarily distracted from the soap opera that is becoming my life, I get three waters from the bartender and give one each to Harp and Juan. Good thing I have lots of practice taking care of intoxicated friends. I normally don't like the taste of most alcohol. Then again, I've never had a real piña colada before.

"Let's go dance," I say. Getting away from the bar is probably a good idea, and sweating out some booze won't hurt either. We head onto a dance floor with lit-up fluorescent squares. It's packed and everyone's moving. Time passes in a blur as we bop around like maniacs. Juan and Harp are having a great time. I try not to think of the look on Travis's face. Or Enrique's for that matter.

"There's Kiki and Chrissy," Harp shouts and points at the girls who are dancing with Carlos and Steven. I look around for Travis but can't see him. A slow song comes on as everyone catches their breath and Enrique walks up to me.

"Do you want to dance?" he asks.

I look at Harp and Juan who are swaying together. They deserve some time off from their third wheel.

"Sure." I wipe my damp forehead with the back of my hand.

Enrique's muscular arms encircle my waist and pull me close. My arms go up around his neck. He's a very good dancer. Are all Latin guys born knowing how to move their hips? I still feel the drinks in my system. The dim lights, loud music and large crowd make me feel invisible.

I look up at Enrique to thank him for bringing us here. At the same time he moves his head and his mouth comes down on mine. I freeze like a frog in headlights. His lips are soft and warm but somehow not quite right. I pull away.

"Sorry." He smiles, eyes appearing almost black as they stare into mine. "I couldn't resist."

I struggle to think of something offhand to say and turn my head to look for help in Harp and Juan, who are a few feet away. Instead, I catch Travis's eye. He's standing at the bar, staring at us with an unreadable expression on his face. No — scratch that — it's definitely readable. He looks pissed.

Chapter Twenty-Four

A t that exact moment, Juan proceeds to throw up in the middle of the dance floor.

Harp jumps back in time to narrowly avoid being splattered. A few other people aren't so lucky and one woman shrieks in disgust. Her partner, a big guy three times the size of Juan, starts to puff up his chest and jabs a chunky finger in his face. Enrique quickly takes in the situation.

"*Vamonos*. Now." He grabs my arm. He gives a quick whistle to Carlos who has his arms wrapped around Kiki. Carlos taps Steven's shoulders and nods toward the door. Steven disentangles himself from Chrissy who looks around blinking, like she's just woken up. Or is about to pass out.

"What about Juan?" I say. "We can't leave him." Two burly guys with very unfriendly looks on their faces are barreling toward our group. Harp has one hand on Juan's back and looks around, panicked. In a second, Travis is by our sides.

"Come on," he says, getting one arm around Juan and steering him toward the door. Steven grabs Juan's other arm and we make a hasty retreat for the exit.

"Hey!" one of the beefy bouncers shouts after us. We don't stick around to see what he wants. We race out into the night and along the stretch of beach, sand flying up at our heels. I turn to see the security guards chasing us, out of breath and panting. Lucky for us, it looks like they indulge in a lot of the resort food.

"This way," Carlos motions, running up a path that snakes behind the kitchens. We follow, breathing hard, our faces flushed. We reach the parking lot and sprint toward the vehicles.

"See you back at my place," Enrique says to Carlos, who helps Steven and Travis get a semi-comatose Juan into the back of his Jeep.

"Don't puke in my car, *amigo*," Carlos says to him as the girls jump in Enrique's Jeep. We tear out of the parking lot, tires screeching in our wake.

"That was crazy," Enrique says, whizzing down the highway. Chrissy and Kiki titter nervously. Harp looks pale and fumbles for her inhaler. "Everyone okay?"

I look at Harp who nods along with Chrissy and Kiki. "What would've happened if they had caught us?"

He shrugs. "Probably would've called the cops, then kicked you out of the country."

Harp pales further and sucks back some more of whatever's in there.

"Just kidding." He grins. "Maybe nothing so serious, but best not to find out."

I sit back, my head against the seat. That was pretty risky. And it's not over. We have to sneak back in before Mr. A notices we're gone. I pray he's still on his date with Lola.

We pull into the compound and I see that those prayers are not about to be answered.

Mr. A stands there, arms folded across his chest, an agitated expression on his face. Lola is beside him, looking concerned. Enrique's parents are off to the side, seemingly unsurprised and unimpressed with their son.

"Are you going to get in trouble too?" Chrissy whispers from the back, hiccuping.

"No, I can do what I want." But he looks slightly doubtful as he turns off the Jeep. Carlos pulls in behind us. Oh God. Juan. Mr. A will see right away he's wasted. I try to think of a distraction and come up with nothing.

"Where were you?" Mr. A demands as we step out of the car to face our executioners.

"With me," Enrique says in a confident voice, his head high.

"And where was that?" Carlita says, her eyes flashing.

"A party," Enrique replies.

"It's after midnight." Mr. A's stormy gray eyes drill into the four of us. "Do you have any idea how worried we've been?"

I look around at the other girls. Their heads hang low and they stare at the ground.

"I never thought you'd do something like that." Mr. A's hand runs through his spiky hair in frustration. Lola puts a hand on his back.

"We were completely fine," I say. "Just trying to take in a bit of local color, for, um research purposes," I add lamely.

Travis has gotten out of the vehicle with Steven and Juan. Carlos, being a somewhat perceptive fellow, reverses out of the compound as quickly as possible with a brief farewell honk.

Travis speaks up. "We wanted to throw Jess a birthday party." He doesn't look in my direction and keeps his arm around Juan, who's doing his best to stand up straight but isn't having much success. I hope Mr. A doesn't smell the fumes wafting off of him.

"How thoughtful," Mr. A says, his cheeks stained red.

"At least you are all back safe," Lola says, her hand still on Mr. A's back.

"Do you know what can happen when your parents find out about this?" he says.

"We won't say anything." Kiki sniffles.

"That's not the point. They entrusted you to my care and I've done a pretty poor job of it." Mr. A deflates suddenly. The anger leaves him, replaced by disappointment, which of course, is much worse.

Hector clears his throat. "Well, they are back and, as Lola said, safe. Why don't we finish talking about this tomorrow?" He sends his son a look that says, *'This is why we told you not to mess with the tourists.'*

"You know I'm going to have to call your parents," Mr. A says, reluctant.

Crap and double crap.

"Do you have anything to say for yourselves?"

"Yesss," Juan slurs, "I just want to say…" He throws up again before he can finish his thought, this time all over himself. He really does have the worst timing.

"Please, go inside. Now." Mr. A's face is drawn.

We go silently into our villas. Nobody says a word as we wash up for bed.

I lay on my mattress staring up at the ceiling, listening to Harp's snores. I think of Enrique's kiss. I touch my lips as I remember the look on Travis's face. There's a sick curdling in my stomach. I'm not sure if it's the piña coladas or guilt. I roll over and look at the ancient brown alarm clock on the nightstand beside my bed. It reads 1:04 a.m.

Happy birthday to me.

***

"Ohhh." A moan comes from across the room.

I open my bleary eyes as the sound comes again, accompanied by an, "I want to die."

"Are you okay?" I croak.

"I feel awful," Harp groans.

"It's called a hangover."

"I know," she says.

"You'll feel better after some water and a big breakfast." My head is throbbing. "Breakfast?" She turns green, then jumps up and runs to the bathroom. I hear the toilet flush. She comes back into the room and flops down on her bed.

"Why do people drink when you feel so terrible after?"

"Not sure," I say, rubbing my temples.

The bell rings for breakfast.

"Do we have to go?" Harp asks.

"I don't think we have a choice."

We drag ourselves out of bed and get dressed, bumping into Chrissy and Kiki on the stairwell, and they look just as bad. We run into the boys, who aren't much better. There's a fine sheen of sweat on Juan's upper lip, and all three have dark circles under their eyes. Steven and Juan mumble, "Good morning."

Travis doesn't say a word to me.

We stumble into the *bohío* like criminals on their way to sentencing. There are a few boxes of cereal out and some muffins. I pour myself a glass of orange juice and sit down. It's all my stomach can handle at the moment.

"What do you think is going to happen to us?" Harp says.

"We're probably getting sent home." Juan's miserable.

I'm not feeling so hot myself.

We sit in silence, nobody eating much. Mr. A isn't there. He's probably arranging our flights back to Seattle. Enrique is also absent. Most likely his parents told him to stay away for a while.

"Where's Mr. A?" Chrissy asks. At that moment he staggers in to the *bohío*, sweating profusely, glassy-eyed and ghastly white.

"Mr. A, are you okay?" Harp asks.

"Urk." He looks like he's going to yak then and there. "You," he points at us, "stay in compound." He clutches his stomach. "I've called Lola. Hector is taking me to the clinic." Speaking those few words costs him and he turns to flee. Cheeks bulging, he barely makes it to the bathroom beside the pool.

"He looks bad, man," Steven says, to no one in particular.

We look around at one another — pity, with a huge dash of relief, appears on everyone's faces. Poor Mr. A, but at least it looks like our punishment will be momentarily delayed. Thank God, because all I can deal with right now is lounging by the pool.

Mr. A emerges unsteadily from the washroom minutes later, on the verge of collapsing. Hector reaches his side, hands him a paper bag, and assists him to the van. Lola pulls up in her little car just as they're reversing. She rolls down her window and Mr. A does the same.

"Kenny!" she exclaims at his dreadful appearance.

"Must've been our *raspados*." He's too sick to muster much of a smile. "Thanks for coming to keep an eye on the kids."

"Once the doctor gives you something, you will feel better in no time," she assures him.

"How come you're not sick?" we hear him ask.

"My stomach is used to the bugs here," she says. "Don't worry, I will take care of everything."

"Thanks," he mumbles, then bends his head down to dispense whatever's left of his stomach contents into the bag between his knees. Hector speedily pulls out of the compound and Lola gets out of her car.

Carlita comes up to Lola and says something rapid in Spanish. Lola eyes us in our sorry hungover state and responds, also in Spanish. She walks up to the *bohío*, folding her arms.

"Carlita just informed me that your villas could use a good cleaning and that perhaps it is also a good time for you to think about your actions," she says.

I sigh. So much for lounging by the pool.

***

A few hours later, after a lot of sweat and nausea, we finish cleaning. I sprawl on my bed, exhausted, one arm over my face.

Harp walks in the room. "A few of us are going down to the beach. A dip in the ocean might help."

"Sounds perfect," I say. "Are we allowed?"

"Lola's coming with us," she says. "Mr. A's back from the clinic but probably won't be getting out of bed for the rest of the day."

I drag myself up and out of the bed. Maybe the saltwater will clear my head.

Down at the beach everyone is subdued, the tentacles of our hangovers unwilling to completely release their grip on our bodies. The boys and Chrissy and Kiki wade into the water. Juan's barely spoken all day.

"Have you talked to Juan?" I ask Harp. "He seems really quiet."

"I think he feels pretty bad. He's not used to disappointing authority figures." She looks over at the group. "None of us are."

"It gets easier," I crack, but realize I'm dead serious. Somewhere along the way I've gotten used to disappointing people. Teachers, old friends, my parents, even that other part of me I've suppressed for so long. Messy Jessie.

"It was a fun night." She looks out at the water then gasps loudly, hands going to her mouth.

"What?" I scan for a dorsal fin, half-springing up to shout a shark warning when she grabs my arm.

"We forgot your birthday!" she says.

"Oh, that." I sit back down. "Don't worry, I don't think anyone's really in the birthday mood today. Plus, we celebrated last night."

"Well, you certainly did." She elbows me. "So is Enrique a good kisser?"

"He's okay." I shrug, feeling embarrassed by the whole thing.

"No butterflies?"

"Not even a fuzzy caterpillar." Unless you count his top lip.

"I've never been kissed before," she says, her voice wistful.

"Is there anyone in particular you'd like to remedy that?" It's my turn to elbow her back.

"Maybe." She looks in the direction of the boys. Juan's standing in the water, talking to Travis and Steven. He laughs at something Travis says.

"You really like Juan, don't you?"

"Is it that obvious?" She bites her lip. "He's just so into conservation." She looks glum. "I mean, I am too, of course, but I don't think there's any room left over in his head."

"I don't know. I think Juan has a very big brain, with more capacity for that kind of stuff than you think." I look at her. "Why don't you tell him?"

"Are you crazy?" she says. "I could never. Besides I'm not allowed to date until college anyway." She places her chin in her hands, elbows on her knees.

"I have a great idea," I say, wanting to cheer her up. "Let's do a makeover, like the other night, but more!"

She looks at me and raises an unplucked eyebrow.

"Not that you need one or anything," I say, realizing how it sounds. "Sometimes it's just nice to refresh our look…" I shut up, hoping I haven't completely offended her.

"You think I'm ugly?" She pulls at her braid.

"No! I didn't mean it like that…" I feel awful. Harp laughs.

"I'm just messing with you," she says in a playful tone that has me sighing with relief. "I'd love a makeover."

"Perfect! Let's do it tomorrow!" I clap my hands together.

"Deal."

"Time to go, guys!" Lola shouts.

"But I haven't gone in the water yet," I call back to her.

"Then hurry up," she says.

Tearing off the ratty gray sundress worn in reflection of my physical state, I race for the water as the others make their way in, looking like they've come back somewhat from the dead.

I dive headfirst into the salty ocean. The shock of it blasts the last remnants of alcohol from my cells and the coolness of the rolling waves soothes me. Treading water for a minute, I look back toward the shore at Harp. Juan is toweling off, talking to her, and I smile. This trip has been a disaster in so many ways, but it's possible I may go home with a new friend.

Juan holds out his hand and helps Harp up off the sand.

Possibly two.

Travis walks over to them and my smile falters. After last night, maybe not three.

"Jess!" Lola shouts.

"Coming!" I swim back to shore, then get my own towel and wrap it around me. I follow behind everyone as we head back. Travis stops to tie his shoelace and I walk by him quickly. We still haven't spoken since outside the club when he may or may not have admitted he liked me. Right before Enrique kissed me.

"Jess." I freeze as he says my name. Everyone else has pulled ahead.

I close my eyes, take a breath and turn to face him.

Chapter
Twenty-Five

"What's up?" I inject an artificially casual tone into my voice. His green eyes are stormy, his angular jaw tense. "Did you have fun last night?"

"Um, yeah." I bite my left pinky nail.

"That's it?" he says.

"Well, until we got busted, of course," I add, but those don't seem to be the words he wants to hear. He looks down with one of his penetrating stares that peel a layer off me. I shift uncomfortably, not sure if I should broach the kiss with Enrique or not. I decide not.

"Well," he finally says, "happy birthday."

"Thanks." I'm relieved he let me off so easily.

"And I definitely think we can forget about our non-dates." His voice is quiet. The perpetual playful glint in his eyes is gone.

I feel like he's punched me in the gut.

"Fine by me." I look at my chipped fingernails, striving for blasé. "They were your idea anyway."

"Cool. See you later." Without a backwards glance he walks toward the compound and leaves me standing there in my towel staring after him, feeling like a very big pile of frog crap.

***

Dinner is a meal of something called seviche, which is mixed raw seafood cooked in lime. I'm sure it's normally delicious, but definitely not the best hangover remedy. Everyone looks a little green when Carlita serves it with a flourish. I wonder if she made it on purpose.

Afterwards, I grab the computer to check my emails. There are a zillion birthday messages and a few emails from some of my friends. Both Alyssa and Ky have finally sent me emails, but they're devoid of any real message, going on about what a great time they're having and how they don't want to go home. Not one question about me or how things are at my end of the world. I'd probably just depress them to death anyway. Nothing from Miles, of course. An email from my parents says they tried to reach me and to call them back.

I ask around for the phone but nobody knows where it is. Which means one thing: Mr. A probably has it. Crap. My parents will be choked if I don't call. And I always like to thank my mom on my birthday for having me and all that. God knows she'd hated all that weight gain and the stretch marks. I suspect that may very well have been a contributing factor to my lack of a younger sibling.

I go to the boys' villa and knock. There's no answer so I open the door and poke my head in.

"Mr. A?" I call out. No answer.

I walk inside.

"Mr. A?" I call again.

"In here," Lola calls.

I go down the hallway to the living room. Lola sits beside Mr. A on the couch, mopping his sweaty brow with a facecloth. He still looks pale but a lot better from the nasty puce of this morning.

"How are you feeling?" I ask.

"I'll survive." His voice is raspy. "The doctor seems to think it's just a twenty-four hour thing."

"You should be feeling better by tomorrow," Lola declares. Mr. A looks up at her, gratitude shining in his eyes.

"I was just wondering if you had the phone." The words tumble out, aware I'm intruding.

"It's on the table." He nods across the room.

"Thanks." I walk over to get it, taking a deep breath. "Was there anyone in particular you were calling?"

"Like your parents?" he says.

I gulp and turn around. "Look," I say, "it's my fault. Send me home if you have to, but don't punish everyone else. They just wanted to celebrate my birthday."

"It's partly my fault," he sighs. "I shouldn't have gone off and left you alone like that."

I pick up the phone.

"You know, it's the frogs that are going to lose out if we go home." He glances at Lola, then back at me.

"Plus it'll cost a fortune to change all the tickets," I add, my fingers tightening around the phone.

Lola hides a smile.

"I do hate to deliver bad news on birthdays," he finally says. "Tell everyone they'll find out their fate tomorrow."

"Okay, have a good night." Relieved, I turn to go before he changes his mind.

"And, Jess," he calls. I freeze. "It's across the board. What happens to one happens to all of you."

That does not sound promising.

***

I call my parents, who are happy to hear from me and wish me a happy birthday.

"How's the report going?" Dad asks.

"Pretty good. I'm actually finding the research kinda interesting."

"That's good," he says. I can tell he's trying not to sound too pleased.

Mom's voice comes from the other line. "How's your skin, sweetie?"

"Pink and peeling." I can't resist.

I hear a gasp. "Are you moisturizing?"

"Yes, Mom." I try to distract her. "I'm bringing you home this really cool volcanic mud."

This mollifies her a bit and we chat for a few more minutes.

"We'll be at the airport to pick you up next week," she says, her voice catching.

"Why, Mother, could it be you actually miss me?" I joke.

There's a muffled sob on the phone and one of the lines click.

"Hello?" I ask, alarmed. What'd I say?

"Your mom's just feeling a bit emotional," Dad's voice comes across, "with you being away. It's hitting her that it's going to be much harder to say good-bye when you go to college." He clears his throat. "If you go. Whatever you decide, we'll support you."

"Okay…" I say, slowly. "Thanks."

"I better go," he says. "Mom needs a hug. See you in a few days." We hang up.

Is it possible Mom never encouraged me to go Berkeley because some part of her doesn't want me to leave home? After talking with Harp and Juan I've also been thinking that maybe her lack of interest in the academic stems from her feeling a bit … inferior. It must have been tough living up to Dad's genius ex, not to mention Gigi. I suddenly feel a bit more charitable toward her, which triggers homesickness.

I look down at the phone in my hands. On a sudden impulse, I dial a number.

The phone rings. My grip on it gets sweaty.

"Hello?" a voice says.

"Miles?" There's a cinch cord around my chest. "It's Jess."

"Jess?" he says, his voice heartbreakingly familiar. "Where are you?"

"Panama, remember?" I hear water running in the background. I've caught him just before he's getting in the shower.

"Yeah, I just thought you'd be on your way home."

"Hopefully not for a few more days." I can't believe I'm actually talking to him. "What about you?" There are so many things I want to ask him.

"We head home tomorrow," he says.

A familiar voice calls out in the background. "Miles, you have no conditioner!"

The cinch cord tightens a few notches.

"Is that Ky?" My throat closes. I know it's her. "What's she doing in your room?"

More importantly, what's she doing in his shower?

"Uh, look Jess, I gotta go. Happy birthday." He fumbles the phone and the line goes dead.

I sit there holding the silent phone to my ear. Was I hearing things? Is this why Ky hasn't called? She's been hooking up with Miles? Dazed, I wonder how long it's been going on. Because something in my gut tells me it has been *going on*. I knew she had a crush on him a few years ago and asked her about it before we started dating but she said she was way over it. I'd asked because I didn't want to be someone who hooks up with guys their friends like. Apparently, she has no such qualms. I can't wrap my head around this. She's supposed to be my friend. My cheeks are wet when I finally bring the phone down.

This is officially the worst birthday ever.

***

After a fitful sleep, I wake the next morning, nauseous with anxiety. Today we find out our fate. We betrayed Mr. A, my best friend has been hooking up with my boyfriend, and Travis ... well, Travis might very well hate me. Unexpectedly, it's our derailed friendship that makes me feel the worst. I look over at Harp's bed, but it's empty and made.

I pull on jean shorts and a pink tank and put my hair up in a messy bun. Yesterday when we were cleaning, Carlita said we could use the laundry facilities so I decide to throw in some clothes. I stuff every dirty piece of laundry in my backpack and go downstairs. It's strangely quiet. I don't see anyone anywhere. I go to the laundry hut that's just off the *bohío* and dump my clothes in.

The bell hasn't rung for breakfast but I go to the *bohío* anyways. Pastries lay out on a table but there's still no sign of anyone. Just as I'm thinking everyone's been wiped out by the chytrid fungus, Enrique strolls out of his villa. I grab a bran muffin and walk toward him.

"*Hola*," I say. "Where is everybody?"

"My parents are at church," he says, "and I think your friends all went into town."

"Oh." That makes it official. I've been abandoned. I'm hurt nobody came to get me, especially Harp.

"Do you want to come with me for a drive?" he asks. "I can take you to meet them."

I'm not sure if I'm supposed to leave the property. I feel grounded. But if everyone else did, there's no point in sticking around. Plus, I need a distraction from the shit pile that is my life and Enrique always seems to be there when I need one. It's like he has antennae for it. I decide to be forgiving and chalk up his make out attempt to the alcohol.

"Um, sure." We walk over to his Jeep, pull out of the compound and drive down the highway toward town.

"Did you have fun the other night?" Enrique asks, his question echoing Travis's from the night before. The expression on his face when Enrique kissed me appears in my head.

"Yeah, the resort was beautiful," I say, distracted.

"What did you think of the club?" He looks back at the road.

"The cave theme was pretty cool."

"And me?"

I feel my cheeks flame.

"I, um … you're great." Lame. Totally lame.

"I think you're great, too." He puts a hand on my leg and gives another meaningful look.

"Oh, well, that's … great." I mentally slap his hand away. *Why do you get yourself into these situations?* A pair of golden arches springs into view. "Coronado has a McDonald's?" I seize anything to change the topic.

"*Sí*, and I have a craving for a Big Mac." He lets the subject and my leg go as he turns on squealing wheels into the parking lot, narrowly missing several cars in the process.

Unsure of where that conversation leaves us, I hop out of the car and hurry into McDonald's. The door swings behind me and I get chills, and not just from the full blast air-conditioning. It's familiar. A little piece of home. Greasy fast food and supersize combos are things America does very well. A tear springs to my eye at the sight of an enormous McFlurry sign hanging in the window. Enrique and I step up to order.

"How's the vegetarian thing coming along?" a voice says behind me.

I whirl around to face Travis. Juan stands beside him and Harp waves from the corner table where she sits with the others.

"I'm getting a McFlurry, if you must know," I say. So they all came to McDonald's without me. How nice. More betrayal.

"Why don't you hold off on that and come over here. We have some food we can't finish," Juan says.

Harp beckons me over so I walk stiffly toward their table. Enrique and Travis follow. Chrissy and Kiki look like someone peed in their chocolate sundaes. On the table is an enormous cake that reads 'Happy Birthday, Jess' in pink icing, covered in flowers with little frogs in the corners.

I'm shocked.

"Happy birthday," everyone says, with varying degrees of enthusiasm.

I don't know what to say. The single tear that formed upon my entry threatens to turn into multiple salty drops and I blink back hard.

"Surprise!" Harp stands up and claps her hands. "We know it was yesterday, but since that was such a write-off we figured we'd celebrate it today."

I'm speechless.

"Harp planned everything." Kiki's mouth puckers like she's swallowed an extra sour lemon.

"We're just here for the cake," Chrissy says, to be clear.

"Oink, oink," Juan says, seeming like his old self again. Harp cuts the cake and passes me the first piece.

I take it from Harp, stunned that these people I just met went to any effort whatsoever to ensure my birthday did not pass in a haze of hangover and looming punishment.

"Thanks for bringing her," Harp says to Enrique, handing him a piece.

"*De nada*," he says, smiling at me. "My pleasure."

Juan passes me a fork. "How are you feeling?" I ask.

"Better," he said. "Let's just say tequila and I will never be friends."

I laugh, then get sober. "How do you think it looks for us?"

"I don't know," he says, dejected.

I hesitate, then, "Mr. A said whatever happens to one, happens to all."

The table goes quiet listening to us and the mood shifts from celebratory to brooding. Everyone offers an opinion as we polish off the cake Harp bought from the supermarket across the street. Mr. A wouldn't seriously send us home, would he?

"I suppose we better get back for our verdict," Harp says over the crumbs.

Enrique jingles his keys. "Who wants a ride?"

"We do," Chrissy and Kiki chime.

"Jess?" he asks.

"I'm okay, actually." I don't really want to get back in the Jeep, especially not with the biology babes from hell.

"See you later, then?" He winks.

"Um, sure."

The three of them leave and the rest of us clean up then abandon the AC for the hot sun. Juan wants to stop at the supermarket for more Gravol so we all go in. Glancing at the back of Harp's head, I'm struck by an idea. I grab a box off a shelf and a few other items and meet the others at the cashier. We walk to the local bus stop and wait for a minivan to pick us up off the side of the highway. Cars whizz past and the heat from the pavement blasts through the soles of my feet. I sneak a look at Travis, who hasn't spoken to me since his initial flippant vegetarian comment. He's talking to Steven and Juan about a red frog disappearing from one of Panama's Caribbean islands.

"Thanks for today," I say to Harp. "That was really sweet of you."

"I'm a big fan of birthdays." She smiles as a van screeches to a halt and we get in. We find some empty seats as the vehicle pulls into the busy traffic, hurtling down the highway, toward the compound and our unknown fate.

***

"You guys really damaged my trust." Mr. A's voice falters. His eyes focus on each of us as we sit at our tables under the *bohío* after dinner, awaiting our verdict. He clears his throat. "But we came here to do a job and it's not fair to leave without finishing what we started." We let out a collective sigh of relief. "However, I will be informing your parents of your little escapade and leave it to them to deal with you personally. My pay grade doesn't cover that."

Harp gulps and a sardonic expression crosses Juan's face. His parents probably won't care. Not necessarily a good thing, I guess. I have no idea how mine will react.

"Now, get to bed and let's try to enjoy our last few days here." His gray eyes search out Lola, who stands off to the side. "We can't forget to fight for what's important." He looks at each of us. "The frogs."

We nod, chastised, and he walks away, Lola's hand on his arm. We slink off to our villas.

"Jess," Travis calls after me as I'm about to enter the house.

"Looks like someone wants to talk to you," Harp whispers and leaves me standing there alone with him in the dark. Crickets chirp in the balmy night air.

I turn around, guarded. He's been avoiding me all day and I've been trying not to care.

"I was just wondering…" he takes a step closer, looking at me like I'm one of those pictures where a hidden image pops out if you stare hard and long enough. "How would you feel about resuming our non-dates?"

My jaw drops. It's the last thing I'm expecting. "I thought you said it wasn't a good idea."

"Guess I changed my mind." He sucks in the hollows under his cheek-bones, waiting for my response.

"What … why?" I stammer.

"Something Mr. A said. About fighting for what's important." His fingers come up under my chin and lightly close my mouth. "Careful. You'll catch flies."

My heart does a weird skip. I swallow, looking up at his face.

A small smile plays around his lips. "How about tomorrow afternoon?"

"I guess that's fine." I look up at him, not quite sure what to think.

"See you tomorrow, then," he says, not moving.

I turn and walk up to the villa, looking back over my shoulder when I reach the arched doorway. Travis stands there in the moonlight, bold stare unwavering as I open the door. Closing it gently behind me, I lean back against the wood to steady myself.

It's crazy how quickly things can change.

Chapter
Twenty-Six

"Owww!" Harp says as I run a comb through her very unruly and very tangled dark hair. It snags in a particularly gnarly spot. "Sorry!" Full of nervous energy and unable to sleep, I woke her up with the news she was getting her makeover this morning. We're out on the balcony and the breeze gently flutters the ends of her hair. It's cool for the first time since our arrival.

"I hate my hair." She tugs at it. "It's so frizzy."

"Most girls would kill to have such thick hair." I think of my and Ky's over-processed blonde locks. Ky needed conditioner all right.

"You've never dyed it before?" I shake the bottle of hair dye I grabbed off the shelf yesterday in the store.

"Never." She bites her lip. "My parents are going to kill me."

"It'll be fine," I reassure her. "You can just say it got bleached by the sun." It already looks lighter from the developer. The color in the bottle is a lustrous auburn. I coat her locks, trying not to get the messy dye everywhere, then wrap a plastic bag around them.

"Done. Let's move on to the eyebrows." I pull out a pair of tweezers from my makeup bag. Harp squirms and yelps as I pluck. "Stop moving." Standing back, I admire the finished result.

"I want your eyebrows," I say. My own are so light and thin I have to pencil them in.

"So you're saying I should be thankful for the excess of body hair I've always hated?" She arches a now perfectly shaped brow.

"Yes. Let's rinse you out before we start on the makeup." A few minutes later she's back in the chair, wet hair in a towel. My tools are laid out before me.

"Where'd you learn to do all this stuff?" she asks as I set to work.

"I was hopeless before my … friends taught me." Are they still my friends? I wonder if Ky knows I know. If she even cares. Part of me wants to scream and yell at her, the other part just feels sad and drained. Some of the nervous energy leaves my body. I sponge some foundation onto Harp's face. "They're good at this kind of thing."

"They sound nice," she says.

"Sure." My voice wavers. Until they steal your boyfriend.

Harp catches my tone and looks up at me, brown eyes quizzical. "Aren't they?"

I sweep some blush and bronzer over her face, thinking of Alyssa and Ky and how they like to control everyone around them. As long as you do everything they want, things are great. But have a different opinion or idea and watch out. The last time I disagreed with them they didn't speak to me for weeks. I don't even remember what it was about. Just that I felt very lonely and scared I'd never have friends again.

"I guess even crappy friends are better than no friends," I say. Except I'm not sure I really believe that anymore.

"Have you heard from your ex lately?" Harp looks at me.

"As a matter of fact," I say, moving to brush her lids with shadow, "I talked to him yesterday. Close your eyes."

She obliges. "And?"

"It's definitely over," I say, surprised that as I speak the words aloud, most of the sting has melted into sadness at the wasted time I'd put into Miles. Into all of my so-called 'friends.' If Ky and Miles have been going on for a while, the others must have known.

"I'm sorry," she says.

"Me too." Even more so about Ky than Miles. A heaviness settles on my shoulders. Is all this worth it? The effort it takes to repress Messy Jessie is exhausting. And for what? People who betray me as soon it suits them?

"So what's going on with you and Travis?" She switches tracks, batting bare lashes in mock innocence.

"No idea," I say, feeling even more confused. "One minute it seems like he wants to be friends, the next he barely talks to me and the next we're friends again."

"Maybe the problem is he wants to be more than your friend."

I almost smear her carefully lined upper lids. I put the pencil down then grab the mascara.

"Blink," I say. "What are you talking about?"

"Maybe he's confused because he knows things were up in the air with

Miles. Or maybe he thinks you have something going on with Enrique."

"But I don't."

"We all saw him kiss you."

"He was just drunk." Old insecurities flare. "Besides, Enrique's super hot, I'm sure he has his pick of a million girls." Like Miles does. I smooth a soft cocoa-colored lip gloss on her lips.

"Um, Jess, have you looked in a mirror lately?" Harp stares up at me. "You're beautiful."

"Try telling that to my mother." I brush off her remark. "Besides, so are you." I hand her my compact mirror.

"Wow." She makes a move for the bigger mirror on the wall but I grab her arm.

"Sit," I command. "I'm not finished."

I grab my small blow-dryer and start on her hair. After all the work, time and energy I put into my appearance these last few years, I suppose I should be ecstatic Harp thinks I'm beautiful. I look down at her head and smile at the irony. After all, there's nothing wrong with the confidence that comes with feeling attractive. But something about this past week has shown me that it's not enough anymore. That there might be more important things.

I think of Gigi and the picture of her in my bedroom. She's surrounded by a group of friends, her local chapter of The Raging Grannies, an activist group that participates in protests on peace and the environment. They're standing in front of a giant redwood, canes and walkers out in full force. She'd given me that picture right after I'd started middle school. She must have known I was having trouble adjusting. "Anyone can make a difference, Jessica, even a bunch of old ladies with arthritis." Her vibrant blue eyes peered into mine. "Don't be afraid of your gifts, even if others don't appreciate them. You'll find your tribe yet."

I turn off the dryer. Maybe I *do* want to make a difference.

"Almost done," I say, trying not to let Harp see I'm having a revelation. I grab my hair straightener. With the dryer off, we can talk again.

"So what are you going to do?" she asks. I wonder if she's been reading my mind.

"About what?" I say.

"Travis."

"I have no idea." I run the straightener through her hair. "What are you going to do about Juan?"

She blushes. "Nothing."

"He's going to freak when he sees you."

She picks up a smooth strand of hair. Red tones glint in the sleek mahogany.

"You think?" she asks, an unsure tone in her voice.

"I know. You can look now."

She jumps out of her seat and runs over to the large mirror. She's silent as she takes in her transformation. Shiny dark hair falls past her shoulders. Subtle makeup illuminates high cheekbones and makes her caramel eyes, framed by freshly tamed brows, sparkle. Plump lips curve in delight.

"Who is that?" she says in awe, moving her head around to check herself out from all different angles.

"It's you," I say.

"That's not me."

"Sure it is, just a side you've never seen before." A peace settles over me as I come to terms with the realization. "You're allowed to have more than just one, you know."

"Yes." She looks straight at me standing behind her in the mirror. "You are."

The bell rings for breakfast. I turn away, unnerved, and pick up the hair dryer. "Flip your head. I want to give those roots a quick blast before we go." I turn on the dryer and the lights go out, along with the fan. "Oops."

We hear Chrissy shout in the shower.

"I think you blew a fuse," she says.

"Wait 'til everyone sees you." I put down the dryer and we head for the door. "You'll be the one blowing fuses."

"Okay, that's seriously cheesy." She laughs and I join in, feeling lighter.

I grin. "That's me."

***

Harp saunters into the *bohío*, a saucy swing in her hips. I follow at a distance to watch reactions.

Everyone immediately stops talking and just stares. Harp nonchalantly serves herself breakfast and we sit down at our usual table across from Juan. Steven and Travis whistle and Kiki and Chrissy ignore us, talking loudly.

Juan hasn't moved a muscle, his mouth hanging open as if he's beholding a three-headed frog.

"I'm excited to see the animals today," Harp says, as if nothing is out of the ordinary. "The all-white peacocks are so pretty." She flicks her hair over her shoulder. "I didn't even know they existed until we got here."

"What about you?" I ask Juan. I'm strongly tempted to reach out and lift his jaw off the floor like Travis did to me last night.

"What?" He doesn't comprehend a single word I've said.

I can't resist. "Are you excited to see the polka-dot peacocks?" I say with a straight face.

"Um, yeah, sure, very rare species," he says.

Harp and I laugh as Juan looks even more perplexed at his best friend who's unexpectedly transformed into a total babe.

***

I spend the whole morning at the center interviewing Lola, who's turning out to be the perfect source for my paper. She knows everything about frogs and the local legends of Panama. I'm growing fonder of the little guys, and not just because they're the only things that can save my butt from failing bio. The more I learn about them and the other frogs, the more I realize the importance of individual species to biodiversity as a whole, not to mention their place in Panama's cultural landscape.

God, I'm beginning to sound like Juan.

I look over at him with a smile. He's filming some of the interview for his documentary and my report while Harp watches us, cutting up most of the bamboo alone. She looks amazing, her glossy straight hair now pinned back.

I ask my last question. "Do you think that the golden frog and others will ever be reintroduced to the wild?"

Juan focuses in on Lola, who contemplates it with a serious expression on her face.

"Of course I hope to see them in these forests again. And there are new developments every day in the fight against chytrid." She looks at the camera, her voice husky. "But it depends on us. Many species are on the verge of going extinct and the golden frog is only one of them. They are an ambassador species, similar to Sumatran orangutans and tigers or polar bears. People need to realize that once these creatures are gone we can never get them back. They're lost to us forever, and with them we lose a piece of our humanity."

Juan lingers on her sincere face for a moment then turns the camera off.

"You sure know how to work the camera," he says.

"I used to be an actor." Lola dimples modestly.

"Really? That's so cool!" Harp says from behind her massive bamboo pile. "When?"

"Before I went to college in the US. It was just for some silly Spanish *novela*," she says, dismissive. "I think you call them soap operas?"

"What made you go into conservation?" I ask.

"I've always loved animals, but to tell you the truth, it was Kenny," she says. "He was just so passionate. I was really inspired by him."

"It sucks you guys live so far apart," I say.

"*Sí*." She's somber.

"Have you ever thought about moving back to the US?" Juan asks.

"The frogs need me here," she says. "My country needs me. I cannot turn my back on them." Her voice breaks. One hand goes to her mouth to muffle a cry. "*Perdóneme.*" She hurries out the back door with a murmured, "*Un momento.*"

Harp and I watch her go and let out a little sigh at the wrenching sacrifice of it all.

Travis pokes his head in the doorway. "How's it going?" he asks, pushing the hair that's forever falling into his eyes off his face.

"Good." I take a step toward him.

"You ready?" he asks, smiling, and my heartbeat involuntarily picks up tempo.

"Um, I think so." I turn to glance at Harp and Juan.

"We're done anyway," Harp says as we walk outside with Travis. Clouds have rolled in since this morning and the air is refreshingly cool. "Where are you going?"

"It's a surprise," Travis looks at me, green eyes sparkling with their familiar mischief. I feel like I've just stepped off a roller coaster at Six Flags. Something inside me that I didn't even know I was fighting finally and completely gives way.

Shit. I have feelings for Travis.

Chapter Twenty-Seven

I need a minute. "Hang on a sec, just let me get my sweater." I run back inside to grab it, gulping down deep breaths.

Get it together Jess.

"Do you think it's going to rain?" Juan's craning his neck and looking up at the sky as I walk back outside, somewhat composed.

"It hasn't the whole time we've been here," Harp points out.

"It'll pass," Travis says with confidence.

"See you guys later." I tie my sweater around my waist.

"Later!" They wave.

"So what are we doing?" Feeling unexpectedly shy, I follow him to the bike shed.

"Do you like horses?" he asks as we pass Lola, who now looks dry-eyed and composed. I wave and she gives me a wink. I blush. Am I that obvious?

"Not sure. I've never been all that close to one."

"You've never been around a horse?" He hauls a rickety bike out of the shed and hands it to me.

"Unless you count the poor things at the fair, plodding around in circles." We get on the bikes and exit the zoo.

"Well, in case you haven't guessed, we're going horseback riding." He looks to gauge my reaction.

"Oh." I'm momentarily distracted from the halo of invisible birds chirping around my head. "Do we have a guide?"

"At your service." Travis bows.

I roll my eyes but smile. "Because you're so familiar with the area?"

"Trust me, I looked into it. There's tons of easy trails around." Travis turns up a long dirt driveway. "It's just up here." Off to the left is a large enclosure penning in several horses. The closer we get, the more intimidating they look. I eye them suspiciously. I'm supposed to get on one of these things?

"It's easy." Travis's tone is soothing. "They've been ridden so many times they know this area like the backs of their hands. Or hooves." He grins. "Just sit on top, stick your feet in the stirrups and hold on to the reins. A nudge with your heels tells them to go faster, a tug on the reins slows them down." He hops off his bike and walks it over to the fence.

"You make it sound so simple." I get off my bike and follow him. Travis shrugs his backpack off his shoulders and pulls something out. "What's that?"

He holds up an apple. "Just a little treat from our friends at El Níspero." One of the horses ambles over and Travis offers the fruit in his splayed out palm. The brown and white creature noses it, then crunches down with slobbery lips, taking the apple. Travis shakes the horse drool from his hand.

"Ew," I say.

A jacked man with a large-brimmed hat walks over. "You want ride?" he says, a piece of straw between his teeth. He looks like he benches his horses. "Five dollars, one hour."

"*Sí*." Travis gestures to the both of us. "I want this one." He points to the horse who just French-kissed his hand. "And a *bueno* horse for her." He nods at me.

Fifteen minutes later we are saddled and taking some practice walks around an empty pen. I sit stiffly on the horse, squeezing it tightly with my knees, clutching the ropes. So far I've mastered the walk. I'm perfectly content to travel at this pace.

"Give her a little nudge with your heels," says Travis from his horse, Destiny. He looks so natural, sitting tall and comfortably in the saddle.

I give the tiniest squeeze of my heels. My horse's name is Mariposa, Spanish for 'butterfly,' according to Travis. She doesn't seem to register and keeps on at her steady pace.

"Harder than that," he encourages. "Trotting is not scary, I promise."

"I'm actually okay with this speed," I say, not loosening my death grip on the straps.

"We're not leaving the ring until you at least trot."

"Ugh, fine." I give Mariposa a firmer squeeze and she immediately starts to move faster. I bounce up and down awkwardly in the saddle.

"Relax your body," Travis calls. "Move with the horse, not against her."

"Where'd you learn to ride?" I try to follow his instructions.

"Science camp," he says.

"You're kidding."

"No lie." He places a hand on his chest in a mock pledge. "My grandparents paid for me to go every summer."

"A bunch of nerdy science kids riding horses?" I say.

"Being mentally active and physically active are not mutually exclusive," he says dryly.

I realize that's one of the things I like about Travis. He says things like 'mutually exclusive.'

"You're getting the hang of it," he says.

I must look ridiculous, but I do feel more settled on the giant animal.

"What do you say? Are you ready for the open trail?"

I gulp. "Onward ho."

"Atta girl." Travis walks his horse over to the owner, Rodrigo, and speaks to him in Spanish. Rodrigo nods, pointing to a well-marked trail. Travis responds, then deftly turns the horse around and trots back toward me.

"We're good to go," he says.

Travis clicks to his horse and Rodrigo opens the gate, waving us on through. We walk along the trail toward the hills behind the ranch and I relax with each step. Mariposa's definitely done this route before. She moves as gracefully as her namesake and we follow Travis and Destiny, both of us content to let them lead.

I'm riding a horse.

"How you doing back there?" Travis looks over his shoulder.

"Like riding a bike," I say.

Destiny lets out a decidedly un-ladylike fart.

"Phew." I wave a hand in front of my face. "You stink."

In response she lets loose a neigh then proceeds to expel the contents of her last meal directly in front of us, which Mariposa neatly side steps.

"Good girl." I pat her neck affectionately.

We mosey along the trail, taking in the beautiful scenery. The clouds part and the sun shines down as we pick our way over rocks and streams, the forest around us teeming with background music. A thousand and one birds sing to each other, harmonizing with the heavy buzz saw of the cicadas. We cross a wooden bridge, emerging into a field that resembles desert plains.

"They've had fires up here." I nod at patches of charred grass.

"Might have been from lightning." Travis glances up. "So, how's the report going?"

"I've been getting a lot of great stuff," I say. "I'm almost done with my research and starting on a rough draft."

"Nice," Travis says admiringly.

"With a little luck I'll be able to get into Berkeley after all," I say. A hard lump dissolves in my chest.

"And that's what you want?"

"Yeah," I say quietly but firmly, coming alongside him with the horse. "I really do."

"So spending the week with the freaks and geeks hasn't been the worst thing in the world?" He looks at me as our horses plod side by side.

"Well, some of you I can take or leave." I think of Chrissy and Kiki. "But I'm actually growing quite fond of others."

"Which category do I fall in?"

"Depends on the day, I guess." I don't want to give too much away.

"And on your other options?" he says, lifting an eyebrow.

"Miles and I are finished, remember?" I tell him, and he looks up. "Look, about the other night at the club—" I begin, just as a fat raindrop lands on my forehead.

Travis stiffens in his saddle. "I get it," he says. "You dumped him for Enrique. I'm not your type." He holds out a hand. "Looks like Juan was right about the rain. Maybe we should head back." He turns Destiny around and I pull on Mariposa's reins to stop her. We face each other on horseback.

"That's not it at all." I want to make him understand I don't have feelings for Enrique. Another raindrop falls on my bare leg. Then another. Mariposa shifts uneasily under me. "The kiss didn't mean anything."

"So you just go around kissing guys who don't mean anything?" he says, abrupt. The rain starts falling harder.

"What's that supposed to mean?" I'm indignant. "For your information, Enrique kissed me." A sharp wind comes up, stirring the dry grass and raising the scent of scorched earth.

Travis looks around. The sky has gone from gray to black in seconds. Wind whips at my hair and the horses' manes, creating instant tangles. Mariposa lets out a loud snort at a flash of lightning that brightens the sky. An instantaneous crack of thunder has Destiny whinnying uneasily, her nostrils flaring.

"Let's talk about this later. We need to get back to the ranch." His tone is urgent. "Now."

The next boom of thunder has Mariposa rearing and I clutch the nob at the top of the saddle, my irritation turning to fright.

"Whoa," Travis says as Mariposa goes wild underneath me. "Jess, get off her."

My voice is as shaky as the horse. "And how do you propose…"

A slice of lightning hits somewhere close and the acute stench of sulfur fills the air. Mariposa screams and takes off at a speed that's most definitely not a trot.

She gallops through the field at a breakneck pace, heading straight for a patch of trees. Ignoring the branches slapping at my face, I focus solely on hanging on. My thighs and legs are iron-locked around the horse and I feel her shudder underneath me at the next crash of thunder. Apparently Mariposa is not a fan of thunderstorms.

I don't know if Travis is behind me or where I'm going. The trees slow us somewhat and I hazard a glance up just in time to see a large branch directly in our path. There's no time to react and it clotheslines me, sending me sailing through the air as all the oxygen leaves my lungs.

Chapter Twenty-Eight

I tumble off Mariposa in what feels like slow motion, landing with a hard thump on my back.

I lay there staring up at the gloomy sky, treetops going around in circles. A blurry face appears above me, accompanied by another whiff of sulfur.

"Jess! Are you okay?" Travis jumps off Destiny and quickly tethers her to a nearby tree. I haven't regained complete sensation of my body but there isn't much pain. I wonder if that's a good or bad sign.

He kneels down beside me and helps me sit up. I wheeze and cough as air whooshes back into my lungs.

Mariposa stands up a ways, rearing off to the side, reins tangled on one of the branches. Her wide eyes are accusing, as if everything is my fault.

"Jerk," I rasp. It hurts to breathe.

"Me or the horse?"

"Both."

We're drenched, hair plastered against our faces.

"Can you stand up?" he says.

"Not sure." He helps me up slowly and I lean against his shoulder, clutching at my ribs. Shockingly, nothing seems to be broken, but everything aches.

"Where are we?" I wince at the soreness in my body.

"Not sure. As soon as your dumb horse bolted I didn't take my eyes off her. I didn't want to lose you."

"So we're stuck out here in the middle of a thunderstorm with no idea where we are or how to get home?" My chest feels tight.

Travis looks up and opens his mouth. "At least there's no shortage of water," he says. He shrugs off his backpack and pulls out a bottle of water and a few granola bars. "Rations." He looks at me, green eyes twinkling. "If things get really bad, we can always eat the horses."

Destiny nickers loudly.

I give him a dirty look. "This isn't funny."

"Relax, we'll be fine." He pats my shoulder, reassuring. "Do you feel like getting back on the horse?"

"Absolutely not." I eye Mariposa, who's giving me the same suspicious look.

"They should be able to lead us back." He walks over to her and makes soothing noises.

The rain seems to be subsiding but the sky is still dark and the wind gusts strongly through the thin trees.

"Do you think we should just wait the storm out?" I say. "Isn't the first rule when you're lost to stay where you are?"

"That's if people are looking for you," he says. "Nobody knows we're missing."

"What about Rodrigo?"

"Rodrigo probably thinks we're making out under a tree somewhere."

"In this weather?" I ask.

Travis leads Mariposa back toward me and puts her reins in my hands. He pushes wet hair off his face. "What? You don't think it's romantic?" He leans over and wipes a smear of something off my cheek. I look down at his hand. It's blood.

I feel short of breath and attribute it to the aftereffects of my less-than-elegant dismount. It's not because Travis is standing mere inches from me. Not because his face is bending slowly down toward mine in expectation. I rise slightly on my toes, lips pursed in anticipation.

A funny look crosses his face.

"What?" I whisper.

"Don't move."

"Why?" I look over my shoulder, there's nothing there. My eyes scan down to the forest floor.

Then I see it. A slender green snake, two feet behind us.

"Oh. My. God." I breathe.

The snake is poised, ready to strike. Mariposa prances nervously beside us.

"Get behind me," he says softly, "as slowly as you can."

I obey, quietly placing one foot in front of the other, leading the quivering horse.

One step. Two steps. *Crack!* A clumsy hoof comes down on a big stick.

The echo of the splintering wood reverberates through the forest. Mariposa, jumpy creature that she is, neighs loudly, and reverses. Her big behind knocks Travis off balance, sending him stumbling forward. That's threat enough for the snake.

It strikes so fast, I'm not sure if I imagine the whole thing. A very bad word from Travis assures me it's all too real. He goes down, clutching his leg. I let go of Mariposa, who doesn't waste any time and bolts for the hills. The snake, affronted at being disturbed, slithers off.

I run to Travis, who grips his ankle, grimacing.

"Oh my God, oh my God, oh my God." I say, kneeling down beside him.

"Jess," Travis puts his hand on my arm. "It's okay."

"Let me see." I pry his other hand away from his leg. Two angry red puncture wounds in his lower calf dribble a small amount of blood.

"It stings like a bitch, but it's not poisonous." He smiles, then winces. "At least, not very."

"Not very?" My voice rises. "What's that supposed to mean?"

"It's just a green vine snake, their venom is mild. At most my leg will just be sore for a few days."

"How can you be sure?" I try to tamper down my panic.

He closes his eyes, not responding.

"Travis? Are you going into shock?" I shake his shoulders. "Answer me!"

He looks up, exasperated. "Can you please stop shaking me? I'm fine. Just embarrassed."

"Why the hell would you be embarrassed?" I stare at him.

"Because I look like an idiot every time we hang out." He makes a frustrated noise, hitting the ground with his fist.

"What are you talking about?" I say. "I'm the one who always looks like an idiot."

"You could never look like an idiot," he says, lifting his hand to touch my cheek. "There's nothing even remotely idiotic about you."

Disconcerted, I look at the snakebite again. It's slightly swollen. "Look, on the off chance you're wrong, I'd feel a lot better doing something about this bite." I undo my belt and wrap it snugly around his calf, but not too tight.

"Taking your clothes off at a time like this?" he quips.

"Ha-ha." I say, but am relieved. He wouldn't be making jokes if the bite was venomous, would he?

"You're going to be fine," I reassure him, giving him an impromptu hug.

"I know." His breath is warm in my ear. "Well, this hasn't gone exactly as planned."

"You mean you didn't mean for us to get caught in a storm and attacked by a snake?" I say into his shoulder, not wanting to end the hug.

"Well, no, but if that's what it takes to get your arms around me." I feel him smiling.

"Are you saying you like my arms around you?" The rain is still falling. Lighter now, but we're both soaked.

"What do you think I'm saying?" His voice is low. "What I've been trying to say for a while now."

My brain is having trouble processing his words.

"Jess? You're killing me with suspense here." He puts his hands to my shoulders and gently pushes me away from him, eyes searching my face.

Steam rises from our wet clothes. Slowly leaning forward, Travis presses his lips to mine. They're soft, warm despite the cold, and my brain explodes. Everything comes together in flashes, like the lightning illuminating the landscape.

Breathless, I pull back, a million sensations racing through my body. "We should be getting back to get your leg checked out." Despite his reassurances, I'm still worried about his leg. "Do you think you can stand?"

His green eyes dance. "Of course I can. I was just enjoying the moment, you know?"

I help him up and we hobble over to Destiny and attempt to get Travis on the horse. But she's skittish from the fading thunder and is in no mood to stay still. After a few tries, we give up.

Travis leans back against the tree for support. "You're going to have to go for help."

I so do not want to leave him in the rain after just getting bit by a snake, mildly venomous or not. My chin juts out and I open my mouth to protest. Travis pulls me close for another kiss. Its sweetness sends warmth from my brown roots to my crimson toenails.

We break apart. "I'll be fine," he says.

"I'll be right back." I say, threading my fingers through his.

"I'm not going anywhere," he promises solemnly.

Chapter Twenty-Nine

I guide Destiny through the trees as fast as I can, feeling a sense of urgency despite Travis's theory about the snake. I let her have her lead, hoping she takes us back to the stables. The elation sparked by his kisses is tempered by my worry. *What if he's wrong?* No, he'll be fine. He's going to be alright. I repeat the words in my head like a mantra as I clutch the reins.

I see a stream that looks familiar. Next is the bridge. I'm going the right way. Relief floods my body. We crest a small hill and I see the ranch in the distance. A shout goes up when I'm spotted. I ride Destiny to the fence where Rodrigo waits with Mr. A, Lola, Juan and Harp. Mariposa prances around restlessly behind them.

"Jess, what's wrong?" Mr. A takes in my sodden state. "Where's Travis?"

"Back in the woods, there was a snake—" I jump off Destiny. Rodrigo turns and heads for the stables. Lola gets out her phone and calls someone, her voice low and rapid.

"What did it look like?" Juan asks, forcefully pushing his glasses up his nose.

"Green. Thin. Long." I focus on getting air into my bruised lungs. "A little yellow on the underside. Travis said it's not dangerous."

"Sounds like an arboreal vine snake," Juan's shoulders relax a bit. "He should be okay."

"Should? Should?" The drama of the last few hours hits me full force and I burst into tears as Rodrigo comes back with three horses. Harp comes up and puts an arm around me.

"Jess," Mr. A says, "can you take us to him?"

"Yes, I remember the way." I try to calm down. "It's not too far."

"Harp and I will stay here and wait for the doctor," Lola says.

"Juan, you should stay here too," Mr. A says, getting on his horse.

"No can do, Mr. A," he says, eyes flashing behind misty glasses. "Besides you might need my help."

Mr. A shakes his head but doesn't argue.

The four of us jump on our horses as they wave us off. Mr. A and Rodrigo head in the direction I just came from. Juan and I follow their quick trot. He too looks like a professional equestrian.

"Let me guess," I ask, "science camp?"

"Nah, private lessons," he responds, his eyes scouring the land. The rain's almost stopped.

Rodrigo turns his head, questioning.

"Over the bridge," I point.

We make our way to the wooden structure.

"How did you know we were here?" I ask Juan.

"Travis told me what you guys were doing," he said. "When the storm came up Harp and I got Mr. A and Lola and told them where we thought you went."

We reach the field quickly. I lead them through trampled bushes and broken trees. Mariposa's crazed path is easy to follow.

"There!" I shout, spotting Travis, against the tree where I'd left him. His eyes are closed.

Then he opens them and his smile shines like the sun coming out from the clouds.

"My princess in soaking wet armor," he jokes.

Rodrigo and Mr. A jump off their horses and help him up. The two of them are able to get him on the back of Rodrigo's horse with only a few grunts of pain from Travis.

"*Oxybelis fulgidus?*" Juan says from his horse, referring to the snake's Latin name.

"You know it, brother," Travis says, his face looking a bit pale.

"Drama queen," Juan snorts, but I can tell he's relieved.

"Everyone all set?" Mr. A asks, looking at Travis, who nods from behind Rodrigo.

We ride.

***

I lay in the dark, wide awake. The ring of a phone downstairs has me sitting up and clutching at my thin sheet. I hear Lola murmuring.

"*Sí, sí …* I will tell them…" I can't catch the rest of the conversation.

I get out of bed and creep downstairs, my ribs protesting. Lola hangs up the phone and sits there, her head in her hands, long dark hair spilling through her fingers.

"Lola?" I whisper, terrified despite everyone's assurance that the snake's venom is indeed mild.

Her sigh of relief has me realizing I'm not the only one who was worried. "He's going to be just fine, Jess."

"He is?" Tears fill my eyes, falling down my cheeks. I don't bother to wipe them away.

"The doctors have wrapped up his calf and are keeping him overnight just in case."

"So he's going to be okay?" My nails bite into my palms.

She smiles at me. "He's a strong boy. His leg may be sore for a few days, but it's nothing some rest can't fix." She walks over and gives me a hug. "You were very brave, Jessica," she says, her voice soothing. I realize I'm holding my breath and I exhale and inhale again. Lola smells of sunshine and the mild antiseptic we use when handling the frogs.

He's going to be alright.

***

I wake to sunlight streaming through sheer curtains. There's movement beside me on the bed.

"Good morning, Princess," Travis says, lying on his side, his head propped up on one hand, elbow on my pillow.

I'm so shocked to see him I don't even worry how I must look.

"What are you doing here?" I ask, my arms going around him in a delighted rush.

"Catching up on my beauty sleep." He rolls his eyes. "Waiting for you to wake up. It's one in the afternoon. Everyone else is at the center."

I'd finally passed out sometime around 4:00 a.m., emotionally and physically exhausted. Everyone must have let me sleep.

"They let you out of the hospital? You're okay? Let me see your leg," I demand.

He obliges, holding up a bandaged calf. "Didn't even need antivenin."

I become very aware our bodies are pressed close together in the twin bed. Suddenly shy, I lower my eyes.

One hand comes up to lift my chin. "And despite the venom being mild, they also said that whoever put on the tourniquet was really thinking." His beautiful eyes look into mine.

"I can't stand to think of anything happening to you," I blurt.

"Why?" he teases. "You stuck on your report?"

"No." I look into his eyes without flinching. "Because you *are* my type."

"Really?" He lifts an eyebrow. "I'm very glad to hear that," he murmurs.

He lowers his mouth to mine and kisses me. Tingles course along my entire body, like an electric current just under my skin. My mouth is made for his and there's nothing in the world more right than this.

"Ahem." A throat clears.

We pull apart, flushed, and look up to see Carlita standing in the doorway, arms crossed, a wry expression on her face.

"Are you two hungry?" she asks.

Travis looks at me and smiles. "Starving."

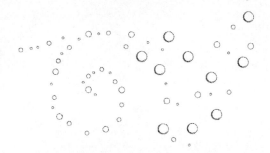# Chapter Thirty

"These guys are too cute," Harp says as we look at the frogs. "I'm really going to miss them."

"I know," I say. We're finishing up our second to last day at the center. Have we only been here just over a week? Juan's out front giving a guided tour to some visitors. He's memorized everything there is to know about each of the exhibits.

"So what's happening with you and Travis?" Harp asks as we cut up bamboo. He sat with us at dinner last night, much to Kiki's fury. I'd felt her eyes on my back all through the meal and again this morning in the van. Travis's calf is feeling a lot better, so he came up with us to the center today.

"I'm not sure." I don't want to get too ahead of myself. "I mean, I really like him and the chemistry's great, but we lead pretty different lives." The truth is, I don't exactly know what's happening. We haven't had any time alone to talk. Everyone keeps asking us to retell our adventure. Plus, he had epic phone calls with his mom trying to convince her she didn't need to fly down, that he's fine and will be home in a few days. Then this morning he went for an early appointment at the clinic to get his leg checked out. I snip another piece of bamboo. "Who knows what will happen when we go back home."

"Opposites attract," Harp says. "Besides, I think you're a good match in the areas that count."

"Like what?" I ask.

"Well, you already said you have chemistry." She holds up her thumb, counting off her fingers. "You're both intelligent." She holds up an index finger.

"Him, more so," I say. Harp waves away my comment.

"You share similar interests." Up goes the middle finger for three.

"Like what?"

"Conservation?" She looks at me hopefully.

I can't help but smile. "Definitely a new interest, but sure, I'll give you that one."

Looking pleased with herself, she continues, holding up her ring finger. "You both want the same things."

"Travis wants to pass biology too?" I clasp my hands together earnestly, all wide eyes and more than a little sarcastic.

She ignores me. "You want to go to college, which Travis also wants to do. You have the same goals — that's important."

"Except he's a lot closer to accomplishing his," I say.

"Face it, Jess, you're made for each other," she says. "And what do you mean? You're going to rock out your report, pass bio with flying colors, and get into Berkeley, no problem. Which is only a few hours from UCLA, I might add."

"Just like that? Oh, well then, easy peasy lemon squeezy."

Up goes her pinky. "I forgot to add you're both a little cheesy." She smugly holds five fingers up to my face.

I throw a piece of bamboo at her and she ducks, giggling.

Juan walks in, flushed with triumph from his tour.

"How was it?" Harp asks.

"He did great." Lola comes in behind him. "Juan, why don't you help Harp with the bamboo and let Jess give out the vitamins today?"

"Sure," he says, generous.

I'm jittery as I walk over to the cages with Lola. Taking a deep breath, I pull on a pair of gloves and set to work under her watchful eye. I very carefully distribute the tiny calcium coated insects into the cages, keeping a close eye on the frogs. The last thing I want is to be responsible for the loss of an entire species.

Coming to the last exhibit, I feel more confident. "You're looking a particularly festive shade of yellow today," I say to the golden frogs as I open the latch. "Lunch time!"

"*Fantástico*, Jessica," Lola says. "Now, how do you feel about cleaning out their tank?"

"The golden frogs?" I gape at her. It's massive.

"*Sí*. Once every few weeks we clean out their exhibit." Lola puts a hand on the glass and peers in, scanning for the creatures. "We put them in one of the transport terrariums in the back while everything is made nice and fresh for them."

"Um, sure," I gulp.

Lola grins at the look on my face. "Don't worry. I will help you catch them."

Ten minutes later, I gently deposit the two frogs Lola wrangled into a tiny glass terrarium in the back room. Harp and Juan are finishing up the bamboo and Lola is pulling out the cleaning supplies we need. I stare at the frogs. How could I have thought they were disgusting? They're delicate and lovely, their vivid yellow-gold skin flecked with ink-black spots.

"Hey, buddy," I whisper. One lets out a noise that sounds like a low whistle and I give a start.

"Did you hear that?" I ask Lola. "He's talking to me!"

She laughs. "They have a nice little whistle. But since they love to be around waterfalls and streams, sometimes it is difficult for females to hear their vocalizations."

"That's why they wave, right?" I ask.

Lola beams at me. "Jessica! We have a budding biologist, I see." My chest swells. Harp and Juan smile at each other.

"Sorry about the cramped quarters guys, but it's only temporary," I whisper to them, sympathetic.

I hear the front door of the center open and Kiki bursts into the back room. "Lola, the caiman's eggs are hatching!"

"*Si?*" she says excitedly, putting down the misting bottle and sponge. Juan grabs his camcorder and the three of them run out the door.

"Wait for me!" I yank off my gloves and race out the door behind them.

***

"That was so cool," I say to Harp as we walk back to the center to grab our things. "They look like baby dinosaurs."

"They basically are," Juan says from her other side. "Crocodiles have been around two hundred million years."

I notice Harp keeps glancing at him. After his initial reaction to her makeover, he seems to have regained his composure around her. This boy definitely needs a push.

"Hey, Juan, can you show us the square trees you guys saw the other day?" I ask. "We really want to see them."

"We do?" Harp looks at me. I jab my elbow into her side.

"Sure," he says, "but we need the bikes to get there."

Ten minutes later we're wheeling bikes out of the zoo, and I make a show of patting myself down, one hand still on the bike. "My ring!" I exclaim. "I think I left it by the sink after washing my hands."

"We'll wait for you," Harp says.

"No, you guys go on ahead, I'll catch up."

"Are you sure?" She looks uncertain.

"Positive." I wave them off. "I don't think Travis and Steven are doing anything, one of them can show me the way." Before either of them can protest, I turn and wheel my bike back toward the center, ring safe in my pocket. "See you later!" I call over my shoulder, suppressing a grin.

Whistling, I walk back to the center feeling lighter than I have in a long time. Despite telling Harp that I'm not exactly sure what's going to happen with Travis, a contented certainty had infused my body while watching the caiman's eggs hatch with her and Juan. They're going to end up together, just like me and Travis.

"There you are," a frosty voice says to my left. I stop walking and look over to see Kiki standing with Chrissy, both sporting matching accusatory looks.

The goofy smile fades from my face. "What's up?" I say, wary.

"You are in so much trouble." Kiki doesn't bother to keep the spite out of her voice.

"Why?"

"You really messed up," Chrissy echoes, hands on her hips, "big time."

"What'd I do?"

Kiki takes a menacing step toward me. I shrink under the malevolent intensity of her gaze. "You, Miss Incompetent of the Year," she says, her voice pure acid, "forgot to shut the latch properly on the golden frog's transport terrarium."

"Oh, no," I whisper. Both hands fly to my face and the bike falls to the ground.

"Oh, yes," Chrissy hisses, crossing her arms. "They're gone."

Chapter Thirty-One

I race to the center and burst through the back doors, my heart pounding. I hurry over to where I left the frogs, hoping this is all some terrible joke. But the terrarium is empty.

The world drops from under my feet as Chrissy and Kiki rush in behind me.

"We have to find them!" I turn to face them, blood roaring in my ears.

"It's too late, they're gone." Kiki is vehement. They stand there, glaring. And for once, I can't blame them. She takes a few aggressive steps toward me. "Nobody's going to want you around after this, so why don't you just go too?"

Oh God. What have I done? Am I that much of a careless idiot that I've managed to lose some of the last survivors of an endangered species? I feel like throwing up.

I turn and push by them, running out of the building. I don't know where I'm going. I just have to get out of here. I run and keep on running.

I pass by Travis and Steven, who are sitting on stumps by the entrance. There's a bike by Steven's feet.

"Jess?" Travis calls as I fly by. "What's wrong?"

Oh God. Travis. I can't bear the look on his face once he finds out I've wrecked everything he's fought so hard to save. What everyone here has fought so hard to save. I keep on running, out of the zoo, down the dirt road, in the opposite direction Harp and Juan went. I run hard, until my breathing is ragged and there's a stabbing in my side. I look up. I'm at the market. I stop to catch my breath in the heat when a hand grabs my arm.

"Jess?" It's Enrique. My mind dimly takes in the grocery bags in his hand. "What's wrong?"

I can't speak. Words won't form.

"Do you want to go somewhere and talk?" he asks, concerned.

I stand there numb, unable to answer, my breath still coming in gasps. He steers me around the market stalls, toward his Jeep, which is parked off to the side.

He helps me in. I've yet to utter a word. Pulling out of the parking lot, we turn down a bumpy gravel road. Tears begin to flow down my cheeks at the magnitude of what I've done.

"Here." Enrique reaches behind him into the back seat and pulls out a beach towel. "Use this."

I dab my eyes with the towel. We pull off onto the side of the deserted road.

"Now are you going to tell me what happened?" He turns to me as he shuts off his Jeep, a concerned look on his face.

"Nothing," I finally hiccup. "I'm useless. I suck at everything."

He searches for something to console me. "You were good at surfing the other day."

"Fluke." I hiccup again.

"What is that?"

"An accident. Good luck." This reminds me of the golden frog, and tears well again.

"Why don't we go for a walk?" he says after the worst of the crying subsides. He gets out of the car and comes around to open my door, helping me out of the Jeep. I'm too drained to argue and we start off on a trail alongside a river.

"Where are we going?" I sniff, not really caring. I pick my way over the rocky trail, past rapids and tiny cascades of water. The tears have stopped, at least.

"To see The Three Sisters."

"Who?"

"You'll see," he says with his trademark wink. A few minutes later we reach a stunning waterfall. *This used to be prime golden frog habitat*, I think. Now they're all gone.

"This is the first of The Three Sisters," Enrique is saying. "Legend has it three beautiful sisters of a rich Panamanian family were in love with the same man from the nearby town of Penonomé."

"Awkward," I say dully. A haze of depression has settled around my shoulders. I stub my toe on a rock. "Ouch." Flip-flops are not ideal hiking shoes. Enrique places a hand on my lower back to steady me.

"It would have been, if he'd loved one of them back, but his affections were for a local girl from his town."

"So, what? They all drowned themselves here?" That doesn't sound like such a bad idea.

Enrique laughs. "Not exactly. When the eldest reached the first waterfall she gazed into the pool below. She looked around at the beauty in nature and realized that her happiness was not dependent on a man's love. Overjoyed with this newfound realization, she dived into the pool below."

"I'll bet," I say, peering into the frothing water below with sharp rocks jutting out.

"The other two sisters held hands and jumped in as well."

"Tragic."

"Normally it would've been, but it was a special day — Easter Friday. The waters appreciated the admiration of the young women and so received them safely, where they still swim as mermaids today when no one is near."

"Sounds like a fancy way of saying they drowned themselves," I say, morose.

Enrique laughs again and sits down on one of the rocks. "Come sit." He pats the spot beside him.

I feel unsteady looking down into the teeming waters, so I obey. We're silent for a few minutes.

"And about the other night — I'm sorry I got you and your friends into trouble."

"They're not all my friends." I think of Chrissy and Kiki's faces when they told me about the frogs.

"Am I?" He looks at me intensely and I sigh. Despite him being gorgeous and somehow always around for my damsel in distress moments, his isn't the shoulder I want to be crying on.

"Yes, you're a good *friend*." I emphasize the word. "And I appreciate you trying to make me feel better and all, but maybe we should be getting back."

"But you seem much calmer out here in nature, like the eldest of the three sisters."

"And like the three sisters, maybe my happiness is not dependent on a man's love." I inject a firm tone into my voice, standing up.

"Can I try to change your mind about that?" Enrique's voice is low and husky. His hand reaches for mine.

Oh boy.

"Enrique," I say, "Look, you're great, but…"

"You're great too."

Gently, I extricate my hand from his and step back.

"Um, I don't think…"

Just then I hear laughter on the trail. Two ladies in their mid-fifties appear, cameras hanging around their necks, binoculars at the ready.

"Look, Helen," the taller one exclaims excitedly, holding the binoculars up to her face. "An orange-bellied trogon!"

"Ooh, I see it!" the shorter one squeals. "And there's a white-ruffed manakin!" She points off to the left somewhere over our heads.

"Don't look now, Betty," Helen whispers to the taller one, "but I see a pair of lovebirds." She nods in our direction.

Relieved at the distraction the birders afford me, I start walking down the trail. "*Hola, señoritas*," Enrique says, all charm, as he passes by the women. "Jess, wait."

I glance over my shoulder.

Smash! I walk into a broad white T-shirted chest. Travis's chest.

"Jess?" he says, his voice relieved. Then he looks up to see Enrique behind me and his face darkens like the sky when the storm clouds swept across.

"What's going on?" he asks, taking in my disheveled appearance. I'm not sure which one of us he's talking to. I'm hot and dehydrated from all the crying.

"Jess was upset," Enrique says. "I was trying to make her feel better."

Trying to hit on me is more like it. I am grateful to see Travis and give him a trembly smile. He does not return it.

I notice he's favoring his bad leg. His face is blanched.

"What are you doing here?" I ask.

"I could ask you the same thing," he says shortly. "I saw you run by so I followed you on a bike. Then I saw you get in Enrique's car." He crosses his arms over his chest and widens his stance, eyes narrowing. "I thought I'd better see if you were okay." Enrique also crosses his arms and returns Travis's cool look.

"She can go where she wants, *hombre*."

"Me?" I interrupt, incredulous. "Who cares about me? What about the frogs?"

"What about the frogs?" Travis looks confused.

This is it. He will never forgive me. Good-bye, Travis. I take a deep breath and look up at him, utterly shattered, utterly wretched. "I lost, um…" My voice trails off. I can't bear to see the look on his face. I'm such a coward. I can't tell him.

"What? You lost what?" He sounds exasperated.

My gaze drops to the ground and I don't say another word as Travis looks at me like I'm someone he's never seen before.

***

It's after dark when we pull into the compound. The tension in the Jeep is all-encompassing. The three of us haven't said a word the whole drive home. I jump out before Enrique even finishes putting it in Park. Travis hops out after me, leaving Enrique with the bike.

Travis follows me and grabs my hand. "Why would you go off with him like that?" he says, angry.

What can I say? That I was too devastated about losing everything we were here for to pay much attention? I could've wandered off to lie down beside Flor del Aire for all I cared, or jumped off one of those rocks. The Panamanians in those legends really did have a flair for drama.

I spot Harp and Juan sitting by the pool. I pull my arm from Travis's loose grasp and walk toward them.

"Hey, guys," I say when I'm a couple of feet away. My voice is hoarse.

"Jess." Harp jumps up, taking in my tousled appearance. "Where have you guys been?"

I shoot a glance back at Enrique who whistles a carefree tune as he walks toward his house. Travis limps up behind me. I want to ask about his leg but he doesn't look like he's in the mood. "Long story."

"Why don't you tell us about it?" Travis's tone is clipped. I haven't elaborated on what I said when he found me with Enrique. "You were saying you lost something?"

"You don't know?" I look at the three of them, my voice barely audible.

Out of the corner of my eye I see Chrissy and Kiki walk toward us. Steven tags along behind. They haven't told anyone. They want me to have that pleasure.

"Know what?" Harp is baffled.

I look at her and Juan's faces. In this place, with these people, I've been able to be more my real self than I have in years. They've become my friends. Travis, maybe almost more than that. That's all over now.

I can't do it. I can't look them in the eyes and tell them I've ruined everything.

"Ask Chrissy and Kiki," I say, my voice breaking as I walk toward the villa, leaving them behind. "I'm sure they'll be happy to explain."

"Jess," Travis calls after me, "wait!"

I ignore him and keep on walking.

Chapter

Thirty-Two

I lie on my bed, the French doors open, listening for the sounds of full-scale panic as the news that I've lost the golden frogs spreads through the compound. It's quiet, eerily so. The sounds of the creatures that normally chatter outside our window have gone silent. I hear no crickets chirruping, no birds tweeting, no frogs croaking. Maybe somehow they know too. Not only have I done something that may have devastating implications up and down the ecosystem, but there's no way I'll be passing biology now, and deservedly so. Good-bye Berkeley, good-bye Travis, good-bye future.

I get up and walk out onto the balcony and stare at the never ending ocean. The sky dims and the sun casts a reddish glow on the horizon.

Smelling something, I sniff a few times and the acrid smell of smoke wafts lazily under my nostrils. I lean over the balcony and peer closely at the compound fence. A mile of thick shrub and brush fan out on the other side of the fence. A flicker catches my eye and I stare in dawning horror.

Sparks fly through the air, an orange blaze about fifteen feet wide bubbles and crackles, enveloping one dry branch after another. Fire. And it's close.

I rush downstairs in a panic, looking for someone to tell. Outside the smell is stronger, and I wonder why no one else seems to have noticed. Probably too distracted over the frogs.

I see Enrique steering a wheelbarrow over to one side of the compound.

"Enrique!" I shout. "There's a fire!" I point in the direction of the burning.

"*Sí.*" He gently lowers the wheelbarrow to the ground. "We get them all the time. It is very common." His face seems to suggest I'm overreacting. As usual. "There is no need to worry."

"But it's really close," I protest. "I can see it from the balcony." He looks in the direction I'm pointing. Smoke billows up and around. The flames have spread even closer to the fence in the seconds it's taken me to come downstairs.

"Where are your mom and dad?" I feel like he's not taking me seriously.

"In town, picking up supplies."

Frustrated, I tighten my ponytail and stare in the direction of the encroaching blaze. "I will go check it out," he says finally. I get the feeling he's only doing it as an apology for what happened earlier. "If you want to do something, maybe go close the windows in the house." With that, he walks away.

I run through the compound, looking for the others. They are still by the pool. Mr. A sits on one of the lounge chairs, speaking to them quietly. Lola sits beside him. Everyone looks serious. Oh God.

Mr. A sees me. "Jess." He beckons me over with a steely gaze and a wave of his hand. "Just in time. We're talking about what you did today—" I swallow as he sends a disapproving look over his metal rims. "—taking off without telling anyone where you were going."

Huh? What about the frogs? But I don't dwell on it. There's no time.

"Um, have you seen the fire?" I look around at them. Their faces are blank.

Lola puts a hand on Mr. A's leg. "I do smell something, Kenny." She glances around. The others start to sniff the air, looking like the baby caimans from this morning getting their first scent of a new world. It would have been comical under different circumstances. The boys stand up, trying to get a better glimpse of the flames. I can't look at Travis.

Mr. A also stands up. "Hector mentioned they get brush fires here all the time. I'm sure it's nothing to worry about. I'll go speak with him."

"He's not here," I say. "He's in town with Carlita."

Lola stands up now too. "There are thousands of little blazes all over the countryside during dry season. I'm sure we are all safe here."

"Um, it looks pretty close," I say, doubtful. "And big."

"Show me," Mr. A says. I lead everyone around the back of our villa. From the ground the flames aren't as visible, but there's no mistaking the smell of burning and the smoke rising from the trees several feet back. Enrique walks briskly toward us with a long garden hose.

"I've called my father," he says without preamble, spraying the fence where parched sticks and brush stick through, "and *los bomberos.*"

"The bomb squad?" Chrissy shrieks.

"*Bomberos*," he says. "The men who fight the fires."

"So it's close, then?" Travis asks.

"Close enough. And the wind seems to be against us."

"What should we do?" I ask.

"First of all, everyone just stay calm," Mr. A says. Lola whispers something in his ear and he nods. "In case of the very small possibility we need to evacuate, I want you to go to your rooms and pack your things."

"How are we supposed to evacuate when Hector has the van?" Kiki's voice rises.

"There's still time. Enrique said the firefighters are on the way." Mr. A tries to look confident, but his shoulders are tense and he keeps glancing at the compound gate.

We obediently go to our villas and straight up to our rooms. There isn't a lot of talking amongst the girls as we hastily throw things into our bags. I listen carefully for the sirens, but can only hear the crackling of the fire as it inches its way closer, growing in size and volume. I look over at Harp, who seems to be unsure of what she's supposed to be doing. She paces the room, her toothbrush clenched tightly in her hand.

"Are you okay?" I ask.

Before she can answer, footsteps thunder up the stairs and Travis bursts into our room, out of breath.

"What is it?" I ask.

"There's no time," he says, loud, so Chrissy and Kiki can hear. "Mr. A wants us out of here now. Grab what you have and let's go."

"But I'm not finished packing," Harp says, dazed, still holding her toothbrush.

"That's okay. I'm sure everything will be here when we get back," I take her by the arm, like I had in the water, leading her out of the room.

"Wait, where's your inhaler?" I ask.

"My top drawer," Harp says. I leave her on the landing and run back for her inhaler, and also grab her passport beside it in the drawer. I throw them in my backpack and sling it over my right shoulder, going to her. We pass by Chrissy and Kiki, arguing heatedly about something on the stairwell.

"Let's go, girls," Travis says, coming up behind them and firmly guiding them down the steps over their protests.

We follow Travis out into the night air, which is thick with smoke. The flames are definitely visible now, the fire dangerously close to the fence. It looks half a mile long. I can't believe how quickly it's spread. There's no sign of the firefighters. Mr. A stands outside with Lola, doing a quick head count, when he sees us. Steven and Juan have their bags and Enrique has a few things from his house piled into his Jeep.

"Let's put our things in Enrique's Jeep and take a walk down to the beach," Mr. A says. "We'll be safe by the water." Chrissy shoots Kiki a pan-icked look.

"So we're just supposed to let the place burn down?" I glance at En-rique, who finally looks worried.

"The firefighters should be here any second," Mr. A says. "Your safety is my primary responsibility."

Enrique opens the gate just as Hector and Carlita pull up in the van. They both jump out. Hector lets out a shout and points, yelling something to Enrique in Spanish. We follow the direction of his finger.

I gasp. One half of the grand tree outside the girls' villa is lit like a torch. Its branches stretch out over the fence, tantalizing the flames. Burning leaves fall to the ground as the fire appears to gather itself and makes the final leap over the fence, eagerly snatching at the shrubs and plants border-ing our villa. Carlita crosses herself and both of them run off in the direc-tion of the house. Enrique throws the car keys at Travis.

"Take your stuff," he says. "I'm staying with my parents."

"Are you crazy?" Juan yells.

"We won't let our home burn to the ground without a fight." He turns and runs after his parents.

Everyone looks at each other. Chrissy and Kiki are close to tears. Mr. A looks torn. "Kids, go to the beach with Lola," he decides. "I'll meet you there when we get this thing under control."

"They know where the beach is," Lola says, "and I've known Hector and Carlita a long time. I must help."

He looks at her pleadingly. "Lola, please don't put yourself in danger."

She whips her hair back, dark eyes shining. "Only you are allowed to do that?" She turns to us. "Children, go to the beach and wait for us."

The roar of the fire increases. Hector shouts something and Mr. A turns and runs in his direction, followed by Lola. Enrique sprays the flames with the garden hose. Hector drags another one out of the shed and over to the pool. Carlita has a spray nozzle in one hand that she uses to drench the bushes around the villa. It all seems pitifully inadequate against the now deafening blaze that is hitting full stride.

Fingers of flame dance along the branches of our tree, crossing from one side to the other, skirting the edges of our balconies. The drapes billow in the wind.

We don't see the spark that ignites the curtains on Chrissy and Kiki's terrace, but they go up with a *whoosh* that leaves us staring, dumbfounded.

"Oh my God," Kiki whispers, one hand flying to her mouth. Chrissy sucks in an anguished breath. The two seem absolutely petrified of fires.

"The frogs," Kiki squeaks, hyperventilating.

"What, what is with the frogs?" Juan asks. "Will someone please tell me what's going on?"

Kiki and Chrissy exchange another horrified glance.

"They're in the villa," Chrissy whispers, then bursts into tears.

"What?" I shriek. "You told me I lost them!"

"What?" Travis echoes, looking back and forth from me to Kiki and Chrissy.

"We just wanted to make you think you did," Kiki wails. "We switched the terrariums while everyone was watching the caimans hatch. We hid the frogs behind the shed and were going to put them back after. But when we went, someone had locked the center, so we hid the terrarium under a blanket in the back of Hector's van and later stashed it in our room…" Her voice trails off as the rest of us gawk at her.

"We were going to bring them back tomorrow," Chrissy finishes for her. "No one would've even noticed they were gone."

"Are you crazy?" Juan is furious. "You risked the frogs to play a stupid prank?" He's yelling. Harp puts a hand on his shoulder. Kiki and Chrissy are crying.

"Do Mr. A and Lola know?" Travis asks. His voice is deadly calm, in complete contrast to Juan's.

"No." Overcome, Kiki drops to the ground, puts her arms on her knees, and hangs her head between them.

"So you didn't tell anyone, except me?" I ask. Chrissy shakes her head as tears stream down her face.

A loud cracking sound makes us look back to where the others are fighting the fire. A large branch breaks off the tree and falls onto Chrissy and Kiki's balcony.

Relief had flooded my veins upon hearing the frogs aren't actually missing. A giant blast of adrenaline flushes it out at the thought that they will be in about five minutes.

"Holy crap," Harp whispers, letting her toothbrush fall to the ground. She sucks smoky air into her lungs and coughs. Chrissy and Kiki are incoherent. Harp looks like she's on the verge of fainting.

"Take them to the beach," I shout at Travis and Steven. I throw my backpack at Juan. "Harp's inhaler is in here."

Then I turn and sprint toward the villa.

A fire truck's siren sounds somewhere in the distance. I pass by Enrique and Hector, the sweat pouring off of them as they alternately point their hoses at the tree and the fence, the fire growling behind it, wanting to be let in. Mr. A, Lola and Carlita have buckets and are racing to the pool to scoop up water and throw it on the fence to soak the flimsy barrier. The wall of flames gives off a shimmery heat, visible through the smoky air. Smelling burning hair, I look down at my forearms.

The sirens get louder and flashing red lights pull into the compound. The *bomberos* are finally here. I look up at the burning veranda. But, they might be too late for the frogs. Not stopping to think, I run up to our villa, open the front door, and slip inside.

I hear Travis shout behind me. "Jess!"

Inside, the villa feels like a brick oven. Enrique must have hit the main electrical switch as a precaution because there's no power. I make my way to the stairs in the dark, my hands groping the wall as I climb the curving steps.

I reach the top and fling open the door to Chrissy and Kiki's room. It's full of smoke. I cough as I enter, eyes watering.

Where would they have put the frogs? The flames have engulfed both French doors, providing some light and a lot of heat. I run to the closet and fling it open.

Nothing.

I race over to their beds. I look under Chrissy's. My hand gropes around, coming up with a lone sock. I roll over to look under Kiki's. Orange flames reflect off glass. The two little frogs chirrup as I grab the tank and stand up.

Glass explodes and I look down at my hands. Amazingly, the tank's still in one piece. Then I feel stinging on the backs of my legs. One of the panes in the French doors has shattered.

"Jess!" I hear Travis yell. He stumbles into the room. "Come on." He grabs my free hand and leads me through the smoke out the room. Glass explodes behind us as the rest of the panes burst, one by one.

We race down the stairs and out into the night air, coughing and sputtering. We both slump to the ground a few feet from the villa, panting from the effort. I shake my head to dislodge the ringing in my ears. I realize I'm not the only one who hears it as Travis looks up, relief on his face as more sirens sound in the distance. Another fire truck careens down the dirt road that passes a few feet behind the fence. The men set to work, unloading their equipment and yelling in Spanish. Firefighters on both sides subdue the worst of the flames as the fire reluctantly relinquishes its grasp on the property line and recedes slowly into charred bush.

"That was pretty stupid, Princess," Travis coughs, grimacing as he grabs his leg. Fresh blood shows on the bandage. We sit on the grass, watching the firefighters.

"That's me," I say, staring down at the frogs in my lap, who are oblivious to the fact they'd almost become a roasted French delicacy. Thank God for the terrarium's air filter.

"Jess, look at me." I do, unsure of what I'll find in his eyes. "I didn't mean that," he says, his expression softens. "You just scared the hell out of me." He reaches for my hand, taking it in his sooty one. "What you did was brave. You saved them."

"Are you guys okay?" Juan runs up, breathless. I see Steven shouting at Mr. A and the others, and pointing at the window. He looks over and sees us, an expression of immense relief crossing his face. Mr. A looks back, alarmed at what Steven is telling him. He glances at the firefighters, who seem to have the worst of the conflagration under control, and drops his bucket, hurrying over.

He's followed by Lola, who's crossing herself. "*Ay Dios mío!*" she exclaims.

"What were you thinking?" Mr. A yells when he reaches us, fear showing in the whites of his eyes. "What could you possibly have needed to save that you'd do something so stupid?"

I hold up the little terrarium, my arms trembling. "Them."

Chapter Thirty-Four

Lola stands by the golden frog exhibit, smiling up at Mr. A as he gazes down at her, open adoration on his face. The frogs are safely back in their exhibit following their adventure, after being closely inspected and pronounced fine. Both seem happy to be home. They hop around their waterfall, soaking up the misty spray.

Lola leans forward and says something to Mr. A. He flushes to the roots of his hair. She turns to us as we circle the glass exhibits, getting one last look at the creatures we came to help. Well, that everyone else had come to help. I just kinda fell into it. I look across the room at Travis. And him.

"I want to thank you all for your hard work and time helping us at Níspero, especially here at our amphibian ark." Lola looks around at each of us. Juan has his camcorder in hand and is moving around to get the best shots.

"It is with your support and awareness about what is happening to these animals that allows for our best chance in saving them."

I look over at the golden frogs. Typically they hide under leafy foliage on a rock. Today, as if sensing our departure, the two of them sit contentedly beside their little stream, basking in the warmth of their artificial sunlight.

I feel depressed. This is quickly becoming the reality of all too many species. Confined to special exhibits, on display to the masses that come to *ooh* and *ahh*, who feel a quick pang of regret at their loss in the wild but then quickly forget, going back to their homes and lives.

Back in the 'real' world, it's so easy to become bubble wrapped in indifference.

I will not be like that, I vow silently to the frogs. *I won't forget.*

"So please, go now and educate others," Lola says, "with your stories, your reports, your films, so they can know what is happening here and all over the world. It is not too late for others to make a difference."

Juan turns from Lola's pretty face and zooms in on the frogs.

"*Adiós, amigos*," he says softly, and turns off the camera.

We're subdued as we walk around the zoo, saying goodbye to our favorite animals. Chrissy and Kiki are especially quiet. Their remorse at endangering the frogs hangs over them like the smoke back at the compound. They were berated by Mr. A for being irresponsible, careless and reckless. He even mentioned something about possible suspension. But I don't think anything he said made them feel any worse than they already did.

Carlita, Hector and Enrique shrugged off the fire like it happens every day.

"That's not the worst blaze we've seen," Enrique boasted. Aside from some fire and smoke damage to our balconies, and Chrissy and Kiki's bedroom, the rest of the property is intact. We aren't sure yet how the tree will fare.

"I can't believe I completely freaked out like that," Harp says, glum, as we stand in front of the crocodile cage. "I'm such a wuss."

"Don't be so hard on yourself," Juan says, patting her on the back. He leaves his hand there and her face reddens. I smile at the ground. Finally.

"Hey, Jess." Travis hobbles up to us. "Can I talk to you for a minute?"

"Sure," I say, my nerves jumping. We leave Harp and Juan cooing at the baby caimans like they hatched them personally.

Travis and I haven't had a chance to talk about anything since the fire. Or since that kiss on my bed. I have no idea if he's still angry at me for taking off with Enrique, or how he feels, or what's going to happen with us, or anything at all. If anything at all.

I follow him to the bike shed. "Where are we going?"

"Surprise non-date," he says as he grabs a bike. "You still owe me one."

I feel my body relax. "FYI, your last few non-dates haven't gone so well." I snort, thinking especially of the horseback riding.

"Exactly. You gotta give me a chance to make up for it." He gives his head a rueful shake as we pedal out of the zoo.

"Come on, it wasn't that bad." I try not to laugh. "How many guys can say they got bit by a snake and lived to tell the tale?"

He smiles. "I'd get bit by a snake any day if it meant I got to spend time with you."

I feel my cheeks grow warm.

"So where are we going again?"

"I didn't say," he looks at me. His eyes are jade today.

A few minutes later we reach El Chorro Macho and park our bikes.

"I thought I'd bring you back to the scene of the crime," Travis says as we walk down to the outdoor natural stone pool where I'd lost my ring. The ring that he'd found.

"It's a pretty spot."

He kicks off his flip-flops and sits down on the stone ledge, unwraps his lower calf, and sticks his leg into the water. "That feels good," he groans.

I sit down beside him, dangling my feet in the cool clear water.

"Can I see?" I ask.

He lifts his leg out of the pool. I squint and see two innocuous-looking puncture wounds.

"I was expecting it to look way worse," I admit.

"I know, right?" He grins, lowering his leg back in the water. "I think I'd feel more like a man if it *was* poisonous."

"Don't even say that." I shudder. "Mildly venomous or not, that scared the crap out of me."

"Talk about being scared." Travis's face clouds over. "I'll never forget the feeling when you ran into the house for the frogs. I still haven't decided if that was the silliest or bravest thing I've ever seen."

"I do lots of silly things." I kick my feet in the calm pool.

"You do a lot of brave things," Travis corrects, patting my leg.

"What about going off with Enrique?" I give him a sidelong glance.

"Well, that may have not been the best idea, but you were upset and there will always be guys who capitalize on that." I know he's thinking of his mother.

"He's not a bad guy." I sigh. "Just … opportunistic?" Travis stays quiet. Enrique does seem to have a sixth sense about when I'm at my most vulnerable. Maybe he just has really good — or bad, depending on how you look at it — timing. "So you're not mad at me, then?" I say in a small voice.

His hand comes up and turns my chin towards him. "I was worried, Jess — there's a difference."

"Oh." My heart is thudding.

"Here, I have something for you." He picks his backpack up off the ground from the other side of the ledge and unzips it.

"A souvenir from the fish market?" I try to calm the butterflies with a lame joke.

"Ha-ha." He turns back around and grins unabashed, holding a square object.

It's a small carved box inlaid with intricate designs. The wood is polished and shiny, the artistry in the details stunning.

"Travis." I run my fingers over the designs. "It's beautiful." The carvings are of frogs resting on lily pads at the bottom of a waterfall. I make out a rainbow in the top right corner.

"I got it for you for your birthday, but things have been a little, uh, busy, since then, and I never got a chance to give it to you."

"Thank you," I say, clutching it to my chest. "I love it."

He gives me a look I've never seen before. "It's, ah, a jewelry box — this way you don't have to worry about losing your ring." He seems almost shy. "Although I'm glad you did."

"Why?" I look up at him.

"Because if you hadn't, then I wouldn't have had a chance to get you to change your mind about me."

"Who says I've changed my mind?" I tease. But I have. I've changed in a lot of ways on this trip.

"So you still think I'm an annoying know-it-all?" Emerald eyes dissect me.

"A know-it-all? Yes. Annoying? Maybe not so much." I put the box in my lap and rest my head against his shoulder. Very sturdy. Definitely a shoulder a girl can lean on.

We sit there, listening to the sounds of the forest, as tranquil as my heart.

"So what happens when we go back?" Travis says, interrupting my new-found serenity.

"I finish my report, stay involved with the frogs, hopefully pass bio and get into Berkeley."

"So you still really want to go?" he asks.

"Yes, I really do." Badly.

"And us?"

I look up at him, faintly making out the sound of the roaring waterfall in the background. I take a deep breath and stare at Travis, the boy that had teased me all those years ago. The boy who is nothing like any other guy I've ever met. In the best way.

"Our fairy tale is just beginning," I whisper.

He smiles at me and brings his mouth close to mine. He stops an inch from my lips. "Do you know that you're a serious cheeseball?" he whispers.

"So I've been told," I whisper back and grab his shirt, pulling him down the rest of the way for a kiss that's one for the storybooks.

Epilogue

M y fingers shake slightly as I pull the envelope from my backpack. We're in the lab after school. Juan's just finished screening the first edit of his documentary. I fidgeted through the entire thing, not because it isn't good — it's amazing, actually — but because of the envelope I'd brought from home this morning. An envelope holding the key to my future.

"Ready?" I glance over at Travis, who's patiently waiting for me to open the letter. As are Mr. A, Harp, Juan and Steven. Chrissy and Kiki try to look like they couldn't care less, but I see them eying it. We've reached a mutual cease-fire. They still feel terrible about the whole frog episode and are trying their hardest to be nice. I'm letting them.

When we got back to Seattle it seemed like things changed without me having to do anything at all. Sure enough, Alyssa spilled the beans that Miles and Ky were now dating. I was relieved to have an excuse to not hang out with them anymore. They're still friendly when I see them in the halls, especially Alyssa, but it's incredible how easy it was for those relationships to evaporate and for new bonds to strengthen with these people who sit around me now.

I hear Gigi's voice: *You've found your tribe, Jessica.*

"Just open it already, you're killing us," Harp says. She sits beside Juan. They've been together since we returned from Panama, just like Travis and me.

"I have complete faith in you, Jess," Mr. A says. "Your report was among the best I've seen. Definitely one of the most interesting to read."

"Thanks to all of you," I say, looking around, my gaze lingering on Travis. Travis stayed up late every night helping me with my report. Having a steady study partner who awards me kisses at every right answer has even bumped up my already good grades. "Whatever happens, I want you all to know I'm really glad that I was almost failing biology."

"I wouldn't go that far," Mr. A says, grinning from ear to ear. He's been doing that a lot since Lola told him she's coming for the summer, having found a temporary replacement to watch over the ark. "But we're glad you came on the trip too."

I pick at a corner and gently pull the flap. It tears slightly.

"C'mon Jess," Juan urges. "Like a Band-Aid."

I slide my finger in the hole I made and slit it all the way up. I pull out the piece of paper and scan it quickly.

"Well?" Chrissy says impatiently.

"I got in," I whisper. Reading the words over and over again to assure myself it's not a hallucination. *We are pleased to offer you acceptance to the University of California, Berkeley.*

Cheers erupt and Travis swings me up in a full hug. "I knew you'd get in," he says into my ear. "I'm so proud of you, Princess."

I know Gigi is too. And my parents. And Messy Jessie.

"I couldn't have done it without the frogs," I say, "or you."

"Yes, you could have." He puts me down, his hands still around my waist.

I smile up at his handsome face. "You're right, I could have."

"I can't believe we're almost finished with high school," Harp says, sounding wistful.

"Trust me, guys, there are many more adventures waiting out there for you," Mr. A says.

"Speaking of which, my next documentary's going to be about the disappearing orangutans in Indonesia," Juan says. "What's everyone doing for summer vacation?"

Acknowledgments

So many people have contributed their time and energy to help make this book possible. I'd like to thank my superstar agent and friend Ali McDonald and my former boss and mentor Sam Hiyate for all their encouragement and support. Elizabeth Prats, intern extraordinaire, for her in-depth assistance with edits as well as dear friends kind enough to take a look at early drafts and provide their feedback: Christine McIntyre, Laura McCallen, Angela Plante, Cheryl Munson, Artie Chumpol, Alexandra Jenal and Jacquelyn Abraham.

I'd also like to thank my wonderful editors and publishers at Swoon Romance (US), Mandy Schoen, Allie Kinchloe and Georgia McBride, as well as Fierce Ink Press's (CND) incredible Colleen McKie and Kimberly Walsh. You ladies are amazing! Thank you for making the manuscript the very best it could be.

A special thank you to Pierre-Louis Beranek for his fabulous videos and warm hugs to my lovely Latin ladies for help with the Spanish translations: Maryann Calderon, Juanita Hermida Gutierrez and Cristina Fondevila.

To my parents and all my family back home, you mean the world to me. Thanks for always supporting and loving me.

Finally, to my own prince Aaron Unterman, without whom this book would not have been possible. Thank you for all the big and little things: from sharing your love of travel and introducing me to so many beautiful places around the world, to taking the baby for walks so I could write. I could not have done it without your endless encouragement. You're a phenomenal husband and father and I'm constantly blown away that I get to spend the rest of my life with you.

Xoxo
Alisha

A Word About the

Golden Frog

The fate of the golden frog is becoming all too common nowadays as we are currently experiencing what some call a Global Amphibian Crises. Chytrid, habitat loss and pollution are causing hundreds of species of frogs to disappear at an alarming rate, some even before they've been discovered. Although all the characters in this book are works of fiction, El Valle and the conservation center at Nispero Zoo is real and the various people and organizations connected to EVACC and other centers like it are working hard to make a difference. If you'd like to find out how you can support their efforts in helping the golden frog and other amazing amphibians during this critical time, please check out http:// amphibianrescue.org.

Bio

Alisha Sevigny holds a degree in sociology and professional Writing from the University of Victoria, is a film school graduate, former literary agent and current social media and Communications Director for an award-winning English school. A shameless romantic, Alisha and her husband have travelled the world together. On a recent trip to Panama with their new daughter, Alisha fell in love with the country, culture, and their national emblem, the golden frog. She was inspired to write her first young adult novel, Kissing Frogs. Born and raised in Kitimat, British Columbia, Alisha has always had a strong connection to the environment and conservationist spirit. She now lives in Toronto with her family.

(Photo © Joanna Helli)

From Alisha

Hello Dear Reader,

Thank you for purchasing the Collector's Edition of Kissing Frogs. We've included some extra content here exclusively for you. So many things about a book evolve and change during the writing process. Scenes get cut, two characters might merge into one and a complete reversal of events can occur.

In one of the earlier drafts, the big climactic scene was actually when Travis was bitten by the snake on their last date and it turned out to be poisonous. The fire scene came earlier, and was much less dramatic. Jess losing the frogs wasn't even a part of it, but rather just a minor event. The scene below is one that originally took place after Chrissy and Kiki tell her the frogs are missing and she takes off with Enrique, who tries to kiss her but then drops her off with the group after she rebuffs his advances, which were more aggressive in earlier drafts. It's also still early days in her relationship with Travis as they haven't had their riding date yet.

Deleted Scene:

At that moment I don't care what he thinks. I look over at Harp. "After what I just did, you're worried about me missing dinner?" I ask, incredulous.

"What you do on your own time is your business," Travis says, staring after Enrique.

"Yeah," echoes Steven. "We don't need to hear about your love life."

"What are you talking about?" I'm confused.

"What are you talking about?" Juan asks, looking equally mystified.

Just then Chrissy and Kiki walk out of our villa towards the pool, smirks on their faces.

"The golden frogs…" I start, looking from one baffled face to the next. "They're not gone?"

"Why would they be?" Travis asks.

"But I thought ... Chrissy and Kiki said…" The girls reach the group, victory oozing from their pores.

"They said what?" Harp narrows her eyes at them.

"Just a little misunderstanding," Chrissy says, pushing back her cap of blonde hair. "Jess thought she forgot to do up the latch on one of the exhibits."

"Because you told me I did.," I turn to face her.

Kiki stands beside Chrissy. "Relax Jess, it was just a joke."

"Hilarious." I whirl around and take off for the beach.

"What did you guys say?" I hear Harp ask.

I reach the empty stretch of sand a few minutes later and sit down, utterly wiped. First, I think I've single-handedly decimated an entire species, then I have to fight off an over-zealous Casanova, and now it turns out the frogs are fine and it's all a big prank. I lay back and stare up at the stars, sand in my hair the least of my worries.

"Jess?" A voice calls out searching for me in the dark. It's Harp.

"Over here," I call out, reluctant.

"Are you OK?" She plunks herself down and lays on her back beside me.

"I'm fine," I say.

"Don't let them get to you," Harp says, staring up at the sky as well.

"Trying."

"You just make them feel insecure."

"I could say the same thing about them." The waves lap rhythmically at the shore, soothingly meditative.

She changes the subject.

"What happened with Enrique?"

"Let's just say he tried to get real friendly and I wasn't appreciating his timing."

She turns her head and looks at me.

"Did he ... do anything?"

"Nothing serious," I say. Thanks to the birders who'd stumbled across us. "Don't say anything to anyone, it's not a big deal."

"Sure."

"I thought I'd really screwed up," I say, fingers tracing outlines in the sand.

"Well, you didn't. In fact, I heard Lola telling Mr. A. today what a great job you're doing."

"Really?"

"Really."

A warm glow slowly diffuses its way through my body, replacing the fear and doubt of the last few hours. I sit up, sand falling from my hair. "We should be getting back I guess."

Harp stands up and brushes the sand off her butt.

We start to walk back to the villas, when I remember something.

"How were the square trees?" I say, curious about how things had gone with Juan.

"Very educational." She sighs. "You know how he likes to talk about everything?"

"Yeah, he's a walking encyclopedia. Why?" I ask.

"Let's just say when he's nervous he really turns it up a notch."

"So no dirty details?"

"He wouldn't shut up!" I smile at the exasperation in her voice.

"Maybe you need to make the first move."

Harp looks at me like I'm crazy. "I'm not good with that stuff."

I sigh. "That makes two of us."

"I think you do just fine," she says with a sideways glance at me. "I forgot my ring," she mimics.

I laugh. "That obvious?"

"Maybe not to Juan." We reach the compound door and give it a hard yank.

"I might need to forget about guys for a while and just focus on the frogs," I say.

"Science is way easier to understand than boys anyways." We walk into our beautiful garden paradise, floodlit by a bright moon.

Travis stands outside our villa, leaning back against the brick wall like he's waiting for someone.

"Jess," he says when he sees me. "Can I talk to you?"

"Looks like someone else may have other plans," Harp whispers in my ear. "Night Travis," she calls as she walks into the house, leaving me standing there alone with him in the moonlight.

***

So that's it! Thanks again for buying the book! I hope you enjoyed it and I'd love to hear from you. feel free to contact me on social media or on my website: alishasevigny.com.

All my love,
Alisha